CALL
OF THE
CAMINO

OTHER TITLES BY SUZANNE REDFEARN

Where Butterflies Wander
Moment in Time
Hadley and Grace
In an Instant
No Ordinary Life
Hush Little Baby

CALL
OF THE
CAMINO

a novel

SUZANNE
REDFEARN

LAKE UNION
PUBLISHING

This is a work of fiction. Names, characters, organizations, places, events, and incidents are either products of the author's imagination or are used fictitiously.

Text copyright © 2025 by Suzanne Redfearn
All rights reserved.

No part of this book may be reproduced, or stored in a retrieval system, or transmitted in any form or by any means, electronic, mechanical, photocopying, recording, or otherwise, without express written permission of the publisher.

Published by Lake Union Publishing, Seattle

www.apub.com

Amazon, the Amazon logo, and Lake Union Publishing are trademarks of Amazon.com, Inc., or its affiliates.

EU product safety contact:
Amazon Media EU S. à r.l.
38, avenue John F. Kennedy, L-1855 Luxembourg
amazonpublishing-gpsr@amazon.com

ISBN-13: 9781662530203 (paperback)
ISBN-13: 9781662530210 (digital)

Cover design by Kathleen Lynch/Black Kat Design
Cover image: © Vicenfoto, © Svetlana Sarapultseva / Getty

Printed in the United States of America

For all those whose footsteps I followed, and for all those yet to come.

Yesterday is history.
Tomorrow is a mystery
But today is a gift
That is why it is called the present.
—Bil Keane

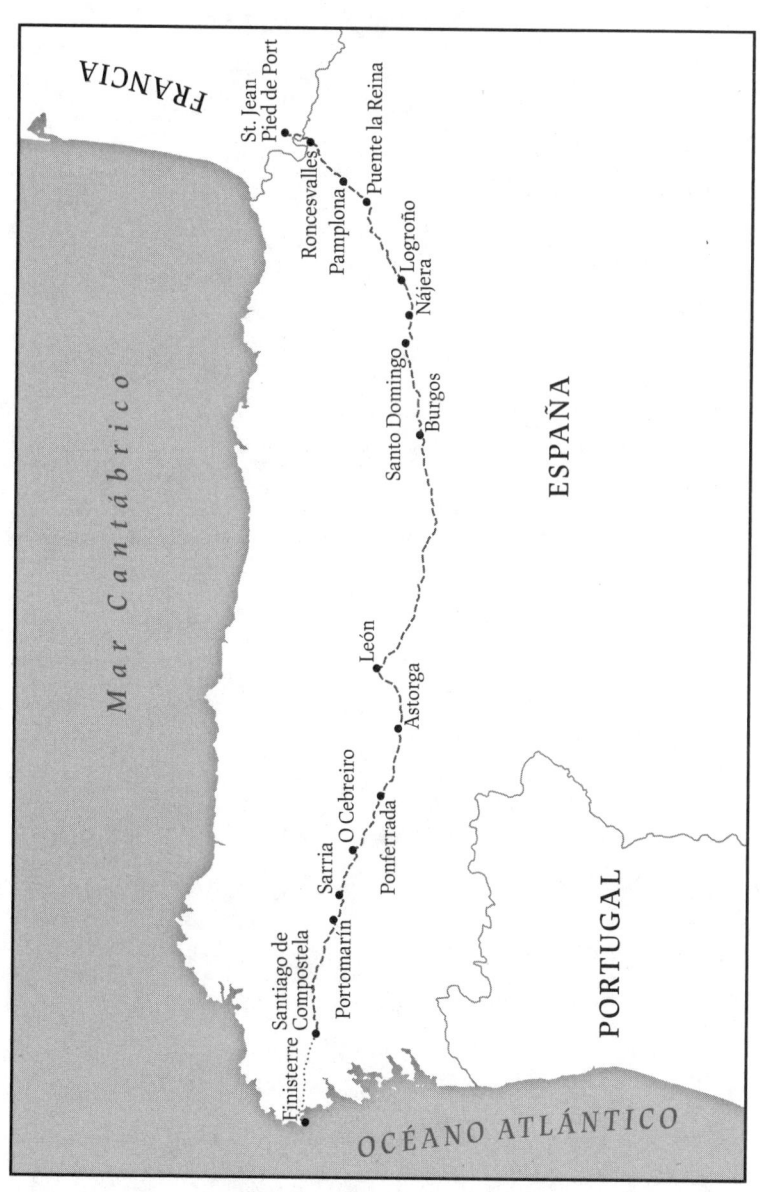

1

ISABELLE

1997

Gemma is laughing. And I would join in her merriment if not for the fact that I'm the one who will be getting the switch if we don't get this situation under control.

"I'm glad you're so amused," I say as I continue to wave my arms up and down, hoping the stupid cow will take the hint and move her half-ton body from the mud pool she's contentedly bathing in.

The sewer swamp formed overnight from a break in a pipe near the road, a puddle one foot deep and twenty feet wide with long blades of grass sticking up through the sludge. The rank smell probably attracted the old girl, and the coolness of the water is what's keeping her there.

"She looks happy," Gemma says, lips still curled in amusement.

"Hay-yah! Hay-yah!" I hoot like an American cowboy in an old Western and wave my arms faster.

If my pa could see me, he'd throw his head back and laugh. Of course, if he were here, he would simply stomp into the mud and swat the heifer on her rear to move her along. Then, after the cows were in the barn, he'd walk to the house and kick his muddy boots on the stoop for my ma to clean. But I'm two hundred miles from home and wearing sneakers along with my favorite jeans, and the only one getting swatted if I walk in the mud is me. Mother Superior would like nothing more than a reason to pull out her lethal steel ruler and let me know, once again, how much she disapproves of me.

"Dang it, cow, move!" I yell in frustration.

The cow's marble eye rolls toward me, letting me know she heard me and is plainly choosing to ignore me. Blithely, she bends her head, yanks off a hunk of grass, and chews, her long lashes hooded as if happy to stay in the mud forever.

"Moooooo-ve!" Gemma bellows, causing me to smirk.

Gemma still wears her school uniform—starched white collared shirt, green-and-navy pleated plaid skirt, knee-high white socks, and her signature clunky Doc Marten Mary Janes. The only addition to what she had on in class is a floppy sun hat, neon pink with bright-yellow sunflowers to protect her fair, freckle-prone skin.

Though we're both on herding duty, I'm the one who mostly deals with the cows. When we started secondary school, Gemma asked to be reassigned from her job in the library so we'd have an excuse to spend time together. Gemma is like royalty, the only child of a senior French minister and notable jewelry designer, while I'm the lowly daughter of an untitled Andorran cattleman. Which meant, after primary school, we were no longer in the same dorm or classes. After our graduation in three weeks, Gemma will be off to university to pursue a career in international law, while I will be returning to Dur to help my family.

Gemma's parents were appalled at the idea of their daughter traipsing through manure-ridden pastures, chasing after cows. But what Gemma wants, Gemma usually gets, and what she wanted was time with her best friend. So for four years, every afternoon, floppy sun hat in place, she has provided the comic relief while I deal with the beef.

My eyes latch onto hers, and knowing my thoughts, she grins wide, and together we lift our faces to the sky and howl, "Moooooooooooo-ve!"

When our air runs out, we look down to see the cow chewing her cud, completely unimpressed.

"I'll go grab some apples," Gemma says. "Maybe we can bribe her out of there."

Gemma walks toward a row of crab apple trees near the road, and I turn to the stubborn, stupid animal. "Listen here," I say, fists on my hips, "enough is enough. You've had your fun, and now it's time to get out. If you don't, we're both going to be late and will miss our dinners."

The cow rolls her marble eye, then, mocking me, yanks off another bite of disgusting grass.

"Ugh!"

"Iz."

I turn to see Gemma walking back, her hands empty.

"Where are the apples?" I ask before noticing her expression, her brow furrowed and her mouth tight.

She flicks her head toward the stone ruins beside the road. I squint against the glare of the late-afternoon sun to see a thick silhouette in the shadows that I instantly recognize, and my throat closes tight.

"I'll take in the others," Gemma says, "and tell the sisters you're trying to get this one out of the mud."

She takes the herding stick from my hand and steps toward the cluster of cows huddled in the shade of a tree a hundred meters away. Now that the herd is clumped together, it's no big deal to encourage them to the corral and the feed they know is waiting.

Reconsidering, she turns back and flings her arms around me. "I love you, Iz."

I stand numb, eyes still on the shadow of my brother in the ruins.

2

REINA

2024

"Moving on to the August issue," Brenda says.

She wears her war room suit today, the one that makes her look like a general—a starched white long-sleeved shirt with gold detailing at the shoulders, tucked into tailored black slacks. I think the impression is intentional. It seems everything Brenda Scythe does is with forethought and purpose. Known as the white tornado because of her shock of white hair and her blizzard approach to turning out magazines on time, she is revered, reviled, and feared throughout the publishing world.

"Our focus will be Spain."

I straighten in my chair, and Liam nudges my knee with the back of his hand, causing me to look down to realize it's jiggling. I force it to stop, and he smiles and knocks my leg again, this time in encouragement. My best friend, he's as excited as I am for what is hopefully to come.

"As we've discussed, we're revamping *Journey*, and our new approach will be to provide immersive, in-depth coverage of a single destination with each issue. Our intent is to make the magazine a cross between travel magazine and adventure guide. We want our readers to not only learn about the destinations through our lens and pens, but for them to feel confident enough to embark on the experience themselves. August will be our flagship issue and will feature the new cover design and logo."

She gives a nod of acknowledgment to Liam, and there's a light round of applause. Liam deserves it. His redesign is perfect. He created his own Journey font, and the magazine's new look is now as iconic and cool as *Rolling Stone*.

"This issue needs to sing," Brenda goes on. "I can't emphasize how important this is."

Her dark, nearly black eyes scan the room, locking on each of us in turn to drive home the point. Over the past decade, magazines have had a rough go of it, and the inflation of the past few years has driven up the hard costs of traditional print magazines and put a final nail in the coffin of many of our competitors. Stellar Publications is one of the last magazine publishers still standing, and Brenda is the reason. Thanks to her, we transitioned to digital ahead of the curve and managed to keep the magazines relevant. *Journey* is our cash cow, with our largest subscriber base and online following. But renewals have been on a steady decline, and this revamp is Brenda's last-ditch effort to reverse that. *Journey* will no longer just be a magazine. Each article will have a QR code that brings the reader to more in-depth coverage online and will include a host of links to related products and travel sites, the most prominent of which will be our subsidiary company TravelWise.com, where you can book flights, hotels, and car rentals. If it works, it's genius and will save the company. If not, I, along with everyone else in the room, will be updating my résumé.

Silently, I pray I'll play a role in its success. It's been a week since Brenda suggested it might be possible. It was nearly eight p.m., and the office was empty except for the two of us. She was working on the final proof for *Cat Story*, our second-most successful magazine, and I was doing a last-minute copyedit on an article about a celebrity who had passed away and had left their estate to their six cats.

My heart pounded as I walked the pages to her office, knowing I couldn't put the moment off any longer. The sky through her window was bruised black, and the lights of Times Square in the distance glowed.

"Good to go?" she asked, leaning back in her chair and bending her neck side to side as if working out a kink. Her desk was strewn with cut sheets, and the only personal item was a mug that read *World's Greatest Grandma*. The mug surprised me each time I saw it. It was hard to imagine Brenda as a grandmother, crawling on the floor with children, molding playdough with her meticulously manicured nails.

I nodded and set the sheets on her desk but didn't turn to leave as I normally would.

Her perfectly teased left brow arched. "Did you need something?"

My mouth went dry, and despite all the rehearsing I'd done, I completely forgot everything I planned to say.

Her brow arched again, this time in impatience.

I almost turned to leave, but the mug stopped me. Three days before, I'd had dinner with my aunt in Ithaca. I try to visit at least once a month. She was worrisomely thin, and when I went to make tea after dinner, I was stunned to discover her cupboards bare and that she'd replaced her favorite ginseng tea, which she always buys from the small Asian market downtown, with generic dollar store Earl Grey. I knew things were tight but had no idea they were as bad as they obviously were. I needed to help but couldn't do that on my measly copyeditor's salary.

"I write," I blurted.

Brenda tilted her head. "You write?"

"I went to school for journalism. It's what my degree is in. Journalism. From Columbia." Aware I was blubbering and coming off like an idiot, I slammed my mouth shut before I could embarrass myself any more.

Brenda laced her hands together on the desk, and I couldn't decide if the expression on her face was humor, pity, or consideration.

Finally she said, "I'll think about it." Then she returned to her work, letting me know I was dismissed.

And now, seven agonizing days later, here we are, the team assembled, and I am about to find out what she decided.

She nods to the man beside her. "Matt, this is your baby, so I'll let you take it from here."

And just like that, my hope deflates. Liam gives my knee a consolatory squeeze, realizing it as well. Matt Calhoun has been the bane of my existence since the two of us started on the same day three years ago.

Matt stands and flashes his double-dimple smile around the table, causing all the women and half the men to swoon.

Turning to Brenda, he says, "Thanks, Chief." He's the only one who calls her that and is the only one who can get away with it. Brenda is as charmed by the two-faced snake as everyone else. "But I'm sorry to say, I'm walking."

There's a united sharp intake of air, and the color drains from Brenda's face.

Yes! I cheer. *There is a God! My prayers have been answered!*

"Walking the Camino de Santiago, that is."

Brenda huff-laughs and puts her hand to her chest like she's been spared a heart attack as my own chest clenches with the one-two punch of his words. First, that he's not leaving, and second, that he is walking the Camino.

Someday, Bug, we'll walk it together. The Camino de Santiago, the reason for you and everything that came after.

My eyes move to the conference-room window and clear blue sky. Whenever I think of my dad, I think of him being among the clouds.

He died in an airplane crash when I was eight, and my little-girl mind somehow equated that with him being permanently in the sky.

Liam smacks my thigh, and I jolt.

I look at him, and he nods to the room, and I realize everyone is looking at me. Matt is back in his seat, and Brenda is standing.

"Does that work for you?" she asks, black eyes fixed on me, and I realize she's repeating herself.

My skin flushes red hot as I nod, having no idea what I'm agreeing to.

"Well then, I think that wraps it up. Matt is lead, and his updates from the Camino will inform the issue. Remember, this is meant to be an immersive experience, so make sure you're working collaboratively and in sync."

She leads the way from the room, and I look at Liam in bewilderment.

"Food," he says with a grin. "You're covering the food for the issue."

My eyes bulge, and he smiles wider, his warm canine-brown eyes wrinkling at the corners.

"You did it, kid. Good job."

My heart skips and pounds and leaps. *I did it!*

"You're going to kill it, and I volunteer"—Liam raises his hand—"to be your guinea pig for every recipe."

"I wouldn't choose anyone else."

"And I volunteer Jake as well."

Jake is Liam's live-in partner and my second-best friend. The two gay middle-aged men adopted me like a pet when I moved to the city. At least once a week, I join them at their Chelsea apartment for dinner and to binge-watch old movies. They provide the ingredients and humor, and I do the cooking and provide fodder for their jokes.

"Food," I say, almost in disbelief.

I love food, not only eating it but everything about it—restaurants, chefs, ingredients, appliances, farmers' markets, gardening, cooking, cookbooks. I grew up cooking—first with my dad and then with my aunt. My dad said my mom was brilliant at it. It's one of the few things I know about her, which is perhaps another reason I love it so much.

"Congratulations, Velma."

I sigh silently through my nose before turning from Liam to face Matt, who stands in front of me with his trademark smarmy grin on his face.

"Thanks. But the name is Reina. I know you're slow, but I believe if you try *really* hard, you can get it. Rei-na. R-E-I-N-A."

The week I started, I made the fateful mistake of wearing a mustard turtleneck with a mid-thigh pleated skirt and a pair of clunky loafers. Matt took one look and said, "Ruh-roh, Velma's in the house!"

It wasn't that funny then, and three years later, it's still not funny. But he insists on continuing with it, calling me Velma with so much persistence that half the people in the building think it's my actual name.

"Maybe you can include a recipe for Scooby Snacks with a Spanish twist."

"And maybe you can do the world a favor and trip over your shoelaces, fall off the Pyrenees, and we'll never hear from you again."

He chuckles and saunters off, walking in the slow, exaggerated way he does, which irritates me almost as much as his twitchy dimples.

"Ugh, I hate that guy."

Liam nods. Like me, he knows the truth about Matt and how he got to where he is. Karen, the woman whose career he hijacked, was our friend.

Liam and I head out of the conference room. Liam turns left toward the art department, and I continue toward the copyediting pool.

Matt leans in the doorway of the cubicle of one of the new advertising sales reps, a petite blonde with nails so long she needs to use her knuckles to operate her phone.

I ignore them as I walk past and am nearly to my cubicle when the whistle hits me from behind, the incessant earworm tune to *Scooby-Doo*.

The sales rep giggles as my hair follicles stand on end, knowing, for the rest of the day, I'll be putting up with Velma quips and *Scooby-Dooby-Doo!* howls.

3
ISABELLE

1997

The first thing I notice is how much he's grown. My sixteen-year-old little brother now towers at least six inches over me.

"Xav?" I say, a question choked with worry.

I've not seen him or any of my family since Christmas, nearly five months ago. And the fact that he is here, alone and hiding in the shadows, carries a distinct omen of dread.

He shifts from one foot to the other, his hands shoved deep in his pockets, still a boy despite his height.

His motorbike leans against one of the walls. Beside it is his old school backpack. Xavier ended his schooling when he turned fourteen. Book learning was never his thing. He never got the hang of reading or doing math, though he's the most mechanically minded person I've ever met. He can fix a combine or a dishwasher, and he practically built his motorbike from spare parts.

He blows out a breath, and the bad feeling grows.

"Is everyone okay?" I ask.

He nods, then his head switches direction to loll in a slow, drooping shake. My family members spiral through my mind in a whirl of panic—Ma; Pa; Ana, my sister; my aunts; uncles; and my cousins.

"Miguel and Manuel," he mumbles, a hitch in his voice.

"The twins?"

He nods.

Miguel and Manuel Sansas are the youngest sons of the Sansas clan, a family with ten children who live across the river. I went to school with the boys until I turned eight and my pa sent me here so I could learn languages to help him with his business in the future.

"They're dead," Xavier says.

I tilt my head, the words not making sense. The twins are my age, seventeen.

"A car accident. On the pass. You need to come home. I came to take you back."

It takes a moment for the words to register, my mind still catching up.

"Take me back?" I say, followed by "oh," as the implication of the twins' deaths, and how it relates to me, becomes clear. "The vote," I mumble to myself, and Xavier nods.

The next thought comes uninvited into my head. "Pa?" I say, praying I've got it wrong. "Did Pa have something to do with their deaths?"

Xavier toes the dirt, something he does when he's upset.

"Who was driving?" I ask, knowing it holds the answer.

Xavier knows it as well and mutters, "Miguel."

Although Miguel and Manuel were twins, they couldn't have been more different. Manuel was a rebel with a reckless streak. Miguel was an artist and a poet, devoutly religious to the point of piety, and he drove like an old lady. It was the reason Miguel nearly always drove. He used to say, "I'd like to live to someday have children."

In the winter, the pass over the mountain can be slick with ice and dangerous, but in May, it's no trickier than driving down the street to the store.

"Senor Sansas is on his way," Xavier says. "He left a few minutes before me with Enric and Jesus." Enric and Jesus are the two oldest Sansas boys. "I took the back way so I would get here before them."

By car, the trip from Dur to my school, which is in Pau, France, takes around four hours, but if you go over the mountain on a motorbike, it's faster. Which explains why Xavier is here instead of my pa and why he came alone.

My pulse ticks up as the puzzle continues to fall into place. *An eye for an eye.* It's the Dur way. If Senor Sansas believes my pa had something to do with his boys' deaths, he is on his way to exact his revenge. I look at my brother, then back at the ground as my mind whirs. And the reason he's coming after me instead of just taking the lives of Xavier and Ana is because of my vote, which, with the twins dead, now suddenly matters.

Ten years ago, a developer named Castor came to Dur with the idea of converting our remote, sleepy little village into a world-class ski resort. Our mountain's north face and flat basin make it an ideal location. No range in the world gets as much year-round snow.

My pa, self-declared lord of Dur, agreed to the proposal without consulting the other families. He claimed the mountain belongs to us because our cattle range abuts the mountain and because we've lived in Dur the longest.

Senor Sansas made a similar claim. He owns the timberland, which wraps around the mountain, and upon hearing my pa's plan, came up with a plan of his own. His idea was to lease the mineral rights of the mountain to a mining company. It would bring jobs and revenue to the village as well as a railroad, which would be a huge boon for his timber business. He claimed his ancestors were the original settlers who carved out the smuggling route, which made him the rightful owner of the mountain.

Dur, which translates to *tough*, was originally nothing more than an outpost for a rugged mountain pass used to illicitly transport everything from drugs to silk to tobacco to people from Spain into Andorra and eventually France. Sometime in the twelfth century, thirteen families settled there permanently, including my family and the Sansas family. Founded on lawlessness, it remains a feudal, independent place, where nearly all its disputes are settled without any sort of government or outside interference.

But the disagreement between Senor Sansas and my pa could not be resolved. No one could agree. So finally, a year ago, the issue went to court. My pa and Senor Sansas each produced questionable records that showed title to the land and lineage going back to the settler days of Dur. The judge, after hearing both sides and reviewing the documents, decided both men were lying and decreed the mountain was communal and belonged in equal parts to each permanent citizen born in Dur before 1979, the year Dur was incorporated. The twins and I were the last villagers to make the cutoff, but we couldn't vote on the future of the mountain until we turned eighteen. The judge made it clear this would be Dur's last chance to resolve the matter independently. If there were any more problems, the Andorran government would step in, a fate neither Senor Sansas or Pa wanted. If the federal government got involved, both men would lose their power, and the crooked deals they'd made with the developers would go up in smoke.

When the vote took place four months ago, the twins and I weren't concerned, certain the issue would be decided without us. But when the results came in, it was a tie—256 in favor of the ski resort and 256 in favor of Senor Sansas's mining plan. My pa was enraged, certain Senor Sansas had played dirty and bribed a dozen turncoats to change their votes.

The twins had two votes, and I only had one, which meant, in a month, when the twins turned eighteen, Senor Sansas would win.

But now the twins are gone.

"We need to go," Xavier says anxiously. He picks up his backpack, pulls out a spare helmet, and holds it toward me.

I don't take it.

Two deaths. An eye for an eye.

I look again at my brother, my nerves on fire. Senor Sansas will kill me and then either Xavier or Ana.

"I need to leave," I say.

"Yes," Xavier says and again pushes the helmet toward me.

"No. Here. You. Now."

He tilts his head in confusion.

My vote. So long as I'm alive, the vote remains deadlocked and the future of Dur unresolved. It isn't much, but at the moment, it's the only leverage I have to keep my brother and sister safe.

Senor Sansas is a smart man, the smartest in our village. Unlike Pa, he is not impulsive, and he will understand the reason I fled. It's the reason he's coming after me first. He wants to nullify the threat before exacting his full revenge. Next to losing the vote, the second-worst-possible scenario for him is that my vote remains uncast.

It was my ma who figured out the loophole. My ma is far more clever than my pa or any of the men in our village give her credit for. The judge's order was very specific. The village stakeholders were to vote on February 15, and the twins and I could not vote until after our eighteenth birthdays. The twins' birthdays were in June, and mine is in July. But the judge did not specify how long the twins and I had to cast our vote after we hit that milestone.

"But what if you, Miguel, and Manuel simply don't vote?" Ma said to me on the phone the day after the vote was tallied.

Ma often poses suggestions as questions, making you believe the idea is your own. Like many of the villagers, she hates both plans and wants things to remain as they are.

"What if the three of you just leave things alone?"

I remember wondering if the twins might do that, the three of us making a private pact not to vote. I knew instantly that they wouldn't. Their pa, like my own, was simply too dangerous. But once my ma put the idea out there, people started talking about it, amused at the idea of the three of us kids thwarting both men's grand plans.

"Iz—" Xavier starts.

"It's the only way," I say, heart pounding.

"But where will you go?"

My ma or God guiding me, the smallest ember of an idea glows at the edges of my overwrought brain. "Je n'ai pas peur, car Dieu est avec moi. Je suis née pour ça," I answer.

My brother's French is not as good as my own, but all Andorrans speak some French, and Joan of Arc's words are better spoken in her native tongue.

I am not afraid, for God is with me. I was born for this!

Before Xavier can respond, I reach up, touch his cheek, then spin and race for the trees.

4

REINA

2024

My phone buzzes, and I look away from the recipe I found online for Spanish tortilla, a staple of the Camino de Santiago.

> R u on your way?

I look from my phone to the clock on my screen, shocked to see it's 7:18 p.m. I look back at the phone and blink several times. *What day is it? Friday! Crap!*

I hit dial, and John picks up on the first ring. "Hey, babe. I got us a table on the patio."

"Uh. Wow. That's great. Except I don't think I'm going to make it."

Long beat of silence.

"I'm sorry. I should have texted. It's just I got caught up at work. I have an assignment. A *writing* assignment."

"It's Friday," he says, not picking up on the significance. "And we agreed."

We sort of agreed. When we first started dating, John suggested we should meet every Friday for happy hour at Muldoon's, an Irish pub near Grand Central Station, to hang out with his best friend, Craig, and Craig's girlfriend, Meghan. I shrugged because, at the time, I thought: *Why not? I have nothing better to do.* And also because I know how much John likes his friends and his routines. He's the kind of guy who keeps in touch with every acquaintance he's ever had, along with every cousin, aunt, and uncle. It's sweet, and I want to be supportive, but having grown up an only child with only my aunt, I'm not used to having so many social obligations, and sometimes I miss my free time or enjoying life without a plan, simply heading out and seeing where the night leads.

"Sorry," I repeat, my eyes wandering back to the recipe and the photo of glistening potato egg pie. "It's just that Brenda's given me the chance to cover the food segment for the next issue of *Journey*."

"That's great, babe. If you leave now, you can still make it for cards."

I could, but I really don't want to. "I need to nail this, so I'm going to stay and work." To soften the news, I add, "Liam and Jake volunteered to be my tasting guinea pigs, and I was thinking you could be my test subject as well."

He chuckles. "That's not fair. You're preying on my weakness."

"Is it working?"

"It is. My stomach forgives you, and since that is the biggest part of me, I suppose we will get through the night without you."

I laugh with him. He's a hardy man and growing hardier by the day.

"Love you," he says.

I parrot him back, "Love you too."

It's not a lie. I do love him. He's a good guy, a *really* good guy, and I'm lucky to have him. Stable, kind, loyal—John ticks the boxes, a rare trifecta in today's dating world.

My eyes slide to the photo of my dad on my desk, a shot taken a few months before he died. We're standing in front of his Cessna, caught in a moment of laughter. His arm is around my shoulder, and I'm looking up at him as he smiles at the camera.

Not everyone can have what you and Mom had, I think as I look into his sky-blue eyes that stare at me from the frame.

I return to the recipe. I'm discovering the trick to good tortilla is drying the potatoes before they go in the pie. But that's not enough. I want to give the reader something more, a surprising dash of wow, a tortilla recipe so special they clip it from the magazine to keep in their recipe box.

An email notification pops up in the upper corner of my screen.

On the final day of production for any of our magazines, I log into Brenda's email in case there are any last-minute tweaks by the editors or contributors. *Bird Life* goes to press Monday, but the email isn't for *Bird Life*. It's for *Journey*. And the sender is Matt.

> Re: SOS!

I should ignore it. It's obviously not about copyedits.
But it does say "SOS!"
My finger hovers over the envelope icon, but only for a second.
Click.
The email opens:

> F!!! I was mugged on my way to Soho. I'm okay, but the guy got my wallet and phone along with my backpack, which had my laptop and PASSPORT! My flight is Sunday. I need to postpone.

My dimples twitch. "Karma's an itch," as my aunt likes to say. Finally, some just deserts. I think of Karen and nod with satisfaction. "That's what you get for stealing someone's story and stampeding over the final chapter of their career," I say to the screen.

Unlike most of the reporters at Stellar Publications, Karen Lindum cared about the copyeditors. When I started, she took me under her wing and encouraged me. "Find your voice," she would say, "and people will listen."

She'd been with *Cat Story* since the magazine's inception. Tall and colorful, she had outrageous style, and her stories were quirky and full of heart, especially her final year's work, which made what happened that much worse. She was at her peak when Matt cut her down to forward his own career.

From the day we started, Matt flirted shamelessly with Karen so she would request him to copyedit her stories. He brought her chocolates and her favorite tea and visited with her for hours in her office, leaving the rest of us in the copyedit pool to pick up his slack.

The day she got sick, I was the one who noticed and insisted she let me take her to the hospital. She had acute appendicitis. Liam was the one who went to her apartment to get a bag for her. And we were both at the hospital the next day when the email arrived from Brenda informing the staff that Matt would be taking over Karen's "Dear Cat Lady" column for the next issue.

A week later, the next *Cat Story* released. The issue focused on the therapeutic benefits of cat companionship. Karen was passionate about the topic and was particularly excited about the feature article she'd written about the psychological and physical benefits of purring. Scientists had recently proven the hertz of a purr beneficial for everything from lowering stress and blood pressure to helping cure illnesses and infections. She'd been working on the story for months, and it was her favorite topic whenever we went to lunch.

I brought the issue to the hospital and was with her when she opened it.

"Oh," she said, and I watched as the smile dropped from her face.

"What?"

She shook her head, closed the magazine, and set it on the table beside her.

"If you don't mind," she said, "I'd like to rest."

When I got back to work, I opened the issue to see what had upset her.

The feature article was titled, "Cat-a-tonic," and the byline read, "by Matt Calhoun." Karen got no mention at all. She also never returned to work. Matt was suddenly permanently on the "Dear Cat Lady" column and took over as editorial director for the magazine, and Karen was out of a job.

Two months later, Karen passed away in her apartment from a heart attack. Liam and I both agreed it was heartbreak. She'd given close to forty years to *Cat Story*, and the thanks she got was having her career stolen out from under her.

Six months later, Matt transferred to *Journey* because he wanted to write about travel adventures, and he had never owned a cat and never intended to.

I stare at the email, the words **PASSPORT** and postpone vibrating on the screen.

I go onto ChatGPT and ask how long it takes to get an emergency passport. The quickest turnaround for non-life-and-death emergencies is five working days. Monday is Memorial Day, which means, best-case scenario, Matt would get it by the following Monday and could fly out Tuesday—nine days after he was scheduled to leave. The Camino takes a minimum of thirty-three days. Matt gave himself thirty-six so he could spend an extra day in the cities—Pamplona, Burgos, and León. Even if he gives up the rest days, he won't make the deadline.

I feel familiar warmth on my spine and look again at the photo of my dad.

Go on, Bug. The Camino de Santiago! Our someday is here.

Turning back to the computer, I click "Reply All" and type:

> I was working on the copyedits for *Bird Life* and saw this email and was worried it was important. Sorry to hear about your troubles, Matt. My passport is in the top drawer of my dresser, and I can be ready to go

on Sunday. I've always wanted to walk the Camino.
Best, Reina.

I press send before I can lose my nerve and, heart pounding, stare at the screen where the email had been, terrified and excited by what I've done.

5

ISABELLE

1997

In front of me is a tavern, the smell of grease and meat wafting from the open door, causing an ache in my hollow stomach. Over the past two days, I've foraged a few mushrooms and berries and forced myself to eat a handful of unripe crab apples, but it's done little to stave off my hunger, and I'm dizzy with starvation.

I stare at the glowing light within, trying to decide whether I'm far enough from my school to take the chance of showing myself. It's dusk, which makes it the ideal time to ask for work. My ma never said no to hungry travelers looking to trade labor for leftovers.

I take a deep breath and am about to step from the shadows when a truck driving down the street stops me. I move deeper into the alley and watch as Carlos, one of Senor Sansas's cousins, drives past, eyes scanning through the windshield.

I whirl and race back for the woods, tears stinging my eyes with fear, hunger, and rage. I don't know how I thought I could do this, alone on the run from a pack of desperate men. No food. No money. How could Pa have done this, put us in this situation? He must have known the danger the twins' deaths would put us in. Was he powerless to stop it? Or did he simply not care?

The ski resort started out as a fun, almost fanciful idea. Pa talked about the tavern becoming a five-star chalet, with noble people—dignitaries and celebrities from all over the world—visiting and making us rich. I was seven, Xavier was six, and Ana four. I remember sitting around the table as his eyes glowed with the possibility. He pulled Ana onto his lap and asked her if she wanted to learn how to ski. He told Xavier he would be in charge of driving the grooming machines up and down the mountain. Even then, Xavier loved anything with wheels. I would be his right hand, master of languages and numbers. My job would be to translate for the guests and make sure no one was trying to pull a fast one. His nickname for me was Petit Geni, little genius.

Then Senor Sansas came up with his plan, and the wondrous dream turned into something else altogether. Powerful people got involved, the stakes were raised, and it was no longer just about Dur and famous visitors and skiing. It was about investors and developers and railway magnates. It was about money and power and rare, precious metals, possibly even lithium and gold. Neighbors stopped talking. Fights broke out weekly at the school and at the tavern.

If you lived at the base of the mountain, the ski resort was going to make you rich. Your property would be bought for chalets, businesses, and the resort. If your home was across the river or near the woods, you would prosper more from the mining and rail line.

I didn't care about either plan. While we weren't rich, our cattle ranch and the tavern did fine, and I never wanted for anything. Like my ma, I mostly just wanted things to go back to the way they were.

I stop to catch my breath and wipe the tears from my face. It's cold, and I shiver through the thin cotton of my T-shirt. I wish I'd thought to ask Xavier for his leather jacket or for any money he had. I feel like I don't stand a chance. I'm only a girl, seventeen and alone, without even a sweater.

Self-pity helps no one, least of all yourself.

My ma was very clear on the subject. I think how sick with worry she must be. For me, and for Xavier and Ana.

I look up at the sky through the trees to be sure I'm continuing west and do my best to push down my emotions.

I find it ironic that it was Mother Superior who planted the seed for my escape. It was in her history-of-religion class two years ago that I first learned about the Camino de Santiago. According to her, there is a trail that leads from a small French town on this side of the Pyrenees, over the range, and then across Spain to the great city of Santiago de Compostela, which is where the remains of the apostle Saint James are buried. The journey is a religious pilgrimage that has been undertaken for over a thousand years by millions of devout Christians. According to the legend, anyone who completes the journey is granted plenary indulgences. Which means your sins are forgiven and any punishment relating to them in this life or eternal life is pardoned.

And while having my slate wiped clean of all my wrongdoings sounds nice, that's not the reason I chose it as my destination. The part that gives me hope is what the mother said about the pride Spain takes in caring for the pilgrims. She went on and on about the good Christians and missionaries who make it their calling to protect the sacred passage and to care for those who undertake the journey. She herself had spent several summers as a young nun at one of the hospitals on the trail, and she said with pride, *No matter how poor, the Camino provides.*

6

REINA

2024

What have I done?

Impetuous, impulsive, ludicrous.

I have no more business setting out on a five-hundred-mile trek across Spain than a penguin. I'm not athletic. I don't camp or hike. I'm accident-prone. And I'm allergic to bees.

"Do they have bees in Spain?" I ask Liam, whose stunned expression hasn't changed since I pounded on his door this morning, an hour after receiving the email from Brenda that said:

> Attached is your ticket. Prove I'm not insane giving you this chance.

She is insane. I'm insane. And this is a terrible, insane idea.

Before Liam can answer my question about bees, Aunt Robbie says, "Found it," as she climbs down the attic ladder in the hall.

Liam leaps from the couch to take the backpack slung over her shoulder. Aunt Robbie's Boston terrier, Rex, leaps forward as well. The dog is half blind and almost deaf, but his sense of smell still works, and he circles around Liam, excited by the moldy, musty scent.

Liam sets the pack beside the coffee table and frowns. It's olive-green canvas and coated with dust and cobwebs.

"I think this pack was already a relic when your dad carried it," Liam says.

The aluminum frame is dented and speckled white with corrosion, and the canvas is faded and moth bitten. My dad walked the Camino twenty-seven years ago, but the backpack looks like it could have served in World War II.

"Between the pack and the shoes, you're definitely going to make a statement," Liam says.

The only shoes I had in my closet that even slightly resembled hiking boots were a pair of flower-embroidered Doc Martens I wore for a brief period in middle school when I was going through a rebel-artist stage. I had to choose between the Docs or my Converse Chuck Taylors, and even Liam agreed Chucks are no match for a five-hundred-mile trek through mountains and forests.

"Should we go to the sporting goods store?" Aunt Robbie asks, her face screwed up with concern as she looks at the ratty backpack.

I shake my head for two reasons. First, I like the idea of carrying the same pack my dad did. And second, I can't afford to buy a backpack and hiking shoes I'm only going to use for a month.

"I could get you an early birthday present," Aunt Robbie presses.

"I told you, all I want for my birthday is one of your flower paintings."

Aunt Robbie dabbles in art, and her favorite subject, other than Rex, is flowers.

I level my eyes on hers. "I mean it. If you get me anything else, I won't be happy."

It's the truth. The last thing I want is for her to spend money on me. Life has been unfair to Aunt Robbie. A fourth-grade teacher, she was saddled with an eight-year-old who wasn't hers when she was in her forties, then bore the financial burden of taking care of her mother, who got dementia and lived ten years in a memory care facility. The house is mortgaged to the hilt, and she's still paying off my grandmother's medical bills. Aunt Robbie is sixty-one. She should be looking forward to retiring, but instead, she has started tutoring in the afternoons and works two shifts on the weekends at Starbucks.

"Fine," she says with an eye roll, then uses a tissue to dust cobwebs and what looks like mouse droppings from the pack, which causes a large scallop shell that dangles from a string to sway. "I remember when your dad and David were getting ready to do this. They were so excited."

David is Uncle David, the younger brother of my dad and Aunt Robbie. He was the one who had been flying the plane when a bird flew into the engine, causing it to stall. The plane rolled during the emergency landing, killing my dad and seriously injuring Uncle David. He broke his leg and suffered a major concussion. A few days after the accident, he hobbled out of the hospital on crutches, and no one has heard from him since.

I remember Aunt Robbie telling me he would be back, that Uncle David did this sometimes, went off to work things out. My grandmother said the same thing.

The Uncle David I knew never went off. My entire life up to that point, he had always been around. He lived in our house, and he and my dad worked together, doing aerial surveying and photography. He flew the plane while my dad sat in the open door taking the photos. He was there each morning at breakfast and most of the time when I got home from school. He usually had dinner with us and never missed a single one of my soccer games.

He never did come back.

Aunt Robbie moved from Syracuse back to her childhood home in Ithaca to take care of me because my grandmother was already starting to forget things. Which meant, she went from her independent, carefree life in a city she loved, to living in the small town she'd fled at eighteen and to being the sole caregiver to a kid she barely knew and an angry, bitter mother who increasingly forgot who she was.

"There's something inside," Aunt Robbie says.

She uncinches the drawstring and reaches in, and I crinkle my nose when she brings out a crumpled yellow clump.

"Looks like that might have been a rain poncho at one time," Liam says, taking the unidentifiable yellow object from her by two fingers and dropping it on *The New York Times* on the coffee table.

Rex sniffs at it and gives a single high-pitched yelp of warning. I scruff the old dog's ears. Aunt Robbie brought Rex home three months after the accident. She said we both needed a bit of happy in our lives.

Next, Aunt Robbie pulls out a grimy blue bottle. "Ew," she says and drops it beside the yellow clump. "Sun lotion, I'm guessing."

She reaches back in and pulls out a Walgreens flat paper bag.

My pulse quickens when she dumps it out on the table to reveal three photo envelopes.

My mom and dad met on the Camino, and if these shots were taken while my dad was on the trail, it's possible they are of the two of them. I have only a single photo of my mom, the one my dad kept in his wallet. For reasons I don't fully understand, when my mother died when I was two, my dad wasn't able to go back to our home in Portugal for our things. He and I were here, visiting my grandparents for the holidays, when she died suddenly of a pulmonary embolism.

"Only negatives," Aunt Robbie says, lifting the flaps one at a time.

Liam holds out his hand. "I can digitize them at the office and email them to you in Spain."

Aunt Robbie reaches back into the pack and pulls out a plastic baggie with a white folded cardboard booklet inside. I recognize it as a Camino passport—the booklet every pilgrim carries that documents their journey and proves they are doing the walk. She spreads it open, and the three of us lean close to look at the rainbow of colorful stamps. Each represents a place my dad stopped on his journey.

"It's like a treasure map," Liam says as I think the same thing, my pulse ticking up at the thought.

"One last thing," Aunt Robbie says, her arm deep in the pack all the way to her armpit.

She pulls out a black moleskin journal, and her eyes lock on mine. All his life, my dad recorded his thoughts and chronicled his photos in journals just like the one in Aunt Robbie's hand. He kept the journals at his office near the airport. Unfortunately, the landlord, on hearing about my dad's death and unable to get ahold of Uncle David, cleared out the space, and the journals were lost.

Aunt Robbie sets the journal beside the Camino passport.

"Looks like a story to me," Liam says. "Follow the yellow brick road or, in this case, the white cardboard road, and see where it takes you."

I lift the journal and open to the first page.

June 1, 1997

St. Jean Pied de Port, France
The taxi dropped us off at the foot of the bridge that leads across the River Nive as the sun was rising, and instantly I was in love . . .

Someday, Bug, we'll walk it together. The Camino de Santiago.

I close the journal, not wanting to get ahead of myself. Tomorrow, our journey begins.

7

ISABELLE

_1997_

I stop to still the dizziness. The incline is endless, and I'm so tired and hungry my mind has started to play tricks. I feel like I must be getting close. I've been hiking three days with hardly any rest, and the air is breathlessly thin, which makes me think I'm near the peak.

I take a gulp from the near empty Evian bottle I've been filling in the many streams I've passed, then I put the top back on and force myself forward.

Minutes or hours later, when I look up again, I see lights, and tears of relief flood my eyes. The town of St. Jean Pied de Port, "foot of the pass," twinkles below. A meandering town of pale buildings with red tile roofs snaking around a river—it looks like a storybook. The dusky dawn paints it like a dream, and all of it is so charming and wonderful that, despite my exhaustion, I start down the hill at a trot.

When I reach the river, I stop to refill my bottle.

Two middle-aged men with backpacks pass behind me.

"Bonjour," I say.

They respond in English.

"Can you tell me where the start is?" I ask, reverting to their language.

"Do you already have your passport?" one asks, causing my heart to stop.

"You need a passport?" I ask.

"Not an actual passport." The man reaches into the side pocket of his hiking pants to pull out a white folded cardboard book. He opens it to show me a grid with the first square stamped in blue ink. "It's how you record your journey. And you need to show it to stay at the hostels."

"The albergues," I clarify, hostel a word I'm not familiar with but that sounds like hotel.

"Yes. It proves that you're walking the Camino."

"It's also what you need to get your certificate at the end," the other one adds.

"Does it cost money?" I ask.

"No. It's free."

I smile in relief.

The man looks at his watch. "But the office doesn't open for another couple of hours. You'll need to wait."

They give me directions to the pilgrim office and continue on their way. I return to filling my bottle, then follow the river to the town. Hunger propels me toward the smell of baking bread. The boulangerie I find is closed, but the back window glows. I knock on the screen door, and a woman with a kind, tired face appears.

In French, I ask if I might help in the kitchen to earn some breakfast, and her expression brightens. She opens the door wider to let me in then points to a sink full of bowls, pans, whisks, and spoons.

When I finish drying the last bowl I grab a broom, but the woman shakes her head.

"You've done enough to earn your breakfast." She hands me a just-baked baguette along with a jar of preserves. "Buen Camino."

I carry my treasures to the river, devour half the bread and most of the jam, then carefully wrap the rest for later and walk to the pilgrim office.

A couple dozen people are gathered in front of the door. As I get closer, I hear the delightful mix of languages. There is Spanish, French, German, and English, all of which I know, as well as some Asian and Scandinavian conversations, which feel like secrets yet to be unlocked.

"Hello!" a woman in her twenties says brightly.

"Hello," I say with a small wave.

She is slight as a pixie with a black ponytail tied high on her head and a backpack so large she looks like she could topple over at any moment.

"Is that all you're carrying?" she asks, sizing up my baguette bag and water bottle.

"She's probably a hell of a lot smarter than us," the woman beside her says.

Far more solidly built, the woman looks around my ma's age, and her pack sits comfortably on her shoulders. She has white-blond hair cut in a bob to her chin, and there is a bright-purple streak through the bangs.

"Jen," she says pointing to herself. She thumbs her hand at her friend. "Erika." Then she nods to a tall, grinning thirtysomething man with glasses. "Joe. Nebraska, Ohio, Wisconsin."

"I'm"—I hesitate a beat before finishing—"Joan," the name coming to me in the moment.

The door to the pilgrim office opens.

"Here we go," Erika says. "Off to conquer the world!"

She raises her fist in a salute, and Jen, Joe, and I punch the air as well.

8

REINA

2024

I have my Camino passport, and I am ready to go. It was no small thing getting here—two flights, a bus, a train, and a taxi. But thirty-six hours after Liam dropped me at LaGuardia Airport, I'm here, standing on a cobbled street, looking through the stone archway of Saint James Gate that begins the journey into the Pyrenees.

I open my dad's journal to read the first entry. In honor of the idea of my dad and I walking the Camino together, I've decided to read the journal in lockstep with my own journey. That way I will experience it in my own way before being influenced by his words, and it will also be as if we are facing it for the first time together, a generation apart:

> The taxi dropped us at the foot of the bridge that leads across the River Nive as the sun was rising, and instantly I was in love. As Lao Tzu said, "The journey of a thousand miles starts with a single step." I suppose that is true of a pilgrimage of five hundred miles as well. Today, David and I set out from this stunning

village to climb the Pyrenees and trek in the footsteps of the countless others who came before us.

I'm so excited I bounce. I tuck the journal into my pack and shrug the pack onto my shoulders. It's barely past dawn, but already pilgrims funnel past, their excitement palpable, bright scallop shells swinging jauntily from their packs as they bound forward. The scallop is the symbol of the Camino and is featured on every trail marker, souvenir, and T-shirt.

"Buen Camino!" a friendly trekker says as he passes.

"Buen Camino!" I echo back gaily, feeling like a superhero.

I'm about to set off when my phone buzzes. I pull it out to see a text from John:

You're going to slay it babe. Good luck.

It's eight in the morning here, which means it's two in the morning in New York, and the fact that he stayed up or set an alarm to text me causes a well of affection. It's possible he feels bad for how he reacted when I told him I was doing this.

"You're what?" he said. "That's ridiculous. You don't hike."

"My dad did it," I responded weakly, self-doubt niggling. "And it's a chance to write a feature."

"But it's June. You'll miss your birthday, and our anniversary."

John is very big on holidays, birthdays, and anniversaries.

"We'll celebrate when I get back."

"It's not the same," he said, pouting.

"I promise I'll make it up to you," I said at the exact moment Liam and I arrived at my aunt's, so I said goodbye quickly and hung up.

I text back:

Thanks. Leaving now. I'll text soon.

I set off across the bridge. According to the Brierley guidebook, the undisputed reference for walking the Camino, the first leg of the thirty-three-leg journey is twenty-five kilometers. At ten kilometers, there is a refugio where pilgrims can stop for lunch. Last year, I ran a 5K Turkey Trot, which took about a half hour, so I figure this first leg won't be too bad. Accounting for carrying a pack and going uphill, I should reach the refugio in a couple of hours and finish the day in Roncesvalles, the town where the first leg ends, around two o'clock.

The pack tugs at my shoulders, and I try to tighten the hip strap to transfer some of the weight to my legs, but the buckle is calcified and won't budge. Giving up, I trek on.

I'm surprised how quickly I get winded. The high altitude makes it feel as if I'm sucking air through a straw, and now that the morning fog has worn off, the sun beats down relentlessly and it's very hot. Sweat trickles down my back, and I think how I should have thought to have worn a hat and should have put on sunscreen.

I squint up at the road in front of me. It winds upward through a smattering of small houses set back from the trail, and in the distance, as far as I can see, pilgrims trudge along it like ants. Some are alone, but most are in pairs or small groups.

Two cyclists struggle past, working hard to pedal up the hill.

"Buen Camino!" the one in the back wheezes.

"Buen Camino!" I gasp back.

I think of my dad and wonder if he was as breathless. Probably not. I never knew my dad to get tired, and he was a planner, so it's likely he trained before he came. He probably ran miles and did dozens of flights of stairs each day for months in preparation. My twice-a-week Pilates class definitely isn't cutting it.

A middle-aged couple saunter past, chatting in a language I don't recognize. They're at least twice my age, and I'm amazed how easily they amble along, like they're on a leisurely stroll through the countryside. They're outfitted to the nines with aluminum walking poles, high-tech hiking boots, and sleek purple hiking packs that look like they were designed by NASA, and I credit their impressive speed to the superiority of their gear.

I fix on the bright Barney color of the woman's pack and heave myself after her, determined to keep up. A goal that falls apart immediately.

For a bit, I tug the shoulder straps forward with my thumbs to relieve some of the pressure. When my forearms cramp, I lean forward so I'm bent over and walking like a zombie. Then, when my back starts to ache, I straighten, and the weight falls back to my shoulders.

Dozens of pilgrims pass me, each with a cheery "Buen Camino," and the couple is now so far ahead I can barely make out their purple packs. My T-shirt is soaked with sweat, my legs ache, and my Doc Martens are chewing painfully on the outside of both pinkie toes and the heel of my left foot.

I swear at the sun, at God, and at John Brierley who grossly understated the difficulty of this first leg, his phrase "undulating path" entirely inadequate for this relentless, torturous uphill slog.

Another group of bicyclists struggle by, weaving side to side to lessen the grade and wobbling to keep their balance. They look miserable. A man in the back, heavyset, lets out what sounds like a string of expletives in what I think is Chinese, then after two more grunt-filled pedals, gives up, climbs off, and pushes his bike up the hill.

I no longer look at the scenery. Eyes on the asphalt, I plod forward and, to distract myself from the pain, focus on Matt's indignation. His email arrived minutes after Brenda's:

> NO! Do not take me off this. I will walk two legs a day to catch up and will still make the deadline.

Fortunately, Brenda wasn't convinced. She didn't want *Journey*'s future left up to the capricious whim of the New York Passport Agency.

"Do you mind taking a photo?"

I look up to see a tall man with tight-cropped gray hair and a neatly trimmed goatee. The man beside him is the same height but three times as wide. His curly brown hair sticks up every which way around a large jowly face beaded with sweat. At first glance, they look nothing alike, but when they smile, their large, toothy grins are exactly the same, and I realize they must be brothers.

I take the man's iPhone and step back to take the photo as the two men pose, both bending and pointing to what I realize is a distance marker—a concrete obelisk with the ubiquitous Camino shell embossed on it and a yellow arrow pointing the way.

It's only after I snap the photo that I register the number engraved beneath the arrow: 796,0 km.

I tilt my head then look at the men. "How far have we gone?" I ask, certain the number must be wrong.

The man looks at his phone. "According to Wise Pilgrim, four kilometers."

Four kilometers!

"Are you sure?" I say, only hearing the outrage in my voice after the words have left my mouth.

He laughs. "Afraid so." He tucks the phone in his pocket.

I look at my own phone to see I've been hiking nearly two hours. Two hours, and I'm not even halfway to the rest area! Which is not even halfway to Roncesvalles!

"Certainly no stroll in the park," the brown-haired brother says.

"Certainly not," I agree.

The three of us start up the road together.

"Where are you from?" the brother with the goatee asks.

"New York."

"I'll try not to hold it against you."

I smile. "You?"

"Canada. Alberta. I'm Ted, and this is my brother Ned."

I lift a brow.

"Yep. We still haven't forgiven our parents for that."

Walking with company helps. Ted keeps the conversation going, while Ned and I grunt one-word responses. The brothers are here for Ned. At his annual checkup after his fiftieth birthday, his doctor told him, if he doesn't lose at least forty pounds, he likely won't make it to his sixtieth.

"What goes up must come down," Ned wheezes as we huff up a particularly steep stretch.

"Except the clouds, the moon, smoke, steam . . . your age," Ted says.

My laugh comes out a gasp, and Ned's comes out a groan. Ted doesn't seem nearly as affected. He is slender and refined, a shaken-not-stirred-martini sort of guy.

It's strange how the brothers fit their similar but different names. Ted looks a little like Ted Danson from *Cheers*, a debonair fox, and he's thoughtful and gracious like Theodore Roosevelt. While Ned is ruddy faced and round like Ned Beatty, and good natured and cheery as the Simpsons' next-door neighbor Ned Flanders.

"Buen Camino," a man who looks like Moses says easily as he walks past with a tall wooden staff, his long white hair and beard an odd contrast to his bright, modern hiking clothes and pack.

"Buen Camino," the three of us echo, and Ned grumbles, "Are you kidding me? That guy's got to be at least eighty."

After that, the chitchat stops, each of us intent on continuing to move forward. Ted and Ned use hiking sticks, and the steady rhythm of the clicks on the dirt is like a metronome I use to time my steps.

When I glance up, the lady from the purple-backpack couple is only a few meters away.

I give a petty cheer of triumph and, as we stagger past, chirp, "Buen Camino!" as if I'm fresh as a daisy.

She glances up but doesn't answer.

A dozen steps later, the incline eases slightly, and Ted belts out, "Oh what a beautiful morning, oh what a beautiful day!" as he spreads his arms wide and twirls in a circle.

Shockingly, Ned joins in, booming in a great big voice, "I've got a beautiful feeling, everything's going my way!"

Inspired, I join in, adding my raspy alto to their tenor–baritone mix. Aunt Robbie is a big show tune fan, so when Ted or Ned falter on the words, much to the brothers' delight, I carry us along.

Halfway through our third rendition, Ted exclaims "Hallelujah!" and I look up to see a stone building a hundred yards ahead with a large deck with tables and umbrellas to the left of it. The refugio of Orisson! We made it!

The three of us collapse onto one of the picnic tables, and I lay my head on my arms.

Ted pats my shoulder. "Good job, little buddy. Cerveza?"

I nod and start to push myself up, but he pushes me back down. "I've got it."

I put my head back on my arms. Ned is flopped in the exact same position across from me.

A few minutes later, Ted returns with a tray laden with three beers, three packages of OREOs, and three plates of tortilla—the delicious egg-and-potato pie I'd been researching for the magazine.

I grab the cookies.

"To almost making it halfway through day one!" Ted says, lifting his beer.

Ned and I glare.

"Fine," Ted says. "To sitting down and drinking."

"I'll toast to that!" I clink my cookie to his glass, then take a bite, and never has a cookie tasted so good.

"Not too shabby," Ned says, and I turn to look with him at the view.

My breath catches. Never have I seen anything so spectacular. The deck is built into the side of the mountain, so the three of us are literally sitting on the edge of a precipice that appears to descend into nothing. Stretched out before us is endless blue sky with wisps of clouds drifting across it, and far off and far below, peaks of mountains form a hazy, dreamlike horizon.

"Astounding," Ted says.

I agree, stunned I am here, in France, sitting on the edge of a mountain eating OREOs, so high up it's as if we've ascended above the earth. And I'm utterly amazed it was my two paltry legs that carried me here.

Around us, bedraggled, defeated-looking people slump, lean, and lie in various states of exhaustion. It's a motley mix. At the table behind us, Moses sits with three men equally as old. Resting against the wall of the refugio is a mother–daughter duo, their legs stuck out in front of them and their faces tilted toward the sun. The Asian bicyclists who passed me earlier are sprawled out on their stomachs in a row beside the deck like a line of corpses waiting to be claimed. And across from me, a woman complains in what sounds like French to the man she's with as she tends to her blistered feet. Gingerly she applies Neosporin on each tender, pulsing wound before patching it with a Band-Aid.

My own feet throb, but I don't dare take off my shoes, knowing to do so would risk never getting them back on. Each pinkie toe stings, though it's the rupture on my left heel that concerns me most. I'm fairly certain blood is oozing from it and soaking through my sock.

We finish our beers.

"Another?" Ted asks.

"My turn," I say.

He shakes his head. "Save your meager journalist stipend. I've got this. Consider it my donation to the arts."

He walks off before I can protest.

Ned pushes to his feet as well. "I see a couple friends from last night." He walks toward a pair of middle-aged women resting on a bench.

With both of them gone, I pull my dad's journal from the front pouch of the backpack and read the entry labeled, "Heaven, Vista in the Clouds."

> We've reached a glorious summit and sit on the
> edge of a mountain overlooking a panorama of peaks

straining for the clouds. Below us, verdant-green hills roll, specks of beige among them that I barely recognize as cows. It gives me the sense of being both insignificant and vital at once. At the exact moment I am wondering if this is heaven, I turn to catch the glimpse of an angel, her long copper hair glinting in the noon sun as she walks, carrying nothing but a water bottle, toward the trail.

9

ISABELLE

1997

"Are you kidding?" Erika exclaims almost angrily before plopping to the ground beside the post and dropping her face to her hands like a petulant child.

She reminds me a little of Gemma, though she's at least fifteen years older and far less curvy. But both possess ageless cuteness, which is somehow both bratty and endearing at once.

"Is math different in Spain?" Joe asks, looking at the offending distance marker.

The yellow arrow points down the trail, and the number reads, "4,1 km," which is point one kilometer more than the last distance marker we passed some time ago.

Jen sloughs off her pack, sits on it, then stretches out her left leg. Her knee started bothering her halfway up the trail, and I can see it's swollen.

Erika mutters unintelligibly into her hands, while Joe sits against the post with his feet stuck out in front of him and his eyes closed. His feet are enormous in proportion to his body, especially considering how skinny he is. Everything about him is lanky, loping, and wonderful.

"The good news is there's no more uphill," Dan says.

Dan and Emily, a father–daughter duo, joined us when we stopped to rest near a small Mother Mary statue a few meters off the trail.

"And the bad news?" Erika mumbles into her palms.

"Downhill is harder than up."

This is Dan's fourth Camino. Emily is getting married at the end of summer, and she wanted one last "hoorah" with her "Pops" before she walks down the aisle. I needed to ask the meaning of "hoorah," and when she told me, I found it fitting for a girl so bright. Because of Dan's extensive Camino experience, he is a fount of knowledge, and it's been wonderful having him along. Had he not been with us, I might not have realized I had crossed into Spain. The cattle grate that marks the border was completely unremarkable and easy to miss.

"Welcome to Spain," he said, when he and I, the fastest of the group, walked through the opening in the fence.

I stopped and craned my head back. "Really?" I said.

"Really." He nodded in front of us. "Spain." Then nodded behind us. "France."

I was so excited by the idea I returned to hop back and forth several times. Spain. France. Spain. France. Just like that, I'd left France behind and had entered another country altogether.

He and I sat down "in Spain" to wait for the others. Dan generously shared his dried apricots and peanuts, and I added him to the list of people I would thank at the end of the journey, a Camino tradition.

The others finally caught up, and they looked so exhausted it made me wonder why they were doing this when it seemed to make them so miserable. There's not a person from Dur who would even consider walking eight hundred kilometers across a country for no reason. And they certainly wouldn't spend money or take time off work for such a thing.

I thought about home a lot today. It was impossible not to when so much of the walk reminded me of Dur—the mountains, flowers, wild horses, and black-faced sheep. I'm having a hard time wrapping my head around the idea of never returning. When I fled, my only thought had been on protecting Xavier and Ana, but today, with endless hours of walking through this strangely familiar world, there was time to consider the rest of it—my ma, cousins, friends, Gemma—and the idea of never seeing any of them ever again is horribly distressing.

Innately, Dan seemed to understand, and he walked silently beside me as we forged ahead of the others, not pressing me, even when I cried.

"The Camino has absorbed many tears," he said at one point. "And it is a keeper of secrets."

It was the perfect thing to say, and I loved him for it. He wears a large silver cross around his neck and returns to the Camino whenever he feels his faith waning. He says the walk is restorative and his way of reconnecting with Jesus. I hope he's right. I could use a dose of renewed faith at the moment.

After the group had rested for several minutes, Dan said, "We need to keep moving or we won't make it to the woods that lead into Roncesvalles before dark."

Erika grumbled as she pushed exhaustedly to her feet.

"I could carry your pack," I offered.

She shook her head at the ground and mumbled, "It's a pilgrimage. You're supposed to carry your stuff."

I found the statement amusing.

"It's not funny," she huffed, again reminding me of Gemma.

Gemma hates being laughed at, though constantly she does funny things.

"It's part of it, carrying your belongings so you realize how little you need," she said.

"Really?" Dan said. "You think, a thousand years ago, when Saint James first walked this path, the Lord looked down and said, 'My children, if you follow in the footsteps of Saint James, your sins will be forgiven, but only if you carry your own flip-flops, hoodies, and Walkmans?'"

Joe chuckled and lifted an eyebrow. "He's got a point. I think God would be okay with you letting this little billy goat carry your load for a bit. As a matter of fact, I think he'd appreciate it."

Erika looked at Jen for her opinion. Though the two only met on the bus ride to St. Jean Pied de Port, it turned out they were both teachers from the same part of the United States, so they became fast friends. Jen is older, and Erika seems to look up to her like a big sister.

"Sounds like a good offer to me," Jen said.

So Erika handed me her pack, and I slung it on my shoulders, and Dan and I took off at our natural speedy clip while the others plodded behind.

We stopped when we reached the aberrant distance marker and waited.

I feel bad for Erika. She'd been so excited this morning at the pilgrim office and now seems utterly defeated. The others are struggling as well but have better attitudes. Joe appears to be sleeping, his body slumped with exhaustion but a content smile on his lips. Emily has her shoes off and is rubbing her toes, but she does it with gusto, like she's raring to put her boots back on and finish the day. Jen is rewrapping an Ace bandage around her swollen knee. She does it without complaint, and I sense her resolve.

Dan and I are unaffected. Dan is mountain man strong—stocky and fit with rawhide skin—and I sense he could walk endlessly for days. And I am Andorran and have been walking mountains like these since I could toddle. My only source of worry is my left sneaker. The leather upper has separated from the sole at the toe, and a small blister has formed on the edge of my pinkie toe from the rough edge.

"Upsy-daisy," Dan says. "We need to get a move on."

Emily pries on her hiking boots. Jen holds in a grimace as she stands and pulls on her pack. She cinches the hip strap, then holds out her hand to Erika. Erika has her hands to her face and looks at Jen's encouraging hand forlornly through her fingers and shakes her head.

"You've got this, E," Jen says. "Just a little farther. Remember how excited you were?"

"I must have been delusional," Erika says, but then drops her hands from her face and allows Jen to pull her up.

I gently kick the sole of Joe's boot to rouse him.

"Huh? What?" He startles, blinks, shakes his head. "Oh. Okay. Right. Tallyho."

He rolls to all fours like a dog, then awkwardly pushes to his feet.

"Onward!" He salutes the air with his fist.

Already, I've come to adore him. He's what my ma calls tot bé, which means all good and no bad. Walking the Camino has been his dream since he read about it ten years ago in a book called *The Pilgrimage*. He's been researching and saving since, and he knows all sorts of facts about the walk. Having him with us is like having a friendly, chatty encyclopedia along. I was surprised when he even knew the species of the enormous tan cows we passed, Aubrac cattle, the same breed my family has raised for centuries.

I lead the way into the woods, practically skipping down the path, excited by the prospect of a shower, meal, and cot. It's been three days since I fled from Pau and all those things I took for granted.

The path descends steeply into a dense forest of woods, and the temperature drops and the air grows thick with the deep scent of pine.

Realizing I can no longer hear Dan's walking stick, I stop. It's been difficult forcing myself to stay with the group. All day, my legs have wanted to go faster. But I really like these people, and it's nice not being alone.

Dan comes into view and waves his walking stick forward. "Go," he says. "We'll meet you at the monastery. Leave Erika's pack at the door so she'll have her passport."

I hesitate, but only for a second, my feet feeling like they have wings. Erika's enormous pack bounces against my back as I hurry down the trail, and I reach Roncesvalles, "valley of thorns," in minutes.

Shrouded in fog, the monastery is barely visible through the mist, and it makes me think of Camelot and King Arthur, like I'm a queen from a faraway land who has traveled a great distance to a castle.

I race up the stone ramp, drop the pack beside the entrance, and walk through the arch.

An old nun sits behind a table, a ledger in front of her.

She lifts her ancient face. "Passport," she says in Spanish.

I pull the white card from the back pocket of my jeans, and she opens it, stamps it, and writes the date beside the stamp.

"Eight hundred pesetas," she says, causing my heart to stop.

Noticing my stricken expression, she says, "Everyone is welcome, child, whether they can pay or not."

I drop my eyes and mutter a quiet "thank you."

"Find yourself a bed. Dinner is after mass."

I thank her again, then walk through a set of large doors into a room with at least a hundred beds. Over half of them are occupied with people sitting, sleeping, reading, or writing. I set my Evian bottle on one toward the back then return to the nun.

"If you tell me where the cleaning supplies are, I'd like to repay you."

The nun's rheumy blue eyes soften, and her thin lips curl. "You'll find a broom and mop beside the restrooms."

I offer a small bow, my pride restored.

I am finishing sweeping the entry hall when the others arrive.

"Billy Goat!" Jen cries and hugs me as if she hasn't seen me in years.

When she pulls away, I see tears in her eyes. Day one is done, and she made it.

All of us made it. Unbelievably I am here, safe in a monastery in Spain.

10

REINA

2024

Ned robustly belts out "Dancing Queen," as Ted and I, along with a dozen others, merrily sing along, melody and lyrics be damned.

A ruddy Scotlander named Gordon is the most entertaining. With gusto, he improvises "See that girl, watch her scream, kicking and dancing queen."

Gordon joined us in the courtyard in Roncesvalles. He stood beside Ted, Ned, and me, waiting as if he were part of our group, so we adopted him. His pack got lost on his flight, so he's walking with only a nylon shopping bag with a few things he bought at the train station.

We're nearly to our second destination, a town called Zubiri, and I am incredibly grateful for the singing distraction.

If not for Ted and Ned, I might not be here at all. I went to bed feeling utterly defeated and convinced I'd made a terrible mistake. Hiking the Pyrenees was no joke. Yesterday, it took nearly eleven hours for us to reach Roncesvalles, and we staggered into the monastery as the sun was setting. I barely had time to set my pack beside my assigned bed and rush to the last dinner seating.

An hour later, I crawled beneath the covers unshowered because I could not take another step. My phone informed me I had walked nearly 41,000 steps and climbed the equivalent of 423 flights of stairs. My ravaged feet and throbbing legs pulsed testimony to the feat, and I didn't know how I would possibly go on in the morning.

The whole night I tossed and turned, not sure what was worse, my disappointment in myself or my embarrassment. I'd barely survived the first day and hadn't written a word for the team. The hike was nothing but a hazy blur of exhaustion, and none of what I could recall would have been the least bit helpful for an issue on the Camino. I dreaded the email I needed to send Brenda, apologizing and telling her I couldn't do it.

Gordon belts out, "Anybody could feed that guy!"

I yawn mid-chorus.

Even had I not been stressed over the impending end of my fledgling journalist career, I doubt I would have slept. The albergue was enormous and packed to capacity. One hundred and eighty-three snoring, grumbling strangers slept in bunk beds around me. I have trouble sleeping with John—a single snoring, grumbling person who I know—beside me.

Ted and Ned opted to stay at the hotel beside the monastery. They are "glam-inoing," as Ted calls it—Camino-ing upscale.

At six thirty this morning, the lights flicked on, glaring incandescent overhead bulbs that caused a wave of groans. I pulled the covers over my head.

Five minutes later, the blanket was yanked down, and there were Ted and Ned. Ned had a coffee. Ted had a needle and thread.

"Is that to put me out of my misery," I asked, nodding to the needle.

"Death by a thousand pricks. It's a Catholic thing," Ted said. "They've got torture and self-flagellation down to an art. Now give me your mutilated feet."

I was about to tell them I was throwing in the towel, but they looked at me with such eagerness, like two Great Danes excited to go out and play, I couldn't bring myself to say it. Instead I took the coffee from Ned and pulled the blanket from my feet.

"Ouch," Ted said as Ned said, "Yowza!"

I nodded, and tears formed.

"You're okay, little buddy. The first day's the hardest."

I nodded again and took a sip of my coffee to swallow back the emotions.

"Good thing I'm a doctor," Ted said.

"I thought you were a computer scientist?"

"But I have a PhD."

I groaned.

"Okay, don't look."

Which of course, made me stare intently at what he was doing. My feet were bad. The balls of each sole had a golf-ball-size blister, the sides of my pinkie toes and the back of my heels were rubbed raw, and there were a dozen other blisters in miscellaneous places.

With great tenderness and care, Ted proceeded to thread the needle through each blister, causing a disgusting oozing of fluid. Once the thread was through both sides, he removed the needle and left the thread in place as a wick. He then carefully tied off the thread so it wouldn't pull out and slapped a Band-Aid over it. With each repulsive stitch, I loved him a little more. It's a special person who will tend to the stinky, oozing feet of someone they've known less than a day.

When he finished, bits of red thread and Band-Aids covered my feet, and my coffee was gone.

"Franken-feet!" Ned declared.

"On to Zubiri!" Ted said with a fist salute.

Which is why I'm still here, trudging along and singing with a dozen other revelers.

We're a motley crew from all over the globe. There is Gordon from Scotland, Ted and Ned from Canada, a pair of best friends from Sweden, a grandmother and grandson from Seattle, two Brazilian men, and me.

The threading helped enormously. Each step now only causes a tiny stinging zap rather than a pulse of intense crippling pain.

The most difficult part is starting after stopping. Whenever we rest—for coffee, lunch, a photo, a view—my feet take it as a miscue that we're done for the day and swell to twice their size. And when I force them back into service, it's like walking on shards of glass.

A lot of the trek today was on a narrow trail beside a wide, rambling creek. It was shaded and beautiful, and I liked the idea of knowing my footsteps were falling on the same hallowed ground my dad's had twenty-seven years before.

For breakfast, we stopped at a café with a piano Ernest Hemingway used to play. I drank my second cup of coffee, ate delicious tortilla, and imagined my dad playing "Chopsticks," the only song he knew.

That's where Ted, Ned, Gordon, and I met our new friends, and the ten of us have been together since.

"Zubiri!" Ted says, interrupting the song.

I look where he's looking to see a clump of white buildings with red tile roofs in the distance, and my heart quickens. I pull out my phone to check the time. It's only three fifteen, which means I might actually have time to write!

Our destination in sight, no one sings, and no one talks, determination and the thought of food, drinks, and showers propelling us forward, but like a cruel *Alice in Wonderland* trick, no matter how much we walk, the buildings never seem to get closer. And with each prolonged step, every ache and pain, blister, and sore muscle becomes more pronounced.

The eleven-year-old boy who is here with his grandmother skips ahead. Happily he plucks blackberries from a bush and pops them in his mouth, and I find myself hating him a little for his youth and boundless energy.

Finally we cross the bridge that marks the entrance to the town. A post with a dozen wooden arrows points to the various accommodations.

"We're this way," one of the Brazilian men says, and the two men take off left. They're staying at a private albergue with their own room.

The boy and his grandmother are staying at a hotel and walk the same direction.

The rest of us—Ted, Ned, Gordon, me, and the Swedish best friends—turn right for the municipal, the public albergue designated for pilgrims. We arrived so late in Roncesvalles last night that, much to Ted's chagrin, he wasn't able to get a reservation at the hotel here. Which means he and Ned are relegated to spending a night among the masses and to enjoying the true pilgrim experience.

The six of us weave our way through the cobblestone streets to a long, narrow, nondescript building that looks like it might have at one time been a stable.

A young woman at the desk lifts her head from her novel and in a cheerful British chirp says, "Sorry. All full up."

"Full up?" I parrot.

She nods, a polite smile on her face, looking at us as if she said something as trivial as "Sorry. We've run out of milk." Though that's not what she said. What she said is there is no room for us to sleep in this place we've walked over eight hours to reach.

Ted, the only nondelirious one among us, asks, "Do you know if somewhere else in town might have room?"

Yes! I think. We will stay at a private albergue, and I will write about adapting to the circumstances. I am giddy with the idea. A room to myself, a private shower, and peace and quiet to write.

"Afraid not. You picked a busy time to be trekking. Your best bet is to continue on to Larrasoaña."

Gordon, Ned, the Swedish women, and I groan in unison.

"How far's that?" Ted asks.

"Around another five clicks," the girl says.

Another five kilometers!

Ted, seeing my face, nudges my shoulder. "You've got this, little buddy. We'll grab a bite—"

"And a beer," Ned interjects.

"Two beers," Gordon says.

"And walk to Larrasoaña," Ted says. "The bright side is that's five less *clicks* we'll need to walk tomorrow."

I sigh heavily and nod. If the team is marching on, I will march with them.

The Swedish women—Ingrid and Bettina—shake their heads like we're nuts. In their fifties, they've been friends since they were children and are walking the Camino to reconnect. Turning to the girl, they ask her to call them a taxi, and I swoon with envy.

Ted, Ned, Gordon, and I walk to the bar down the street crowded with trek-weary pilgrims. While Ted gets us a round of beers, I use the bar's Wi-Fi to check my emails.

"No!" I say as I stare in disbelief at the screen. "No, no, no!"

"What?" Ned asks.

I don't answer, my eyes still on the message from Brenda sent two hours ago:

> Matt got his passport and is flying out tomorrow. He'll be a few days behind but is planning on hiking double time to catch up. The two of you can work together to inform the team, though only one of you will get the feature. May the best journalist win!

11

ISABELLE

1997

I am in the Church of Saint Peter in a town called Puente la Reina. I kneel in the front pew, praying for the souls of Miguel and Manuel. It's the first time I've allowed myself to fully think about their deaths. A choral group is practicing, and their harmonic voices echo off the walls of the empty stone nave.

I look at the Virgin Mother set in the ornate altar and think of Senora Sansas, mother of ten, now mother of eight, and of Miguel and Manuel's siblings, and of all the other people who loved them. Their deaths create a hole in so many lives.

Though Miguel and Manuel were twins, they were different as night and day. Miguel was soft spoken and shy. He collected things like feathers, rocks, and leaves. He excelled at school and liked to read. Before things got so bad between our families that we were forbidden to speak to one another, he and I would talk about books, and he would ask me about school in Pau, curious about what I was learning.

Manuel was the opposite. A jokester and an athlete, he was constantly in motion and smiling. The first crush I had was on Miguel, but it was Manuel who I kissed last summer on my way home from the soccer field.

I had gone back to get my sister's sweater, and he was still gathering the cones. Defiantly, we walked back toward town together. When we reached the old milking stable, we stopped. Manuel grinned and lifted a single eyebrow. I knew what he wanted, and it sent a thrilling buzz down my spine. Gemma had already kissed several boys, and I was curious. Plus, I rarely backed down from a dare.

It was awkward at first, neither of us certain where to put our hands. But once we got the hang of it, it was strange and wonderful and unlike anything I'd ever experienced. We tried several different ways of positioning our lips, and at one point, he tried to use his tongue, which cracked me up and then cracked him up. So we went back to smooshing our lips together.

When we heard his mother ringing the dinner bell, we stopped. He left first, and I left a few minutes after.

A single tear leaks from my eye, and I wipe it away with the back of my hand. Tomorrow, I will walk in the twins' honor and lay a cross on the trail for each of them. Over the past four days, I've passed many humble shrines—mounds of stones with stick crosses, hand-painted signs, dried flowers, necklaces, and piles of shells. For Manuel, I will leave a heart-shaped stone. For Miguel, I will leave a feather.

The singing stops, and the older man of the group gives notes to the others. He reminds me of my pa, assuming he's in charge simply because he's a man of a certain age. He comments on a young woman's posture, then tells an older woman, who had been singing beautifully, that she was off-key.

I remember, as a child, loving my pa's confidence. I thought he was the greatest man on earth and knew everything. He adored me back, his Petit Geni, and would brag to anyone who would listen that I was the smartest girl in Andorra.

Then he sent me to school, not realizing the knowledge he was sending me to learn to help him would turn out to be the thing that would also drive us apart. The more I learned, the more I realized how provincial and often ignorant his opinions were. Pa knew it and grew to resent me. He avoided me when I was home and never spoke about anything of meaning when I was around.

The choral group returns to their singing, and I return to my prayers.

Thank you, Lord, for keeping me safe and for guiding me to this sanctuary. And thank you for the gifts you have bestowed on me since I fled. Especially for the people you have put on my path—Joe, Jen, Erika, Dan, Emily, the woman at the boulangerie who gave me work, and the kind nun at Roncesvalles.

I woke the second morning of the Camino to a gift. Beside my bed sat a backpack, and inside was a rain slicker, a sweatshirt, two T-shirts, a pair of shorts, a baseball cap, a toothbrush, toothpaste, a small bottle of shampoo, and three pairs of socks. The note pinned to the top read:

From the lost and found. Buen Camino.

It is turning out that "the Camino provides" is true.

Please continue to watch over me and my family at home.

I slide from the pew, genuflect in the aisle, then turn for the door as two men walk through it. I recognize them from the pilgrim dinner in Zubiri.

"Hey, we know you," the taller one says.

Both are tan and lightly freckled with dark curly hair and striking blue eyes. The taller one is thinner with sharper features, and he is far bolder and louder than the other. During the meal, he made jokes, poked fun at the server, and shamelessly flirted with two women at his table, a pair of sisters at least twice his age. The other didn't say a word. Silently he ate, pausing every so often to lift the camera around his neck to snap a photo. At one point, I turned to find him pointing it at me. Caught, he blushed, dropped the camera, and returned to his soup.

I smile politely but remain quiet out of respect for the sacred space and the choral group who are still practicing.

The shy one, recognizing this, nudges his brother and says, "David, shh."

"Oh. Oops," David says in a loud whisper, causing me to smile again. His energy is like a Slinky, made to bounce and spring.

I walk past, thinking that's the end of it, but they turn and follow me out.

The day is stifling hot, and the town is quiet, still in the midst of siesta—the three-hour afternoon respite in which most Spaniards return to their homes to rest and wait out the hottest part of the day.

"Are you American?" David asks when we're outside.

"French," I lie. "You are American?"

"Guilty as charged," David says.

In the blazing light of the day, I see how truly striking his eyes are, the color of a robin's egg with dark denim at the edges.

"We were just going to get a beer and play some cards. Want to join us?"

I'm not surprised by the offer. The Camino is a very friendly place.

"Perhaps in a bit. I want to see the river."

Mostly my raw left pinkie toe would like to see the river. The slit in my shoe has become a great source of grief. The rough leather edge has worn a hole through my sock and now rubs directly on my toe. I'm hoping soaking my feet in the current will offer some relief.

I leave them with a polite smile and try not to limp.

I pick my way down the bank of the river, sit on a stone, and pull off my sneakers and socks. When I see the toe, I nearly start to cry. The skin is gone, and it's crusted black with blood. With a wince, I put my feet in the water, drop my head to my knees, and pray it's not infected. My Aunt Rosa, my ma's sister, is the only person in Dur with any medical experience. She served nearly ten years in the Andorran army as a nurse, and she has always said infection is the silent killer. While a bullet will kill you quicker, a speck of bacteria can be just as fatal. And I wonder if such a little thing as the stitching on my sneaker could be my undoing.

"Hello."

I crane my head back to see the quieter brother making his way down the bank with a small red bag in his hand.

"I thought you were going to the bar to play cards," I say.

He offers a shrug. "I noticed you were limping and thought maybe I could help." He lifts the red bag. I see the white cross on it, and I wonder if God was listening and has sent another miracle. "I'm Peter."

"Like the apostle," I say.

"Like the rabbit," he answers, causing me to laugh.

He smiles a wonky grin, higher on the left than the right, and I see that his eyes are the same remarkable blue as his brother's but softer, sky blue that darkens to indigo.

He slips off his rubber sandals and sticks his feet in the river beside mine.

"Bonne," he says, which means nice in French.

I ask him in French if he speaks French, and he blushes deeply and says only the tiniest bit. He took a semester in college. He also took a semester of Spanish. Neither stuck.

I notice he's older than I thought. His brother is so animated it made me think they were both young like Miguel and Manuel, but I see now Peter is probably in his mid-twenties.

He asks me questions, and mostly I lie. I tell him I'm on summer break from the Sorbonne, where I'm studying languages to be a translator. I say I'm an only child and that I came on the Camino to figure out if being a translator is what I really want to do. My passion has always been cooking, and my dream is to someday open a café.

He and David are from a small town in New York, and he came on the Camino to have an adventure with his brother. He wants to be a photojournalist but, at the moment, is working for his dad, building houses.

"I'm hoping the trip will give me some good shots to add to my portfolio, and maybe even a good story to go with it." He's about to say something more when someone says, "Enough flirting. It's time to eat."

We look up the bank to see David smirking down at us.

"Give us a minute," Peter says.

David wheels away.

"Let me look at your foot," Peter says.

I'm embarrassed but do as he asks, lifting it from the water and turning it to show him my pinkie toe.

"Ouch," he says as he takes my heel to examine the wound.

Using a tissue, gingerly he blots it dry, and deep heat rises in my cheeks at the odd intimacy of a stranger touching my bare foot. No one but my ma has ever done anything like that before.

"This is going to sting," he says as he pulls a small vial of iodine from the bag.

He dabs the toe, and I do my best to hold in the wince.

"Sorry."

"It's okay," I say, the pain quickly going away.

He pulls a yellow tube from the bag.

"What's that?" I ask.

"Neosporin. It helps prevent infection."

I smile, certain God had a hand in this, my prayer answered in such a timely and specific way.

He bandages the toe with gauze and tapes it to the toe beside it so it will not come undone. "That should do it," he says, admiring his work before setting my foot on the ground.

I reach for my socks, but he shakes his head, then reaches onto the bank and hands me his rubber sandals.

"I think your toe needs a rest from those sneakers." He nods to my offending shoes.

"But you need these," I say.

He stands and holds out his hand to pull me up. "All I need is for you to join me for dinner so we can continue our conversation."

I blush again and give him my hand, and as he takes it, a shudder runs through me similar to when I've hit my funny bone. My eyes snap to his to see a mirrored expression of surprise on his face.

Quickly he lets go, snatches my sneakers from the ground, and leads the way up the bank.

I follow, the strange sensation still buzzing in my veins.

12

REINA

2024

Puente la Reina. I stare at the sign that bears my name. REINA—queen, pure, wise, one of great power. *Ha!*

Never have I felt so unworthy. Day four of the journey, and I am hobbled and nearly broken. Wise would have been never sending that email to Brenda and putting myself in this situation. And now Matt is on my tail—Mr. Hiker, Backpacker, Adventurer.

May the best journalist win! All day, Brenda's words have played like a taunt in my head.

Ugh! Even with my head start, I feel like I don't stand a chance.

Feeling my dad frowning, I look up at the blazing blue sky.

Sorry, Pops. It's been a long day.

The albergue doesn't open for a few hours. Ted, Ned, and Gordon are at the bar. I will join them after I've written my update for the team.

Despite my ravaged feet and stress over Matt's impending arrival, today was a blast. Ted, Ned, Gordon, and I make an entertaining quartet that seems to draw people like a magnet. Today we hiked, ate, and chatted with just about everyone on the trail, meeting people from so many countries, I can't keep track of them all. It's amazing how everyone gets along, considering the only thing most of us have in common is a bizarre desire to abandon our lives and walk for a month across Spain.

I stop to take a photo of a one-eyed cat peering out from a ruined stone building. Every town has a host of stray dogs and cats wandering around. It's a happy place for the four legged. People set out bowls of food and water in front of shops and houses and cafés, and the animals roam where they please.

"Meow," I say in way of goodbye and continue to the river.

I set my pack on the grass and sit on a wide flat rock beneath an ancient tree bent over the water. I wonder how many other pilgrims have sat in this very same spot and if my mom and dad were among them. I was named for this town, so it must have been important. I wish I knew more about my mom. My aunt never met her. I was born and lived in Portugal, until my mom died when I was two. I should have asked my dad more about her, but of course at eight, I thought I had all the time in the world.

I remove my shoes and socks, then the dozen Band-Aids that riddle my feet. Turning my feet this way and that, I admire the progress of my calluses. Only a few pustules remain. The rest of the blisters have healed into crusty yellow leather patches, badges of honor that make me proud.

I set my feet in the icy water and pull a bag of Chips Ahoys from my pack. My eyes close as I bite into the cookie, a moment of pure bliss.

When the first cookie is gone, I open my dad's journal, excited to read what he wrote about the place that bears my name.

> We walked into the cathedral, and there she was, the copper-haired angel I've been glimpsing on the trail for days. She crossed herself in front of the altar, entirely unaware of her captivating beauty, which far surpassed the magnificent church or the Mother Mary before her.

I think of the cathedral I passed on the way to the river and make a mental note to go inside so I can imagine him seeing her there.

Huh?

I read the next words again:

> Her name is Joan, and she is from France. Like me, she is doing the Camino to figure out her path forward.

My mom's name was Isabelle, and she was from Portugal.

> Her dream is to someday own a café. "Food is love," she told me. "It nourishes and makes people happy. Is there anything better than that?" I'm not sure if my stomach or heart reacted more when she said it.
>
> Up close, she was even more captivating than from afar, her eyes a wondrous mix of green and brown, like they couldn't decide which to be. Her nose and cheeks were sprinkled with freckles, and a single dimple on her left cheek lit up when she smiled.
>
> We talked for an hour, and when I helped her to her feet, a jolt shot through me that momentarily stopped my heart, and now all I can think about is that moment and how I want to feel it again.

I shake my head. First because the entry is so sappy, and it's odd reading such crush-mush written by my dad. And second because the woman he's writing about isn't my mom. Which means, my dad was nothing more than a love-hungry boy who had a thing for girls with copper hair. It also means my name, which I've always loved because I believed it held romantic significance for my mom and dad, actually has nothing to do with them at all.

I read on.

Her sneakers have nearly come apart, and her toe was rubbed raw almost to the bone. I don't know where the next town is where there will be a store that sells shoes, so like any fool in love, I am off to do something foolish. Around me, everyone is asleep, the sun not yet up. But if I leave now and walk quickly, I can make it back to Pamplona around the time the shops open and then catch up with her and David in Estella. I only hope the bandage keeps her safe until then.

I blink in disbelief at the words. I am completely done in from today's hike, and the idea of my dad, on a fanciful whim, backtracking twenty-four kilometers over a literal mountain, then turning around and hiking forty-six kilometers back so he can buy a pair of shoes for a girl he only just met is astounding.

I pull my feet from the water and lie back with my arm over my eyes, tears forming hard behind the lids because that's who my dad was, a real-life superhero. Then he died. And no matter how much time passes, I can't get used to not having that in my life, a man who would hike over mountains for a stranger and who loved me more than anything else in the world.

"Hey."

I look up the bank to see Gordon silhouetted in the late-afternoon light.

"The albergue's open," he says.

I pull on my shoes, gather my things, and scrabble up the bank to join him. We walk past the church, and I glance through the open doors but don't go in, defiantly deciding I don't want to see the place where my dad met "Joan," a woman he believed was his true love, and who he ran a fool's errand for, and who obviously then went on to break my dad's young, heroic, foolhardy heart.

We're almost to the albergue when a hair-raising whistle stops me.

"Scooby-Dooby-Doo!" Gordon exclaims, recognizing the cartoon jingle.

I turn to see Matt standing in the street with a dozen other pilgrims, all young and beautiful, an entire crew of Freds and Daphnes.

"Hello, Velma," he says.

It's impressive that he's here. It means he hiked over ninety kilometers in two days.

"That's quite the fashion statement." He nods to my Doc Martens.

All the Camino Zen I've gained over the past four days evaporates.

"I see the muggers unfortunately didn't take your sparkling personality when they stole your passport," I say.

"At least they had the decency not to try to swipe my career."

I narrow my eyes at him, the hypocrisy rich. He was the one who sabotaged Karen and ripped the rug out from under her.

"Afraid of a little competition?" I say.

He guffaws. "Aw, Velma. That's cute, but I think the Spanish sun must be getting to you. You seem to be suffering from delusions of adequacy."

I flinch, the comment catching me off guard. While Matt and I have always bantered, the barbs have never been personal.

He seems to realize it as well, a flash of what looks like regret crossing his face.

Heart pounding, I pivot away and, fists clenched, continue toward the albergue.

"A friend of yours?" Gordon asks.

Behind us, one of the Daphnes asks with saccharine sweetness, "Who was that, Matteo?"

Matteo? Are you kidding me?

"No one," Matt says before raising his voice to add, "No one at all."

13

ISABELLE

1997

Joe bends to pick up a rock.

"Good one?" Jen asks.

He holds it out for us to see. It's too round on the bottom, making it more a blobby kidney shape than a heart. He tosses it into the field beside us. Since we started, Joe has been on the lookout for heart stones. He explained the stones are good omens, and that, if you find one, it means an angel is watching over you and that you're on the right path. He cautions it's important not to keep the stone for yourself. Within a day of finding it, you need to give it to someone who needs it more than you, which will ensure that your good luck will continue.

It's how Joe has come to be known as "Cupid of the Camino." Already he's given away dozens of hearts, each pilgrim he gives one to lighting up at the unexpected gift.

I keep the stone he gave me in the front pocket of my jeans. When he gave it to me on the first day, he said, "Now you'll be carrying more than just a water bottle." I no longer have the Evian water bottle, having found a larger bottle in Zubiri, but I will treasure the stone forever.

It's just the three of us now—me, Jen, and Joe.

Erika left us in Roncesvalles. She woke that second morning and declared, "This is *so* not fun. Love you guys, but I'm taking a bus to San Sebastián to have a real vacation, one with white sand beaches and cabana boys who bring me margaritas."

Dan and Emily separated from us in Pamplona. They are on a spiritual quest and therefore walking a different path, steering clear of the cities to spend more time at the churches and cathedrals in the villages.

This morning, the three of us got an early start. The albergue last night was horribly noisy and stinky. Between the snorers and the pilgrims unable to hold their bladders, it was impossible to sleep. It also seems several of our fellow hikers have decided to give up bathing and washing their clothes. At dawn, we looked at each other in the gray light and nodded in agreement that we might as well get up. Jen is certain sleep deprivation is going to be her doom.

I walk easily, enjoying the quiet, soulful morning and reflecting on my evening with Peter and our easy conversation. I was sad when the night ended, and we needed to go to our separate dorms. I didn't see him this morning and wonder if I might see him today on the trail.

The day is stunning and not yet hot. Around us, endless fields of wheat stretch to the horizon, the edges trimmed with wildflowers—red corn poppies, lilac heather, and delicate lemon sorrel. If my ma were here, she would gather the sorrel for her wonderful sorrel soup.

Home has not left my mind. I think about my family constantly and worry about Xavier and Ana. My fear for myself has ebbed some, now that I am five days out of France. While I imagine Senor Sansas and my pa are still looking for me, I cannot imagine that they have any idea where I am. The Camino is a wonderful place to hide. There are hundreds of pilgrims on the trail, and most of the journey is through remote, isolated towns with villagers who don't pay attention to the endless stream of strangers traipsing through.

My plan is to walk to Santiago de Compostela camouflaged among the pilgrims, and then to continue to the coast, where Joe says there is another trail that leads into Portugal. In Portugal, I will find a job and pray I'm far enough from Dur for no one to find me.

"Morning!"

I turn to see David, Peter's brother, jauntily walking toward us.

"Hello," Joe says, ambassador of our group.

"Mind if I join you?"

"Of course not."

"Morning, Joan," he says to me.

I watch as Jen's expression tightens, believing David is yet another young male pilgrim who is joining our group to flirt with me. While most people on the Camino are here for soulful or spiritual reasons, a fair share of young men seem to be doing it as a way to pick up women.

It's a bad plan, the odds not in their favor. The ratio of young men to young women seems somewhere around three to one; hence the reason I'm receiving so much attention. In Jen's age group, it's reversed. The women over forty greatly outnumber the men.

"Where's Peter?" I ask, hoping it sounds nonchalant.

It's embarrassing how much I've thought about him since last night. Which, of course, is ridiculous. The whole thing is nothing but a schoolyard crush with no possibility of going anywhere. He's from America. I'm going to Portugal. His life is normal. And I'm on the run for my life and can't even tell him my real name.

"He'll be along," David says with a twitchy grin that makes me curious. Everything about him is bouncy—the way he walks, talks, smiles. He is a very springy person.

Joe and Jen introduce themselves.

"Joe, Jen, and Joan," David says. "Three J's, like it was meant to be."

I smile, liking the idea, until I remember he's got it wrong. My name is Isabelle, which means we are not the three J's at all.

We walk along merrily, happier now that David is with us. And the farther we go, the more it becomes clear Jen was wrong about David's intentions. If he's interested in anyone, it's her. He's at least twenty years her junior, but that doesn't seem to bother him. He flirts openly, and she seems to be enjoying it, which makes me happy all the way to my toes.

Jen is walking the Camino because, six months ago, her jerk of a husband of eighteen years left her. She's forty-two and gave up her dream of having kids because he said he didn't want them. I think that is what's hurting her most. Yesterday, we walked through a village square teeming with children, and her eyes grew misty as she watched them.

Joe and I lag behind, giving her and David space.

We continue to search for heart stones. I bend down, pick up a stone that turns out to be a dud, and chuck it into the wheat field, then continue clopping along with the sole of my left sneaker slapping the dirt with each step. The sole is now detached halfway around, and I'm not sure what I'm going to do if it comes apart completely. My hope is that tonight's albergue might have some tape that I can use to hold the shoe together until I reach the city of Logroño, three days away.

While I hate the idea of leaving my friends, it's clear my shoes aren't going to make it to Santiago. So I will need to find a job in the city and work a bit until I've earned enough to buy a new pair.

Jen laughs at something David said, the sound bright as bells, and Joe and I look at each other and grin.

David is nothing like Peter. I watch as his hands move wildly with whatever tale he is telling. It makes me think of my sister, Ana, and how we look alike but couldn't be more different. She is serious and stubborn, while I'm a dreamer who loves to have fun. I miss her terribly and cannot believe I won't be there to see her grow up. Despite our differences, we were extraordinarily close.

"Look," Joe says, and I follow his finger to see a magnificent white stork wheeling above, its black and white wings long as my body.

Joe is fascinated by the magnificent birds and their enormous nests, which they build in the highest spots they can find—usually church towers, smokestacks, and turrets. The storks are rumored to bring babies to new parents, and everyone in Dur knows, if a woman wants a child, she should place sweets for the stork on her windowsill.

I look from the stork to Jen and imagine her returning to Nebraska and putting pies and cookies in her open window each night, and I pray the tradition works and that a stunning baby is delivered to her door.

We reach the village of Cirauqui, a beautiful hilltop town, and stop at a small café with a patio overlooking endless rolling vineyards. Joe gets his daily café con leche. Jen gets a lemon soda and a croissant. David feasts. He buys a chocolate croissant, a muffin, a banana, two hard-boiled eggs, an orange juice, and a coffee. I pull my water bottle from my pack and try not to stare enviously at the chocolate croissant. I've been surviving on the meager pilgrim dinners and the biscuits some of the albergues offer in the morning.

"You okay?"

"Huh?" I look at David and realize I'm staring at his croissant.

I look away and take a sip of my water.

"You want some?" he asks.

"No. Thanks. I'm not hungry."

He shrugs then breaks off pieces and feeds them to some scavenging pigeons. I watch, my stomach growling savagely.

"I vote for a siesta," Joe says with a nod to a grassy knoll beside a church with olive trees spaced every few yards.

"I second the vote," Jen says. "That looks like a much nicer place to sleep than whatever albergue we're heading toward."

I'm not accustomed to sleeping during the day, so when David says, "Fine. You two nap while I teach our young friend here how to play Frisbee," I nod eagerly.

Frisbee. It's a word I don't know but it sounds delightful.

~

Eight of us throw the red disk, and we've made a competition of it. The game is called Ultimate Frisbee, and it's a blast. David is very good, but he says I'm the team's secret weapon because no one expects me to be so fast. I'm terrible at throwing but good at running and catching. It's very frustrating for the four Australians we're playing against.

"Everyone run into the end zone," David says to our small huddle.

Our two teammates are a pair of best friends from Germany who barely speak a word of English. I help by translating what David says into German. They bob their heads and grin. If we score, we win. If we don't, we lose.

"Go!" David says, and we take off in the direction of the two olive trees designated as the end zone. I'm halfway there when the sole of my sneaker catches on the grass, and I go sprawling.

David reaches me first, the Frisbee still in his hand. My face flames with embarrassment as my knee flames with pain.

"Sorry," I say, hating that I interrupted the game and caused our team to lose.

One of the Australians, a man named Oliver, squats beside me. "Let me have a look," he says. "I'm a paramedic."

Joe and Jen stand a few feet away, fretful looks on their faces. Joe holds his water bottle toward the man.

"Thanks, mate."

I wince as he pours water over a hole in my jeans and the scrape on my knee.

"You'll live," he says, "and be back to outrunning us in no time."

He holds out his hand to help me up.

Noticing my sneakers, the left one now completely separated from its sole, he adds, "The real casualty are your runners."

"I think I might be able to help with that."

All of us turn to see Peter striding our way. He drops his pack to the grass, opens the flap, and pulls out a brand-new pair of blue-and-gray hiking boots.

Quiet, so no one hears but me, Jen says, "It looks like Cinderella might have just found her prince."

14

REINA

2024

I'm in the city of Logroño, enjoying a lemon soda on the plaza while scrolling through the photos Liam sent this morning.
   Liam wrote:

> I hope you're slaying it. I've got skin in the game, taking odds on Team Reina. I hope the photos help.

   I appreciate Liam betting on me, though I'm sure he's the only one. I'd like to say Matt's . . . *Matteo's* . . . comments in Puente la Reina didn't get to me, but they did. Captain America versus Pinocchio, I feel like in impostor who doesn't stand a chance.
   It would be one thing if Matt wasn't talented, but that's simply not the case. While I don't appreciate how he got to where he is, stealing an old woman's story and hijacking her career, I can't deny he's a very good journalist. I've copyedited several of his pieces, and all of them have been smart, witty, and insightful. His style is relatable and has an aw-shucks charm entirely unlike his personality in life. Which means, unless I figure out some remarkable angle, he's got this in the bag.

Looking at the photos feels strange, like I'm a time-traveling voyeur. The images are chronological, and some of the shots are remarkably similar to ones I've taken in the very same spots. The view from the refugio in Orisson on the first day is nearly identical, right down to the gauzy blue sky. The Roncesvalles monastery hasn't changed, and neither has the cattle gate that delineates France from Spain. Even the people seem familiar—the same smiles, exhausted postures, and mocking heroic poses.

There's a shot of the bullring in Pamplona, followed by a stunning photo of the church in Puente la Reina.

I stop cold on the next photo, then zoom in close.

The girl is young, barely older than a teenager. She sits on a grassy hill with olive trees behind her, and everything is muted except the bright sky-blue hiking boots with red shoelaces that she is modeling for the camera. Her hair is the deep copper of old pennies, and her eyes the exact moss green of my own.

I look at the back of my dad's journal, where he logged each shot.

Joan modeling her new kicks.

Joan *is* my mom. And the hiking boots *were* for her.

It makes no sense. Was my mom's name actually Joan? And is it possible she was originally from France?

The single photo I have of my mom, which is the one my dad kept in his wallet, is of a pensive young woman deep in thought, and because of that I've always thought of my mom as serious. But in the moment on the screen, she is laughing, flirting with the camera, her head inclined as she gazes mischievously up at the lens. Her feet are angled to show off the boots, and her long legs are cocked to the left. And while she is still magnificently beautiful, she is also cute and playful and fun, an impish flare of whimsy on her face, which stuns me because it's the exact expression I've seen in photos of myself.

The next photo is a group shot. My dad stands beside my Uncle David, his arm slung over his shoulder. A solidly built woman with bright blond hair with a streak of purple in the bangs is on my dad's right, giving two thumbs-ups. A thin man with wire-rimmed glasses and a Milwaukee Brewers baseball hat is on Uncle David's left. My mom stands beside him with her elbow on his shoulder as if using him as a post.

I look at the photo log in the back of the journal:

> Me and the gang in Cirauqui—Jen, me, David, Joe, and Joan

I run my fingers over the names, happy and sad at once. In the photo, they were all so young, and now, at least two are dead, and we haven't heard from my uncle in more than seventeen years.

A few shots into the second roll, I'm stunned again when I see my dad's left arm in a cast. It's sky blue, and he holds it up for the camera as if showing it off.

I stop clicking, knowing I'm getting ahead of myself and not wanting to see what I haven't yet discovered on the trail.

My phone pings with a text from John. A kissy face and two thumbs-ups.

I heart the message and send a kissy face back.

I need to call him. It's been a week, and with the time difference and how busy I've been, I haven't made the time. There's a surprising amount to take care of each day when I get to the albergue. I need to register, get my stamp, shower, do my laundry, and type up my notes for the team. By the time I'm done, it's usually time to meet the others for drinks and then dinner.

Today is Saturday, so I'll call him after I've checked into the albergue, showered, and done my laundry, and before I meet my friends.

It's odd how little I've thought about him since I left. It's as if being on the Camino has transported me away from that world entirely. Each day, I send a group text to John, Aunt Robbie, Liam, and Jake with a brief update and a few photos, but New York and that world feel very far away.

I lean back in my chair, take a sip of my soda, and soak in the scene around me. My dad was here, and so was my mom. It's possible they sat at this very café, possibly sipping lemon sodas and watching the activity around them.

There's something magical about a village plaza in Spain. It's a place where everyone gathers—young, old, couples, friends, musicians, peddlers. There are a surprising number of older people. Some are hobbled and many are crooked, but none of them are alone.

It makes me think of my grandmother and how sad she was almost the whole time I knew her. She'd lost her husband, her sons, and most of her friends. She rarely left the house. She would say she had no place to go.

But here in Spain, old people are still part of things. They know one another, and I imagine they have since childhood, when they came to this same dusty square to play while their grandmothers and grandfathers watched exactly as they do now.

A boy chases an errant soccer ball heading my way, and I leap up and stop it before it hits the table. Nimbly, I kick it back.

"Gracias," the boy says and returns to his game.

I smile as a memory of playing soccer as a girl flashes in my mind. It must have been before my dad died because Uncle David was there. He was playing goalie as I kicked ball after ball and he pretended to miss blocking them. It's been a long time since I've thought of my uncle, the photos stirring up memories and feelings I haven't had in years.

With a deep sigh, I pack up my belongings and head back to the albergue, my mood murky. My dad's been gone from my life far longer than he was in it, but the loss I feel at moments, especially on this trip, is sharp as the day I discovered he was gone.

"You're in the annex," the girl at the check-in desk says. "Outside. Take a right. Three buildings down. Blue door."

When I checked in earlier, it was still too early to claim a bed, and now I regret not waiting for the albergue to open so I could be in the main building. Rookie mistake. In the cities, the municipals get crowded, so you need to be proactive.

I shuffle out the door and follow her directions to a derelict looking building with a peeling blue door.

I slough off my Docs in the entry and groan when I set them on the rack and see Matt's dusty Timberland boots front and center.

I carry my pack into the dorm. There are four sets of bunk beds, all of them taken except for the top bunk beside the bathroom.

Matt sits on the bunk closest to the door, his arm slung over the shoulders of a leggy blonde named Nicole.

Nicole wears leggings and a crop top, and she looks like she just stepped out of a salon. She's what Ned calls a "little backpack person" or "LBP." Each day, she pays to send her enormous pack ahead and only carries a daypack on the trail. This allows her to have a vast wardrobe, blow-dryer, curling iron, and full array of makeup. Ned tried befriending her the second day, but after three minutes of walking with us, she feigned having a stone in her shoe and told us to go on without her. We didn't see her again until four days ago when she showed up with Matt.

"Look who finally made it," Matt says chipperly.

In the other beds are the friends he's been hiking with since he caught up with me in Puente la Reina.

Ignoring him, I dump my pack beside my bunk, rummage through it for my shampoo and a change of clothes, then head to the washroom to clean up and do my laundry. After hanging my clothes on the small patio in the back, I hurry off to meet Ted and Ned for dinner.

It's only as I pull open the door to the restaurant that I realize I forgot to call John.

Ted treated me to dinner at a charming Michelin-star restaurant that might have had the best ravioli I've ever tasted. When we finished, I vowed to someday pay him back by cooking for him and Ned. They were genuinely excited and made me shake on it.

I walk into the albergue a few minutes before lights-out and hurry to the bathroom to brush my teeth. When I'm done, I rush into the tiny kitchen–lounge for the Wi-Fi password so I can finish my update and upload it to the portal.

The password isn't on the corkboard.

"Lights out," a voice calls followed by the sound of the front door clicking closed. The door is now locked from the outside, and it's a strict rule that no one is allowed in once an albergue is locked down for the night.

My nerves prickle as I walk back into the dorm.

"Matt, do you have the Wi-Fi password?" I ask, knowing the answer even as I ask the question.

"I don't," he says brightly.

The setup is so obvious. He asked the hosteler to put me in the annex with him and his friends, and he took down the password and told his friends not to share it with me.

It's Saturday, the end of week one. The *Journey* coordinator is waiting for my update so he can send the final instructions for the week to the supplemental content team so they'll be ready to go on Monday. Sundays, the team is off. Which means, even if I send the report tomorrow, my input on this wonderful and important leg won't arrive in time to inform the issue.

"Goodnight, Velma," Matt says. "Isn't it nice that tomorrow's a rest day?"

I seethe as I climb into my bunk.

Loudly Nicole says, "Matteo, how's *your* article coming along on the issue *you* came up with and that *you've* been researching for months?"

"Fine, Nicole. It's coming along just fine," Matt answers. "Thanks for asking."

I stare at the ceiling, fuming. It's rich, him having a problem with me jumping at the opportunity to cover this story, when what he did to Karen was so much worse. Karen didn't lose her passport. Karen simply got sick.

I swipe angrily at the tears on my cheeks and think how badly I want to beat him, for me and for Karen. I just need to figure out a way to do it.

15

ISABELLE

1997

Logroño is a lively place. We arrived during a festival, and everywhere people fill the streets, drinking, playing music, talking, and dancing.

"This is more like it," David says and bumps shoulders with Jen. "Ready for me to show you my moves?"

The Camino-mance between them is growing, and it's entertaining and sweet to watch. Constantly David shows off for Jen and showers her with compliments, and she pretends to be embarrassed and tells him to stop, but it's obvious that David is the best thing that could have happened to her. It's like something has broken loose inside her, the storm cloud of her husband's abandonment swept away by the sweet attention of another. And for three days, she has been shining bright as the sun.

"You know, I've got some moves of my own," she says with a playful arch of her brows.

David jumps with excitement. He is a very jumpy person.

We're seven days into the walk, and Camino romances are popping up everywhere. I don't know if it's some sort of magic of the Way or simply human nature. It could be that, whenever people are thrown together for long spells of monotonous physical activity such as walking, it creates a sort of animal magnetism that causes relationships to form.

Peter and I are squarely in the magic category, this thing between us mystical and powerful, like I'm caught in a fast-flowing current heading for a waterfall, and there's absolutely nothing I can do about it.

Since he showed up with my beautiful new hiking boots, we've been inseparable. For two glorious days, we've walked and talked and found out everything there is to know about each other.

He is very passionate about photography, and I love how he sees the beauty in the mundane—a dandelion, a stork's nest, a late-afternoon shadow. And he is curious. He wants to know everything about the languages I speak and the food I like to cook. I tell him the truth when I can and avoid talking about things that would require me to lie.

I understand nothing can come of this relationship. He's twenty-five. I'm only seventeen. In just over three weeks, he will return to America, and God willing, I will be on my way to Portugal. He wants to be a photojournalist who travels the world. My only hope is to find a place deep in the shadows where I can stay out of sight.

He has yet to kiss me or even take my hand. Perhaps he realizes it as well, all the sensible reasons we should not be together.

And yet, it is amazing how little all those very sound reasons do not stop me from thinking of him in that way. As we walk, my blue-and-gray hiking boots kicking out in front of me, the thought of kissing him pulses with incandescent brightness, obliterating all the reasonableness in my head.

"There it is," Joe says, interrupting the thought, "home sweet home."

In front of us is a two-story pink-and-gray house that looks like it might have at one time been a mansion.

"I'm going to find a church," I say quickly. "I'll catch up with you all in a bit."

"I can go with you," Peter volunteers.

I smile sweetly before lying, "I want to say a prayer for my family. It's better if I go alone."

"I'll save you a bed."

"Thanks," I say brightly, then veer off down the street.

Each day it grows more difficult to avoid checking into the albergues at the same time as my friends. The first few days, it was easy because I walk so much faster than Jen and Joe. But now that Peter and David are with us, if I took off ahead with the excuse of wanting to save us good beds, Peter would insist on going with me and would easily keep up. Yesterday, I said I needed to run back to the market to buy shampoo. Today, I'm saying I need to pray. Tomorrow I will need to come up with a new excuse. If they discover I have no money, things will become awkward. They will insist on paying for me, and I will repeatedly refuse, which will make things very uncomfortable.

The problem is, Peter is not stupid, and he is going to catch on eventually.

I also can't continue on like this. I am literally starving, which means I need to make some money. Which I was supposed to do here in Logroño. Which means saying goodbye to my friends . . . and Peter. Which I really don't want to do.

The Concatedral de Santa María de la Redonda is a beautiful cathedral with two stunning bell towers. I walk inside and join the dozen others already in the pews. For a long time I sit staring at the altar, hoping God will send me a message and tell me what to do.

When the bells chime the hour, with no great epiphany, I cross myself and walk back into the daylight and then to the albergue.

The hosteler is a ragged man in his thirties with an Eastern European accent. He smells like cigarettes and stale sweat. He harrumphs when I tell him I have no money, then begrudgingly signs me in and stamps my passport.

He looks like an indigent pilgrim. We've met several over the past week—usually young men who walk Caminos endlessly and make ends meet by working at the albergues, busking for tips with guitars, or panhandling.

"Is there perhaps some work I can do here at the albergue to earn some money?" I ask, figuring he might be sympathetic to my need.

He sizes me up before saying, "In the morning, you can clean the bathrooms and showers. I'll give you fifteen hundred pesetas."

"Thank you," I say, feeling low as a beggar pleading for scraps, and I know this is God's way of giving me my answer. I cannot continue like this. In the morning, I need to say goodbye to my friends and to Peter and get a job to earn some money.

16

REINA

2024

This morning I woke to the Wi-Fi sign back in its place. Not that it mattered; I had already missed the deadline.

I sit at a café sipping my café con leche, looking again at the plaza. It's Sunday, and the square is particularly busy. People are out in their church clothes. Fathers kick soccer balls to their sons. Teenagers lounge about, listening to music and looking at their phones. Young couples push babies in strollers. Lovers smooch. And pilgrims eat and drink, conspicuous in their socked, sandaled feet.

Upset as I was last night, this morning I am the opposite. It is a day of rest, and I am content in a way I can't recall.

Languid, I think.

I've always liked that word for the way it sounds exactly like what it is—relaxed, dreamy, lethargic—at ease in the best possible way.

The way I see it, I have two distinct advantages over Matt, and I intend to use them to beat him. His low-down shenanigan last night fueled my fire, and it made me realize what I need to do. It's like Karen said, *Find your voice, and people will listen.*

The first advantage I have is my story is more relatable. Matt is only walking with the young, pretty people, and his group is treating the experience more like a monthlong rave than any sort of spiritual journey. Ask Nicole or any of the others in his group about their experience so far, and I'm sure they'd talk about the cities—Pamplona and Logroño. The hiking is what they do to get to the next big destination and perhaps to achieve their daily steps so they can drink as much beer and sangria as they want. From what I can tell, there's not a whole lot of introspection and very little desire to mingle outside their group.

My experience has been entirely different. In large part, thanks to Ted and Ned, goodwill ambassadors of the Camino, each day I've met dozens of people from all over the world, and I've listened to their stories and their reasons for being here.

Some are here to deal with loss. They carry ashes to sprinkle along the Way or are simply hoping to let go of their grief. They often walk alone or in pairs, and some attend evening mass each night in whatever village or city they happen to be in.

Others are at a crossroads. I've met pilgrims who have recently lost their jobs, are burned out, or are having marital problems. Yesterday, I met a thirty-five-year-old woman from Santa Cruz, California, who is trying to make the very important decision of whether to have children. The day before, I walked an hour with a twenty-one-year-old from England who is about to finish pilot's school but isn't sure he wants to be a pilot.

Ned is trying to lose weight. Ted is trying to save his brother's life. Gordon claims he is on the trip to "die a good death."

The average lifespan of men in his small Scottish village is fifty-four, and he's still chugging along at fifty-six. He's certain walking across Spain will be the end of him and is convinced it's a fine way to go—surrounded by nature, among people who hold no ill will toward him, and drinking and eating whatever he wants.

Each story has been a gift, a morsel to enrich the article I'm going to write, and I know Matt doesn't have that.

The other advantage I have is my mom and dad. This journey is deeply personal for me. I am literally walking in the footsteps of my dead parents, and with each step, their enchanting love story continues to unfold. I have my dad's journal along with his photographs, and I am reliving their experience while having an extraordinary experience of my own.

If I can figure out a way to capture that, it's going to be something remarkable. My dad's entry for Logroño stole my breath with its beauty:

> I believe the last time I was this happy was when I was a small child. I was standing on the shore watching my toes disappear in the sand as the ocean ran over my feet. I've never forgot that feeling, the moment when everything was right.

All I need is to find a way to express myself like that, to paint a picture with my words that allows the reader to feel like they are here, sipping the most delicious coffee in the world as the sun blazes down on a millennia-old cobblestoned square in a faraway city in Spain, muscles spent, mind at rest, and soul filled with a deep sense of satisfaction knowing I earned it—that seven days of walking over mountains and across endless broiling plains brought me to this single perfect moment of peace.

17

ISABELLE

1997

It's a little after eight thirty in the morning, and the last of the pilgrims have been forced out of the albergue, leaving me alone to clean. I decide to get the worst out of the way first and carry the cleaning supplies to the bathroom—two toilet stalls and two sinks—entirely inadequate for nearly sixty pilgrims. But I suppose that's what eight hundred pesetas gets you.

Peter was upset when he heard what I was doing. So was David. He even got angry.

"I asked if you were hungry," David snapped, running his hand through his hair. "You said no. I fed my food to the pigeons!"

I said nothing. My pa yells all the time. I'm used to waiting anger out. I will tell them about needing to stay in Logroño after breakfast; bad news is better received on a full stomach.

As I predicted, Peter said, "Let us pay for you."

I offered a small smile. "It's only cleaning. I've been doing that since I could walk. Go." I shooed them with the back of my hands. "I'll meet you at the café."

Reluctantly they left.

I'm hoping if I do a good job, the hosteler might let me do something else—wash sheets or sweep the dorm so I have a bit extra to tide me over while I look for work.

My ma taught me to clean up to down, so I start with the sinks. I pull the rubber gloves from the bucket as a sound causes me to turn.

"Hello," I say to the hosteler. "Do you need me to leave?" I assume he needs to do his business.

"I wouldn't be here if I wanted you to leave," he says.

I tilt my head, not understanding, but only for a second. My brain seizes, and my saliva turns to sawdust. I take a step back, and he steps toward me. I stumble up against the sink, and he seizes me by the biceps.

"Please," I croak, panic closing my throat.

"Begging for it. I like that."

I drive my knee up, and it catches him in the thigh, but it's a feeble blow and does nothing but enrage him. The slap comes out of nowhere, registering only after his knuckles have ripped across my cheek, and I am stumbling, my knees gone weak.

He throws me to the floor, and I claw and scratch, but he catches my wrists and pins them over my head. Holding them with one hand, his other fumbles with the button of my jeans.

"Please," I beg, panic flooding my brain. "Please, don't!"

He gets the button undone at the exact moment his weight is thrown off me.

I hear a crash and crane my head back to see Peter on the floor.

"Joan! Go!" he yells.

I hesitate, watching as the man smashes Peter's jaw with his fist.

"Peter!"

The man spins and bolts past me out the door.

I scrabble to my feet at the exact moment David races in, followed by Joe.

"Crap," David says, noticing my face, but then he sees Peter crumpled on the floor and hurries past.

Joe averts his eyes from my undone jeans.

My hands shake so bad I struggle to rebutton them.

"Let me see," Joe says softly and turns my chin gently to examine the pulsing welt on my cheek. I see the rage in his eyes, dark fierceness that doesn't belong on his kind face.

Jen appears, breathless. "I called the police," she says. "They're on their way."

The words register in slow motion. *Police. On. Their. Way.*

I glance at Peter who has staggered to his feet and now stands, bracing his arm, then I whirl and race for the door.

18

REINA

2024

The rest day in Logroño has done my body wonders. I woke up refreshed and almost eager to pull on my pack and get on the trail. Ted and Ned, in new clothes and with renewed spirits, met me in the square at dawn, and we set off on what promises to be one of the most grueling legs of the trip—twenty-nine kilometers and three hundred meters of ascent.

Gordon is with us as well. "Slow and steady gets the job done or will deliver a slow and painful death," he said in his lilting Scottish voice as we departed.

When I left, Matt and his cohort were still asleep in their bunks. They stumbled into the albergue loud and drunk minutes before lights-out, then spent two hours keeping me awake, passing flasks and doing other things I wish I wasn't privy to.

As we walk, I think about my dad's journal. He didn't write anything about Logroño after his entry about being as happy as he was as a boy. Based on the photos, I'm fairly sure Logroño is where he broke his arm, but there's no mention of it.

"Navarrete," Ned singsongs as our breakfast destination comes into view, a stunning hillside village golden in the morning sun and surrounded by rolling vineyards.

Ned is in a great mood. Like me, his blisters have healed, and he has found his physical groove. According to the scale in his hotel room, he's already lost eight pounds. A miracle, he says, especially since he's been eating whatever he wants, including OREOs, which he claims are the single source of all his extra poundage.

Ned used to be an athlete. All through high school and college, he played hockey, and Ted said he was excellent. He played center where his size was an advantage, and he got in the habit of eating to pack on pounds.

"I'm giving up the blue bags at the cross," he declared at lunch on our second day, then used his teeth to scrape off the creamy center of one of the felonious treats.

"The cross" is Cruz de Ferro, an iron cross on a tall wood post that marks the highest point on the Camino. It's where a lot of pilgrims make offerings and lay down their burdens.

According to Ted, OREOs have been scientifically proven to be more addictive than drugs, activating the same pleasure center as cocaine or morphine, which supposedly is why it's so hard to eat just one.

"It's true," Ned said, nodding vigorously after Ted told the story.

He held up an empty package as proof, the six cookies gone in the time it took Ted to explain their addictive quality.

"Which is why I need to give them up completely," he said forlornly, looking at the blue package as if mourning the departure of an old friend.

Now that we've been together for as long as we have, I see the competitor beneath the thick strata of weight. Ned is twice my age and at least three times my weight, and yet, step after step, he is climbing mountains with a pack on his back, determined to make it to the end. It's incredibly impressive, and, more than once, watching him lumber up a hill in front of me has given me strength to continue behind him.

As we wind our way into the village, silently I pray we'll find an open café. We've come to realize we can't count on the guidebook when it comes to food availability. It's only as accurate as its last printing. These small family establishments come and go, or sometimes they close to take a day off. Or there could be a festival or a holiday and the entire village is shut down.

We're nearly to the top of the knoll when we come upon a tiny café teeming with pilgrims. Ted and Ned know everyone, and within minutes I'm sitting at a table among several new friends.

As is our routine, I stay with the packs while Ted, Ned, and Gordon go inside to get the grub. While the Camino is mostly safe, stealing is not unheard of, and we keep our entire lives in our packs, so it's best not to take a chance. I always offer to pay, but Ted refuses, sticking with his line that this is his way of supporting the arts. I go along with it because I know it makes him happy. He has no children and refers to me as his Camino daughter. He is also "richer than rich," he says, though he made me promise not to tell.

I think it's obvious whether I spill the beans or not. Ted is the kind of guy who looks distinguished, even on the Camino. His clothes are perfectly fitted and impeccable. His hair and goatee are always neatly groomed. And he smells like expensive shampoo and aftershave. He oozes confidence; quotes poets and philosophers with ease; knows wine, books, and cheese; and can probably dance the waltz, play a mean game of chess, and recite *Hamlet* word for word. He reminds me of a professor I had at Columbia who taught American Literature in the Gilded Age, both of them throwbacks to the golden era of men like Andrew Carnegie and John Rockefeller.

The other reason I accept his generosity is Aunt Robbie. If I save most of my daily stipend, it will amount to a decent chunk of money, and I can either offer to fix the leaky roof in the kitchen or pay for Rex's cataract surgery so he doesn't end up blind in both eyes. Aunt Robbie won't want to accept my help, but I'm going to insist. She's carried the burden alone long enough. It's time we start dealing with things together. This trip is changing me. I feel it, the shedding of old skin and the growth of something new.

The three Brazilians I was chatting with when I sat down have left, and Ingrid and Bettina, the two Swedish best friends we walked with to Zubiri, have taken their place. They're telling me about the wonderful hotel they stayed at last night when Matt, Nicole, and another couple arrive.

"Velma," Matt says with a self-satisfied grin, still peacocking over his Wi-Fi prank.

I ignore him, though my blood boils.

The email I woke to from Brenda, which was addressed to both me and Matt, read:

> The team is working around the clock to get the interactive segments up and running for the issue's release. YOUR UPDATES NEED TO BE ON TIME!

I watch as he and his friends drop their packs beside the café in the shade then head inside to stand in the long line. I look at the packs, then at him, then again at the packs.

"Excuse me," I say to Ingrid and Bettina.

I pretend I'm going to the bathroom but instead continue around the building and squat out of sight beside Matt's pack. I unzip the rain-cover pouch at the bottom, pull out the cover, then scavenge around to grab every rock I can find and shove them one by one into the small compartment.

I'm surprised how many fit, and I smile with each granite nugget I deposit. When the pouch is full, I zip the pocket closed, jam the rain cover in the back of my waistband, pull my shirt over it, and hurry back to the table just as my glorious breakfast arrives—café con leche, a chocolate croissant, a slice of tortilla, an orange juice, and a banana.

"What are you grinning about?" Ted asks.

"It's just such a marvelous morning," I say. "Not a cloud in the sky and no rain in the forecast for days."

19

ISABELLE

1997

It is the dawn after what was almost the worst day of my life. Again and again I replay what happened, and despite knowing I escaped, the terror remains. Peter lies beside me with his left arm, the one with the cast, draped heavily over my hips. We are deep in a vineyard, hidden by the vines, a pale moon above us. David's sleeping bag is below us, while Peter's sleeping bag keeps us warm. At first, Peter laid the two bags beside each other, but after I startled awake for the third time in as many hours, I asked him to lie beside me so I would know he was there.

Shyly, he did as I asked, and now, several hours later, he still sleeps, while I lie awake replaying the past day and thinking about what it means for what comes next.

David was the one who found me after I fled. I was in the cathedral, kneeling on the hassock, my head bent and my hands clasped tight to stop their quake. The bells had beckoned me, clanging nine times as I raced from the albergue.

He sat beside me as I continued to kneel, not so much praying as trying to draw strength.

For a long time he was silent, giving me the time I needed.

Over the past week, a strange transformation has happened to David. Perhaps it has to do with Jen, or maybe it's a little because of me. But he's gone from a guy who could have cared less about the churches and cathedrals to someone profoundly affected by them. It's the only place he is still, like the agitation that incessantly drives him momentarily quiets in the hallowed spaces, and for a breath, he is at peace.

It's what I love about faith, how it touches everyone differently. David acts like a goofball without a care in the world, but it's a thin veneer. To me, he is like one of Peter Pan's lost boys, a man struggling to find a foothold in the adult world and searching for where he belongs.

"Is Peter okay?" I asked as I pushed back to sit on the pew. My voice sounded strange, tinny, as if it came from far away.

"Joe took him to the hospital. He hurt his arm when he hit the sink."

The words caused a fresh wave of distress, my shoulders hiccuping with tears I tried futilely to swallow.

David wrapped his arm around my shoulder. "He's okay. Just a bruised or busted arm. Not a big deal."

I shook my head because it was a big deal. Peter was hurt, and it was because of me.

"He asked me to find you, and I figured this might be where you would come."

I left him injured, and still his first thought was of me.

"How did you know I was in trouble?" I asked.

David blew out a breath. "We didn't. Pete hated that you were cleaning up after us while we were eating. And we all agreed, so we went back to help you."

I cried harder and felt bad for David, stuck there beside me.

"You're okay," David said.

He reached into his shorts and pulled out a navy blue bandanna. I blotted my face and sniffled back my sobs.

When several minutes passed, and finally I was in control, David said, "I need to check on him."

I nodded and held the bandanna out to him.

He shook his head. "You can give it to me when we get back." There was a challenge in the statement, the bandanna a contract that I would not flee without talking to Peter.

I nodded again and gripped the bandanna tight on my lap.

Satisfied, he left, leaving me in the pew with my head bent and my brain on fire.

A group of nuns arrived. Six of them. I watched as they crossed themselves and went through their daily rituals. It was calming, reminding me of school, the sisters, and Gemma. Gemma and I always sat together in church, from the time we were eight, a daily ritual we often mocked but, which it turned out, verse by verse, had built a certain sustaining mettle in my soul.

The nuns were finishing their prayers when Jen arrived. Thoughtfully, she had brought my backpack so I wouldn't need to go back to the albergue.

"Joe's at the café," she said, "and Peter and David are going to meet us there."

I followed her from the church to the same café we'd been supposed to meet at that morning after I finished cleaning. Joe had thoughtfully bought me a tea and a croissant, and I sipped the tea but had no appetite to eat.

"Did the police catch him?" I asked, my voice small.

"The way he bolted," Joe said, "I doubt it. I'm sure he's long gone."

The idea that the man was still out there, somewhere on the trail, was terrifying.

Joe, sensing it, said, "You're safe now. We won't leave you alone again."

Skinny and gentle as Joe was, there was valor and quiet, simmering rage behind the words.

Peter and David arrived an hour later, Peter with a bright-blue cast on his arm from his hand to his elbow, and seeing it nearly destroyed me.

Noticing, quickly he said, "It's nothing. Really. A hairline fracture. I'll be back to fumbling Frisbees in no time."

No one laughed.

"Can you give us a minute?" I said to the others.

Jen, Joe, and David grabbed their packs and headed across the square. Peter took the seat across from me.

His eyes fixed on my swollen cheek; mine fixed on the dark welt on his jaw.

"I never should have left you," he said, his voice trembling with rage.

The words caused me to come undone. My face dropped from his, and sobs racked my body as fear and love and hate tumbled into a frenzied, sickening brew.

Then he was kneeling in front of me, and I was in his arms, my tears soaking into his shirt.

"Oh, Joan," he said.

I shook my head against his shoulder and pushed away to put distance between us.

Eyes still cast down, I said, "My name isn't Joan." I blew out a trembling breath. "It's Isabelle."

When he didn't respond, I dared a glance at his face, expecting to see anger. Instead, I found only confusion and concern.

"My name is Isabelle Vidal, and I'm not from France. I'm from Andorra."

He sat back in his chair and waited.

I told him the rest, starting with the day Castor came to Dur with his proposal to build a ski resort and ending with the day my brother came to the school to bring me home.

As I told the story out loud, the whole thing sounded preposterous—two grown men feuding over a mountain; a pair of seventeen-year-old boys killed over a vote; a mob of money-hungry men hunting me like prey.

When I finished, without a drop of skepticism, he asked, "Are your brother and sister okay?"

"I think so," I answered. Then, determined not to lie again, I amended it to "I actually have no idea. Every day I pray, but I have no idea what's happening."

"Oh, Joan . . . I mean Isabelle." He reached over and took my hands. "We'll figure this out."

I snatched my hands back and stood.

"I felt I owed you the truth, that you deserved that. But now I need to go."

I lifted my pack and slung it onto my shoulder.

"No," he said and snatched the pack away with the hand not in the cast.

"Peter—"

"No," he repeated. "Stay here. I'll be right back."

To make sure I obeyed, he carried my pack with him as he crossed the square to where Jen, Joe, and David were sitting.

A moment later, he returned. He was carrying David's sleeping bag.

"Now *we* can go," he said.

I wanted to insist but knew it would do no good. Though Peter isn't anything like my pa, in that moment, I recognized the same stubborn, intractable determination. If I was going, he was going with me.

We walked until it was too dark to see, then made our way deep into a vineyard. We ate food Peter had bought on our way out of the city—cheese, crackers, apples, nuts, and salami. And after, we talked, and I told him the truth about everything—my life in Dur, school in France, Gemma, my family.

I cried so much my voice grew hoarse, a great expulsion of the grief and stress I'd been carrying since I fled.

When my eyes grew too heavy to keep open, he laid out the sleeping bags.

Before I climbed into mine, I said, "Thank you. What you did, running at that man like that, it was incredibly brave."

He lifted his cast in the moonlight. "Not much of a hero."

Less true words had never been spoken, and not realizing what I was going to do until I was already leaning in, I set my fingers gently on the bruise on his jaw and touched my lips to his.

When I pulled away, he smiled his crooked grin, held up his cast again, and said, "So is that all a guy needs to do to get a kiss?"

"That's it," I said, then I leaned in and kissed him again.

Now, hours later, the sky is lightening to dawn above me as I think and worry about what is to come. I have no money, and I'm terrified now to be on my own, knowing the man who attacked me is out there. But how can I allow Peter to continue on with me, knowing it cannot work out between us and could possibly put him in danger?

He stirs and, when he sees me, smiles. "Morning."

I lean down and kiss him lightly. "Morning."

"I could get used to this."

"Sleeping on the cold ground in someone else's vineyard?"

"You," he says. "Anywhere."

And with those simple words, I know I'm in trouble, my heart already surrendered to the amazing man beside me.

"I have an idea," he says.

I'm already shaking my head before he can tell me what it is, knowing whatever he's going to propose will be something heroic and noble that I can't accept.

"Hear me out."

I give him a look but keep my mouth shut.

"You need money, and I need help with an idea that I have." He lifts his cast. "Especially now that I've done this."

He says it like it's his fault, and I open my mouth to protest, but he puts his finger to his lips.

"Let me finish."

"Fine." I clamp my mouth shut.

"Since I started the Camino, I've been thinking how much we're missing and how confusing things have been. There are arrows to keep us from getting lost, but no real guidance. We hope for villages and cafés. We guess at the relevance of the sights we see."

"We have Joe," I say.

He nods. "Exactly. We have Joe. But most people don't have a Joe, and Joe doesn't know everything."

He's right. Joe knows the history and recognizes a lot of the landmarks and knows their significance, but he doesn't know the trail itself because he's never walked it. When Dan was with us, it was wonderful, like having an experienced trail guide showing us the way. He offered helpful tips and tricks he'd learned on his three previous Caminos that made the journey easier.

"So I'm thinking about writing a guidebook," Peter goes on. "But not just a how-to manual with a map. I want to create something that gives people more than just the basics. I want it to be entertaining and offer insight, to give the history and background for sure, but also anecdotes, jokes, stories, quotes—"

"The things in your journal," I say.

He smiles his wonky grin, his face lit up.

"The practical and the wondrous," I say excitedly.

"And I want to hire you to help."

My enthusiasm deflates.

"I don't want charity," I say.

"It's not charity. It's a job."

"You want to hire me, a person who knows nothing about the Camino and who has never walked it before?"

"Yes. You will be the documentarian and translator. You have an amazing memory, you're exceptionally organized, and you speak every language on the planet."

"I only speak six languages," I correct. "And three of them are very similar."

Catalan, Spanish, and Portuguese are close to one another, and most Andorrans speak those in addition to some French. English, every student at my school learned. And German was what my pa sent me to school to study. My language abilities are not as remarkable as he makes them sound.

"Yes. Six languages! So you will keep notes on the places we visit and translate any information the locals and non-English-speaking pilgrims tell us."

I squint mistrustingly, still not convinced this isn't just a sneaky way for him to give me money.

"I was thinking about asking you even before yesterday. Ask David. We talked about it after dinner in Puente la Reina." He raises his nonbroken hand with three fingers raised. "Scout's honor."

I have no idea what that means, but I believe it is like swearing on something important.

"I'm not good with details," he says, "but you are. I'll prove it. What was the name of the beautiful church we visited in Estella?"

"San Pedro de la Rúa," I say. It's an easy question. The church was one of my favorites, plus Pedro means Peter, so how could I possibly forget that?

"And what was the name of the winery with the wine fountain?"

"Bodegas Irache," I say. It means Angry Wineries, another name difficult to forget.

"I couldn't have remembered that in a million years. We're already eight days in, so we'll need to recount what we can from the places we've already been. But for the rest of the trip, we should keep notes, write down everything—the cafés, albergues, monasteries, points of interest, churches."

He is very excited, and I find myself caught up in it as well, the idea really very wonderful.

"I would be happy to help," I say.

"Perfect."

"But not for money."

"But you'll be working," he says.

"No. I'll be doing something I want to do to help a friend and for the adventure of it."

"I can't ask you to help and not compensate you."

"You're not asking. I'm offering."

He frowns. "No. Enough. I am doing this, and I want to pay for your services. You either accept that I'm paying you, or you can't be a part of it."

I laugh at him trying to be tough.

"I'm serious."

"I can tell," I say and giggle again.

"I have money," he goes on.

"I'll tell you what. I will help you, and in exchange, you will pay for my albergues and food. Anything beyond that, like my shoes, I will keep a tally of and someday pay you back."

"The shoes are a gift."

"Accept the deal, or find yourself another translator." I hold out my hand for us to shake on it.

He ignores my hand and kisses me instead.

When we break apart, he says, "Do you know what I'm thinking of calling it?"

"*Peter Rabbit's Guidebook to Hopping the Camino*?"

He laughs. "That's good, but I was thinking, *Wisdom of the Way*. What do you think?"

Wisdom of the Way, the name so beautiful I lean in and kiss him again.

Our bodies melt together, and as we continue to kiss, I think again of how much trouble I'm in, completely bewitched and with only twenty-four days left to break the spell.

20

REINA

2024

The rejuvenation of our rest day in Logroño was short-lived. I'm halfway through today's hike and on the verge of collapse. It's at least ninety-five degrees, the incline is endless, there's been no shade, and I am alone.

Ted, Ned, and Gordon left me after lunch. Gordon is waiting out the heat. He and most of the other pilgrims at the café where we had breakfast opted for a long siesta in the shade and then finishing the slog later this afternoon.

Ted and Ned chose to take a taxi to Nájera, today's destination. The downhill that comes after this incline posed too daunting a challenge for Ned, and Ted wants to conserve his energy for a side trek he intends to take this afternoon to a village called San Millán de la Cogolla. The remote town, eighteen kilometers from Nájera, has two monasteries and is supposedly the birthplace of written language. Ted minored in Latin and loves ancient texts and words, so the idea of seeing the place where it all started fascinates him.

The town is also home to a restaurant world renowned for their jarrete de jabalí, wild boar shank, and he offered to treat if I agreed to go with him.

"Experiences are better shared," he said when he asked this morning, a plea in his eyes that would have convinced me even without the bribe.

Of course, when I nodded enthusiastically, I was well rested, my blisters were healed, and I was feeling strong. Eighteen kilometers is a lot on top of the day's twenty-nine, but I liked the idea of challenging myself and seeing if I could do it.

But now, after four hours of heatstroke-inducing, thigh-crushing hiking, I am having second thoughts. I'm also in a bad headspace and afraid I will be bad company.

They say time heals all wounds, but I think people who say that have never experienced true, heartrending grief, the kind that eviscerates you so completely it leaves a vacuum in your soul. It's been seventeen years since my dad died, and today, the pain of losing him returned so sharply it was as if it was just yesterday that I was called into the principal's office to find Aunt Robbie waiting.

She did not tell me the news until we were in her apartment in Syracuse, a place I'd never been. She gave me a glass of lemonade at the dining room table. The wallpaper had blue stripes and floating beige leaves. She wore a Nirvana T-shirt with a smiley face that had x's for eyes, and her dark curls were bound up in a sloppy bun on top of her head.

I barely knew her. At the time, Aunt Robbie had a boyfriend no one in the family liked, so she rarely came to visit. And she and Uncle David didn't get along. I remember him saying she was bossy and didn't know how to mind her own business.

The boyfriend wasn't there that day. It was just the two of us, sitting across from each other. She started by telling me there'd been an accident. I thought she meant something had spilled. But then she said something about a bird flying into my dad's plane.

The next part I don't remember.

Sometimes bits and pieces from the days and weeks that followed come back to me. My grandmother holding my hand at the cemetery.

My aunt moving into my grandmother's house and the two of them bickering over where her bed should go. Walking off the soccer field in the middle of a game and telling the coach I never wanted to play again. Rex, the first time I saw him. His squirming puppy body and wet nose.

I know it took a long time for me to accept my dad was gone. I would sit in the living room, staring at the door, certain he and Uncle David were going to walk through at any moment and tell me they'd just been on one of their adventures.

Aunt Robbie took me to a psychiatrist. He said to give it time. He was right. Eventually I learned to accept the impossible truth. My dad was dead. Uncle David wasn't coming back.

I moved on. I made a life. I came to love Aunt Robbie. The two of us became a family.

I thought I'd put the worst of the pain behind me. But it turns out the Camino has no mercy and things you believed long buried have a way of resurfacing in the void of space that the walk inevitably brings. At home I am careful to keep myself busy. I work. I run errands. I cook. I work out. I meet up with friends. I read. I watch movies. But today. The hike was so hard and the time without distraction so great that, step by step, the carefully constructed walls I'd built around my grief crumbled, leaving me defenseless.

I stop to take a sip of water and look back at the great distance I've climbed. The trail is empty except for two pilgrim specks in the distance—fools like me, forging through the blistering afternoon heat. All the pilgrims with half a brain are back at the café. It's where I would be if I weren't going with Ted to the monasteries.

I put the water back in my back and continue up the hill. To distract myself, I focus on the pulse of pain in my left knee, the joint protesting more than the rest of me. When that no longer works, I break out in song—musicals, jingles, pop songs, the national anthem. And finally, when I run out of musical steam, I think about the mysterious entry my dad wrote about this leg of the journey.

> The only thing that trumps fear is regret. How different this glorious day would have been had I hesitated. The lesson: Stand up to what scares you and opportunities you never imagined possible will be revealed.

I assume it has to do with how he broke his arm, but he gives no details. He also now knows my mom is Isabelle, and it's clear that something has changed between them.

> We slept under the full moon, an enormous orb of reflected silver light, Bella in my arms. Her name means beautiful, and she is the embodiment of it. Though Joan is also fitting, a humble hero risking everything for the people she loves.

Seriously, how much more cryptic can you get? I know so little about my mom, and now I am terribly curious. I imagine my dad did something brave . . . or maybe it was my mom . . . or possibly it was both of them. Either way, I'm guessing it's what brought them together.

A sound breaks me from my reverie, and I stop to listen and realize someone in front of me is crying. I hurry as much as my swollen knee will allow up the remainder of the slope.

I reach the top and, for a moment, am stunned by the sweeping vista of vineyards and rolling hills below, but only for a second, another whimper snapping my attention back.

A hundred meters down, sticking into the scorching, rocky trail, I see a patch of blue. I hurry toward it as much as possible, but the trail is steep and treacherous, and several times I nearly lose my footing.

A girl sits on the dirt, her right leg hugged to her chest and her head on her knee.

"Are you okay?" I ask.

She looks up. Tears streak her dusty cheeks, and she says something in a language I don't understand. She is young, possibly still in her teens, with a round, flushed face and sweat-soaked brown hair.

I look at the leg she's hugging to see the knee is bloody and the ankle swollen above her boot.

"How long have you been here?" I ask.

She stares at me blankly.

I pull out my phone.

"No," she says and shakes her head, then points at the sky, and I'm pretty sure she's telling me there's no signal.

The sun on this side of the slope feels impossibly hotter, a spotlight of fire, and the girl looks like she is roasting. Below us, at least a kilometer away, I can just make out a thin strip of gray I believe is a road.

"Okay," I say. "I'm going to help you down the hill so we can get help."

I point and gesture, miming the words, and she nods and sniffles.

"What's your name?" I ask as I slough off my pack. I point to myself. "Reina."

"Petra."

"It's nice to meet you, Petra. We need to take off your pack." I point to her pack and mime my meaning again.

Panic flashes in her eyes. Our packs contain everything we own.

"I'll come back for it." I gesture walking down the hill, then walking up again and then once again walking down.

Bravely she nods and undoes her pack, and I set it beside my own.

I help her up, and she whimpers. I look again at the ankle, see the discoloration above her sock, and believe it might be broken.

She wraps her arm around my neck, and I wrap mine around her waist. She's about my height, short, but a good bit stockier, and this is definitely going to be a challenge.

Stand up to what scares you. My dad's words replay in my head.

Thanks, Pops. I'm seriously terrified. Happy?

"Okay. Nice and slow," I say, more for myself than Petra, since she obviously doesn't understand a word I'm saying.

I position myself so I'm slightly below her, and we shuffle-slide down the trail with her weight leaning into me. The trail is riddled with rocks, boulders, and deep fissures, and each requires careful consideration. We inch our way down, and with every step I'm incredibly grateful for my Doc Martens. While they might not be the best choice of hiking boots in terms of comfort, the gum rubber soles are what is saving us now.

We've made it perhaps halfway down when a wolf whistle causes me to stop and look back up the trail. Matt stands where we left our packs. His buddy from the café this morning is with him, but the girls are not.

"We've got your packs," he hollers.

I nod in appreciation, surprised how relieved I am to see him.

"You're doing great," I say, encouraging Petra as we continue to pick our way down.

"Hvala vam," she says, which I assume means thank you.

We're almost to the road when Matt and his friend catch up. Each carries a pack in front and another in back.

"Thanks," I say as I continue to help Petra along.

"I've got a bar of service," the man with Matt says. "I'll call for a taxi." He's big and young and has a heavy English brogue.

Together, he and Matt look a bit like Woody and Buzz Lightyear. Matt is dark, tall, and long limbed, and his buddy is blue-eyed, square jawed, and thickly muscled.

I help Petra sit on the gravel beside the road.

"Hvala vam," she says again.

Matt's friend says something in what I think is German.

Petra shakes her head, not understanding, then she says, "Croatia," which answers the question of where she's from. It also explains why we can't understand her.

"Are you here alone?" I ask, miming the question.

She holds up a single finger, then points to herself. Yes, she is alone.

She bites her bottom lip and looks like a terrified little girl, and I wonder what possessed her to set out alone on a pilgrimage across Spain without speaking a lick of Spanish or English.

Matt takes his water bottle from his pack and pours some of the precious liquid on the scrape on Petra's knee, washing away the embedded pebbles and dirt. Then he offers her the bottle, and she takes a thirsty gulp.

The taxi pulls up, and Matt helps Petra up.

I grab her pack and put it in the trunk as Matt supports her into the back seat.

He says something to the driver in Spanish, and I'm both impressed and galled to discover he's fluent.

Fresh tears run down Petra's cheeks.

"Would you like me to go with you?" I ask, bending down in the open door and pointing back and forth between me and the seat.

She nods, her eyes furrowed and pleading.

"Velma—" Matt starts.

"Do me a favor," I say, cutting him off, "when you get to Nájera, please tell Ted, he's the one with the goatee, I might be a little late."

I grab my pack, throw it into the trunk beside Petra's, and climb into the cab. We drive away, leaving Matt looking at me through the window, a strange expression on his face.

21

ISABELLE

1997

"Hold on," I say, releasing Peter's hand.

I open the notebook he bought for me and make a small circle on the line I've drawn to represent the road. Inside the circle, I write, "15," then turn to the next page to write down, "15. Fountain. Water is potable."

I love our shared mission of creating *Wisdom of the Way*. I have pages of notes from today's walk and wish I could rewalk the first days so I could be as detailed. Now that we're working on it, I see how helpful the guide will be. We walked today without passing a café or bar. It was hot, and we were out of water and very thirsty by the time we reached Nájera. It would have been nice to know what we were facing before leaving Logroño so we would have carried more water. I also heard about two monasteries near Nájera rumored to be where the first written language was created. And we only learned this because we happened to sit beside a Spanish professor at a café who was talking about it. I think it's something a lot of pilgrims might like to know.

I look up to see Peter slyly taking a photo of a man and woman leaning against each other beside the fountain. They're holding hands and look exhausted and utterly content—dazed, happy smiles on their faces.

This village might be my favorite so far. Nájera, it means "born," which is how it feels, a place of renewal and birth. As we walk, we pass couples strolling hand in hand, sitting in quiet conversation, and smooching on doorsteps. We're nine days into the journey, and Camino couples are forming everywhere. It's stunning how many pilgrims have paired up, the yellow arrow like Cupid's dart striking randomly and often.

We continue on, and I am happier than I think I've ever been. Because we slept in the vineyard, Peter and I walked alone today, and for four glorious hours, I got to see the whole of him—how he carefully avoided the snails making their own slow Caminos across the trail, his easy humor that's often at his own expense, his curiosity, and his passion. Several times, we stopped so he could shoot something with his camera, spending long, quiet minutes waiting for the wind to gust so he could capture the swaying wheat or for a butterfly to take flight from a poppy, his patience and stillness mesmerizing and beautiful. He listens more than he talks and happily acknowledges things he doesn't know. I've never met a man like him, and it's strange how comfortable I feel around him, not scared to give my opinion or to even poke fun at him if he does something funny.

The others—David, Jen, and Joe—will meet us here. Joe has a cell phone, so as soon as we got to town, Peter called him to tell him we were okay and that we were already in Nájera. I listened as he excitedly also told him I'd agreed to help with *Wisdom of the Way*, which convinced me that Peter hadn't made it up as a way to give me money.

We reach the plaza and see the familiar faces of many of our fellow pilgrims. A few wave. Others smile. We are a tribe of nomads traveling across the land, and our camaraderie grows the longer we are together, and with each day that passes, the less singular I feel and the more it feels like I am part of something greater than myself.

A couple from Spain notice our entwined hands, and the man gives a thumbs-up. His name is Carlos. His wife, Helena, waves us over.

Noticing Peter's cast, her head tilts in question.

"Angry nun," Peter says, causing her to laugh.

I'm grateful Peter made a joke and didn't tell the story. All day, I've worked hard not to think about it, and I definitely don't want to talk about it. Injuries are common on the Camino, so Peter having a cast isn't that great a surprise. But as Peter sits down, I watch as Helena takes in his bruised jaw, and then as she turns and sees my swollen cheek.

"That must have been one hell of an angry nun," she says.

"It was," Peter says, then levels his eyes on hers in a way that lets her know that's the end of the conversation.

I squeeze his hand beneath the table, and he offers a gentle squeeze back.

Carlos dumps his and Helena's water glasses in the planter beside him and fills them with sangria from the pitcher on the table. My ma is famous for her sangria. Her secret is that she adds a dash of brandy, green apples, and blueberries—a combination that tempers the sweetness and makes the drink deep, dark mulberry. She allowed me a taste each time she made a batch, and it's one of my favorite treats. This sangria isn't as good as hers but is still delicious, and after the restless sleep in the vineyard and long hike today, it's especially refreshing.

"Where's your brother?" Carlos asks Peter.

"He should be here soon."

As if the words were a wish, from an alley across the plaza, David and Jen appear. Their hair damp from recent showers, they stroll toward us. David's arm is slung over Jen's shoulder, and when Jen sees us, a blush rises in her cheeks.

"Where's Joe?" I ask when they reach us.

"At the albergue, writing notes," David says with an eye roll. "He's seriously into this idea of yours, Pete, and won't stop talking about it."

I imagine Joe yakking the entire walk, rambling on and on about all the things he thinks the guidebook should include. Ten years of studying has led to an enormous wealth of Camino knowledge, and at times it's as if all that information is literally bursting out of him.

"What idea?" Carlos asks.

Peter tells him and Helena about *Wisdom of the Way*, and they respond enthusiastically.

"You should publish it in Spanish as well," Helena says. "The Camino is very important to us. Most Spaniards walk at least some part of it at some point in their lives."

Carlos lifts his sangria. "To beginning, and to getting it done!"

I memorize the saying as I lift my glass so I can jot it down later in my notebook. *To beginning, and to getting it done.* It's a perfect catchphrase for each leg of the walk and for the Camino as a whole.

The six of us clink glasses, and before we take a sip, Carlos says, "Ultreia!"

Peter looks at me for translation. "Onward," I say.

"It's how pilgrims used to greet each other before 'Buen Camino' became popular," Carlos explains.

Peter pulls out his journal, asks for the spelling, and writes it down.

"Keep that open," Jen says, "I have something to add. We found out why the scallop shell is the symbol of the Camino."

Joe is obviously not the only one excited about *Wisdom of the Way*. The enthusiasm of everyone at the table is palpable, a united yearning for the idea to become real and for each of us to be a part of it.

"The story goes," Jen says, "that when the disciples were sailing with Saint James's remains to bring them to Santiago, they came upon a village that happened to be celebrating a wedding."

David jumps in excitedly. "The guests were playing a game where a man on a horse throws a spear then gallops as fast as he can to catch it before it hits the ground."

He grins like a kid, and I imagine he would very much like to try it. I see it in my mind, David as a young man in medieval times on a great white stallion, his black curls flying and his chest bare as he lets out a wild war cry and charges after a sailing spear.

"But the story is a love story, not a sports story," Jen says.

"It's kind of a sports story," David says, still grinning.

"When it was the groom's turn," Jen goes on, "the man hurled his spear at the exact moment a gust of wind blew across the field, catching hold of the spear and blowing it over the bluff. The groom, not wanting to disappoint his bride, valiantly galloped after it, charging straight off the cliff and into the sea."

"He didn't want to lose," David says.

Jen flicks an annoyed look at him, and he pecks her on the cheek.

"The villagers raced to the edge to find the groom and horse gone, drowned in the stormy, raging sea."

"But lucky for him," David chimes in, "at that exact moment, the boat that was carrying the remains of Saint James happened to be passing."

"Yes, very lucky for him and his bride," Jen says. "Because just as the wedding party was about to give up hope, the man and horse rose from the water—"

"Covered in scallop shells!" David says, stealing the punch line, but Jen doesn't seem to mind.

"So in memory of the miracle—"

"And the man's incredible sportsmanship," David interjects.

Jen mockingly punches him on the shoulder.

"Pilgrims carry scallop shells," she finishes.

Peter writes furiously in his journal to capture the tale as a gust of wind blows across the square, God acknowledging the legend and offering his encouragement.

22

REINA

2024

The bright side of going to the hospital with Petra was that I got to skip the last seven kilometers of the downhill hike into Nájera, and I walk into the albergue refreshed. I set my pack on a bunk and go to the kitchen, where I find Ted, Ned, and Matt at the table, laughing like old friends.

"Florence Nightingale returns!" Ned says.

"More like Dr. Quartz," I say, "but here I am."

"*The Flintstones!*" Matt exclaims. "No way! I love that episode."

I startle. I hadn't expected any of them to get the veiled reference. Dr. Quartz was an obscure character from a single episode of *The Flintstones*. Growing up an only child, I have extensive knowledge of afternoon cartoons.

Matt explains the episode to Ted and Ned, which is basically that Barney drinks a soda Fred concocted and turns invisible. Fred then takes Barney to be "seen" by Dr. Quartz, who of course can't help him without being able to "see" what the problem is.

Ted and Ned laugh heartily, and despite myself, I smile in admiration of Matt's grand storytelling.

I turn to Ted. "If we leave now, we can still make it to the monasteries in time for a tour."

"Let's do it!" Matt says, leaping to his feet.

I look from him to Ted and bulge my eyes in question.

"The bloke asked to join us," Ted says with a sheepish shrug. "What could I say?"

No! I think. *You could have said* no!

Matt gives a what-can-I-say-I'm-a-charmer smirk Ted doesn't see. And it's all I can do not to smack it off his dimpled, grinning face.

As we walk into the dorm to grab our things for the walk, Matt asks, "How's Petra?" And my hatred softens a little as I remember that he carried her pack down the mountain.

"Her ankle's broken, so she's pretty bummed. But luckily, she got ahold of her brother who speaks English, and he's going to help her get home."

"It was pretty great of you to go with her."

I shrug and veer off toward my bunk. Petra was a nineteen-year-old kid with a broken ankle in a country where she didn't speak the language. I did only what any decent human would have.

I stuff my sweatshirt, rain poncho, journal, phone, and water bottle inside a string pack and follow Matt out the door to meet Ted. Ted carries a proper daypack. Matt carries only his water bottle with his rain jacket tied around his waist.

Dark storm clouds have rolled in, obscuring the sun and quelching the oppressive heat we hiked in all day. It's humid but nice, and I set off invigorated. While I'm excited about the monasteries, mostly I'm thinking about the wild boar shank, my appetite ravenous.

The trail runs along a wide, fast river and climbs quickly. My left knee protests being drafted into service again so soon, and I feel the fresh blisters I earned on today's steep declines. Tonight, I will need to drain them, and I wonder if I still have Band-Aids or if I will need to buy some in the morning—the menial daily tasks of a pilgrim.

It starts to rain in earnest, and we stop to pull on our rain gear.

I help Ted drape his poncho over his pack, and when I finish, I smile and say, "Ultreia!"

He responds in kind. "Ultreia!" he says and lifts his fist in the air.

My dad wrote that was how pilgrims used to greet each other, and I knew Ted would like that. My dad's photos from this leg are wonderful. There's one of a couple kissing beside a fountain, and another of Uncle David walking into the plaza with his arm around Jen. And perhaps the most stunning photo yet of my mom, a shot of her caught unaware as she looked up at the stunning facade of Monasterio de Santa Elena. It looked to be late afternoon, and the sun glinted off her hair that hung loose down her back nearly to her waist. A single bird flew in the sky above, and my mom seemed to be smiling at it. When I peered closely, it almost looked as if the left cheek was bruised, but it must have been a shadow. When I get home, I'll make a print of the photo and put it on my desk beside the one of me and my dad.

The rain begins to pour in earnest, and I walk with my head down, eyes intent on the trail as I carefully choose my steps. The path is narrow, littered with mossy rocks, and slippery. Several times I nearly lose my footing, and just as I'm about to ask the others if they think we should consider turning back, Ted yelps, and my face snaps up to see him tumbling over the edge.

He lands hard on his side and crashes down the bank, his arms flailing for purchase. But he's falling too fast, and I watch in horror as he smashes into a bramble of bushes then past them into the rapids.

I drop my pack to go after him, but Matt's voice stops me.

"Reina! No!"

I look back to see him already charging down the bank, slip-sliding down like he is snowboarding.

He barrels into the water and after Ted, who is quickly being swept downstream, his rain poncho and backpack tangling and making it impossible for him to right himself.

Matt thrashes toward him, throwing himself over sticks and boulders, and then, in an act of sheer heroism, lunging, his left arm extended. His hand snags hold of Ted's poncho, and with incredible strength, he holds on, then fights against the current to tug Ted to shore.

Both collapse on the bank, and I race back on the path so I'm above them.

Ted rolls to his knees and vomits. Matt remains on his back, sucking air through his nose, his chest heaving.

Ted, still on all fours, wheezes, "What do you say I treat us all to a cab ride to the monasteries?"

Matt huff-laughs, and I smile through my tears.

They claw their way back to the trail, and I fling my arms around Ted so fiercely I nearly send us both toppling back down the bank.

"I'm okay," he says, patting my back.

I sniffle and cry harder. My reaction is over the top, but I can't help myself. In an instant, that's how quickly things can change. One minute you're happily traipsing along, heading to a monastery and daydreaming about a Michelin-star meal, and the next, one of the most important people in your world is nearly drowning in a river. One day you have a dad and a life full of love, and the next, a bird flies into the engine of a plane, and nothing is ever right again.

"It's okay, little buddy. You're okay."

Finally I let go and stomp back the way we came, angry and upset, the horrible moment of Ted tumbling replaying in my head. I've taken a dozen steps, when I stop suddenly, and Ted nearly crashes into my back.

"Sorry," I mumble and start forward again.

Reina! No! The memory of Matt's voice replays crystal clear in my mind.

He called me Reina. I almost smile. It only took a near-death experience for him to acknowledge he knows my name.

"Should we go back and get changed?" Ted asks when we reach the road.

He looks like a drowned rat, his clothes soaked and his hair and beard patched with mud.

"If we do, we'll miss the tour," I say.

"Ultreia!" Matt weighs in with a fist salute and wink, letting me know he also knows about the greeting. He's soaked but doesn't look worse for wear. It's only when I pan down to his shoes that I see the gash on his shin and trickle of blood.

"You're bleeding," I say.

He looks down at the cut, then bends to examine it closer. "A surface wound," he says. "It's fine."

Ted claps him on the back. "Good to hear. I owe you dinner and a beer. I'll call a cab."

He digs into the pocket of his hiking pants to discover his phone is gone.

"Dang it. I just got that phone."

Beside him, Matt's expression also changes, and I watch as he reaches into his shorts and pulls out his waterlogged iPhone, looking at it with what can only be described as horror.

I swallow, also recognizing what it means. Our phones are our lifelines. They hold our photos, updates, and notes. They are how we communicate with the team.

He looks from the ruined phone to me. "Well, I guess that's it, Velma. Game over. It looks like you win."

23

ISABELLE

1997

I stand in the cathedral of Santo Domingo, looking at two poor chickens locked in a cage in the choir loft. Supposedly they are the descendants of a pair of fourteenth-century chickens that were part of a miracle.

As the story goes, a young pilgrim traveling with his parents was framed by a jilted girlfriend for stealing a silver cup. He was tried and hanged but did not die, his life believed to have been spared by Saint Dominic because of his innocence. The boy's parents rushed to tell the town's mayor what happened and to ask to have their son cut down and freed.

The mayor, upset at having his dinner interrupted and not believing the hysterical parents, said, "Your son is as alive as this rooster and hen I am about to eat."

And supposedly, with his words, the two beheaded, cooked birds sprouted feathers, heads, talons, and beaks and jumped from the plates.

Over six hundred years later, the legend of the miracle and the descendants of the rooster and hen live on.

I frown at the forlorn, imprisoned creatures and shake my head at the absurdity of the story. Being Andorran, I was indoctrinated into Catholicism from birth. Religion is a cornerstone of life in Dur and dictates just about everything—routines, rituals, celebrations, marriages, morals, and justice—and it wasn't until I was twelve that I began to question it.

It happened by accident. While the nuns had done a good job teaching me French, Portuguese, Spanish, and English, over the four years I'd attended their school in Pau, only one of the sisters spoke German and only at a very rudimentary level. German was essential to my pa's plans. Many German tourists come to Andorra to ski. So the summer I turned twelve, my pa decided to send me to the Internationale Deutsche Schule in Paris, which specializes in teaching German.

On my walk home from the school on a particularly hot day, I had stopped at the Museum of Natural History to get a sip of water. The exhibit that day was on evolution. Bone fragments dating back eight hundred thousand years had recently been discovered in Spain, and it had created quite a stir. A woman handed me a pamphlet and said the exhibit was free. The path around the enormous bottom level led me through prehistoric times to Neanderthals and then to modern humans. It said nothing about Adam and Eve and made complete logical sense for how people came to exist.

I walked from the museum enlightened and utterly confused.

I can still feel the sting of my pa's hand on my cheek when I returned at the end of summer and asked him about it. "We do not question God!" he roared.

Stupidly, obviously not having learned my lesson, I then asked the Mother Superior about it in front of the class when I got back to school. My punishment was ten lashes on my knuckles with her ruler and three days of solitary prayer in the windowless stone room we called "the box."

In the five years since, I have continued to think about the contradiction and finally found a way to make peace with it. I accept the stories of the Bible as just that, tales meant to teach people the lessons God wants us to understand. I do not take the stories literally and no longer take everything the church or the Bible says as absolute truth. My faith is deep and personal and has nothing to do with headless cooked chickens coming to life and dancing off plates.

The cock's left eye locks on me as if reading my thoughts. *Yep. It's all poppy-cock!* I laugh at my made-up chicken pun.

"Hey." Peter joins me and wraps his arm around my shoulder. "Making friends with the locals," he says with a nod to the bored-looking chickens.

"I was contemplating breaking them out."

"A chicken break. Count me in." He kisses me on the side of my head, and together we walk from the cathedral into the town square.

It's a blindingly beautiful day. A pair of old men sit on a bench, their mouths set in disapproval as they watch a group of teenagers, the girls in skinny jeans and halter tops and the boys in football jerseys. An old woman plays an accordion. A couple with a baby carriage eats ice cream as they walk. All of it a miracle, and Peter and I a part of it.

24

REINA

2024

We pass a distance marker as we head into Burgos: "492 km," and the five of us stop to admire it—me, Ted, Ned, Gordon . . . and Matt.

For the past four days, Matt has walked with us. Since the unfortunate phone drowning, we've been working together, combining our notes and sending a single comprehensive update to the team each night on my phone.

"Wow, less than five hundred kilometers to go," Ted says as Ned exclaims, "Oy! Five hundred kilometers still to go!"

I'm tending toward Ned's reaction. My body is completely done in. My left knee is permanently swollen to the size of a grapefruit. My blisters from Nájera still haven't healed. And I'm dreadfully sleep deprived from so many nights surrounded by snoring, smelly people. I feel like an empty bottle that needs refilling, and we haven't even made it halfway!

Gordon says, "Nearly three hundred kilometers in, and not dead yet," and all of us laugh.

He's only half as curmudgeonly as he was when he first joined us, and I think he might be enjoying living more than he expected.

Though all of us are worn out from the day, we opt to take the longer riverwalk route into the city. It's been a long, hot, uninspiring day. Most of the trek was on asphalt beside highways with cars whizzing by, and the shade and beauty of the park is a welcome reprieve.

When we reach the edge of the city, Matt says, "I'm going to find an electronics store."

"I'll look up directions for you," I say and pull out my phone.

Offering to share my phone wasn't even a question. While I want to win, I don't want it to be because Matt lost his phone saving my friend.

"I'm going to find a beer," Gordon says and walks in the direction of a pub with bright-yellow umbrellas.

"So no more collaboration?" Ted asks with a taunting eyebrow lift and smirk I want to wipe off his meddling face.

"Nope," Matt says as he jots the directions down in his moleskin journal, the exact same type of notebook my dad used. "Back to every man and woman for themself, and may the best journalist win." He points to himself. "Sorry, Velma, no more riding my coattails."

"I don't know," Ted says. "Seems you were doing your share of coattail riding these past few days."

It's true. While Matt has serious writing chops, I am markedly better at the details. He impressed me with his quips, insight, and humor, and the way he can make each day, no matter how mundane, seem like a remarkable adventure. But I'm far better at recalling the facts, history, and practical aspects. I'm also a better photographer.

Ted, possibly feeling responsible for our grudging collaboration, has been acting as moderator. It was a role that proved necessary when we drove back from the monasteries, and I nearly threw Matt out of the moving taxi because he was dictating the story like I was his secretary and not listening to a single word I said.

Now he listens just fine. He even asks questions and, once in a while, will deign to give a compliment. Ted has continued to listen in and add his own ideas.

With an imaginary doff of a cap, Matt saunters off.

"I could accidently almost drown again so he loses his next phone," Ted says, obviously sad the alliance is ending.

If I'm being honest, I'm a little sad as well. It was fun rehashing the adventures of the day each night, the three of us working together and adding details the others missed. Symbiosis—I've always loved that word—the sum of the whole greater than the parts.

"Thanks. But I think I'm going to have to find another way of beating him that doesn't involve destroying expensive electronics."

"You've got this, little buddy," Ned says, always my biggest cheerleader.

"Team Velma!" Ted says.

I glare at him.

"What?"

I bulge my eyes.

"Oh," he says, realizing his mistake. "I mean, Team Reina!"

Ugh!

"I've got to say, though," Ted says. "I kind of like the guy."

I glare again.

25

ISABELLE

1997

We are in the Meseta, an endless plain of wheat stretched to the horizon, and my thoughts are as heavy as the humidity, which hangs thick in the late-afternoon sun. Peter and I walk alone. Jen, David, and Joe decided to wait until the morning drizzle stopped before starting out. Now it is cloudless, and my left side is turning to leather as my right remains in shadow.

I enjoy walking in the rain, and Peter was happy to splash along beside me. I like that about him, how content he is to do what I do, as if my happiness is all he needs to be happy himself.

He is also sensitive. All day, he has allowed me space alone with my thoughts, sensing my melancholy and letting me be. Since we left Burgos two days ago and entered the eerie quiet of the high plains, I've been thinking a lot about my family, desperately worried and missing them. The tranquility of this place is haunting and makes it impossible not to face the thoughts I've been avoiding.

The single narrow footpath snakes through the endless wheat and forces us to walk single file. I lead, and with my back to Peter, knowing he can't see, several times I have allowed myself to cry. Constantly I agonize about Xavier and Ana and pray they are okay, though mostly it's my ma I think about, missing her and imagining how upset and worried she must be.

She and I have always been close, both of us cut from the same colorful, curious patch of cloth. We share so much—cooking, the stars, nature, art, poetry, and books—things no one else around us cares about.

"Ets la meva obra mestra," she would say whenever we were alone. *You are my masterpiece.*

I wipe away the wetness on my cheek.

"Bella?" Peter says behind me with concern.

Bella, it's what he calls me now, short for Isabelle, though he's told the others he uses it because it means beautiful. They still only know me as Joan.

"I'm okay," I say. "It's just this place."

"Yes," he says. "I feel it too. So much quiet, it's like suddenly you're forced to pay attention."

That's it exactly. We've been walking for hours with nothing but our thoughts and footsteps to distract us.

"Can I help?" he asks.

"I miss my ma, and I'm worried about my brother and sister. I wish I knew if they were okay."

For a long moment, he is quiet, the two of us walking silently through the wheat, until finally he says, "I think I know a way."

26

REINA

2024

"Salami," Matt says as I say, "Baseball."

We look at each other cockeyed, then mirrored smiles cross our faces.

Gordon counts down, "Three, two, one."

Matt and I shout in unison, "Hot dog!" then high-five.

"We rule!" Matt says.

I read about the game in my dad's journal. It's called Compatibility, and supposedly it tests whether you're on the same wavelength as the person you're playing with. Which obviously is bunk since Matt and I are killing it.

"Look," Ned says, and I look up to see the glorious sight of buildings ahead.

"Home sweet home," Tuck says. Tuck is the friend Matt was hiking with when we helped Petra, and he's been walking with us since we started the Meseta, the eight-day hike across the "desert" of the Camino, though it's not actually a desert. There is no sand, only endless flat, featureless wheat fields as far as you can see, with a long wide strip cut to the horizon for pilgrims. Featureless. Flat. Endless.

We started this morning before dawn and, for the first four hours, did not pass a town. Despite leaving in the dark each morning to avoid the worst of the heat, each day the sun rises quickly on the south, baking our left sides while the rest of us remains pale.

Ted and Ned, along with most of our other pilgrim friends, opted to take a one-hour bus ride from Burgos to León to skip this part. Ted and Ned plan to explore the two cities and promised to wait for me to catch up in León before continuing on.

"The three compadres," Ted said when he told me the plan. "We started together and will finish together."

So for five days, it's just been the four of us—me, Gordon, Matt, and Tuck—walking the seemingly unending dirt and gravel path to whatever hole-in-the-wall destination is next.

Crunch, crunch, crunch . . .

Each day is the same, a whole lot of nothing. No cafés. No restrooms. No fountains or streams. No stunning vistas or soaring cathedrals. No interruptions or distractions of any kind. Which have strangely made these endless, monotonous days the most profound.

Tuck listens to music through earbuds. Matt listens to audiobooks. Gordon and I walk in silence. The four of us walking together but apart.

Occasionally, usually toward the end of the day, we play Compatibility or break out in song.

Since the boys don't know show tunes, our repertoire has consisted primarily of television theme songs and product jingles—*The Brady Bunch*, *The Flintstones*, *The Love Boat*, *Happy Days*, Oscar Mayer, Toys "R" Us, and Gordon's favorite, the Kit Kat jingle.

Matt has a notoriously bad voice, and the first time I heard it, his tone-deaf cackle made me so happy I kept starting new songs just to hear it. It was like discovering Superman's kryptonite. The guy is tone deaf as a cow and can't carry a tune to save his life. Tuck has made so much fun of him I'm certain he was as happy as I was to discover the Pavarotti-size crack in Matt's persona of perfection.

The town of Terradillos grows closer. The villages of the Meseta are little more than rest stops. Mostly devoid of charm, they exist solely to provide sustenance and lodging to pilgrims. Typically they consist of a few houses, a café, an albergue, a church, and maybe a gas station or small market. Each day, we do our laundry and shower before heading to the lone bar or café for beer and cards. Then we have dinner, Matt and I send our updates, and we go to sleep.

It's very relaxing, like living in an altered reality. The monotony and sameness of the days combined with the dry, featureless landscape creates the illusion of time standing still, as if nothing exists or matters beyond the moment you are in.

Crunch, crunch, crunch . . .

Unfortunately, this stretch has also turned out to be the hardest for me physically. My left knee continues to give me grief, the swelling so bad that, by the time we reach our destination each afternoon, it no longer bends or acts like a knee at all.

Graffiti on a wall at the entrance to the village reads, "**YOU ARE HALFWAY THERE!!!**" Below it is a spray-painted undulating line of mountains. "**ST. JEAN PIED DE PORT**" is labeled at the start, and "**SANTIAGO DE COMPOSTELA**" is scrawled at the end. A smiling stick figure with a round backpack stands in the center, his arms raised like he's cheering. Beneath it, a yellow arrow points west.

"Halfway!" Tuck says, and we all high-five, then we pose for a dozen goofy photos of us imitating the stick figure.

It's early afternoon, siesta, and the town is so deserted it feels like we've walked onto the set of a postapocalyptic horror movie. Swallows pass in and out of doorways, and a large dog lying in a patch of shade lifts its head but cannot summon the energy to greet us.

Fortunately the albergue is open. We register and claim our beds, and I collapse on the thin mattress, my knee throbbing like a heart. Tuck heads off to use the single shower. Gordon shuffles to the courtyard to wash his clothes in the sink.

"Don't get too comfortable," Matt says. "We've got sheep to shear."

On our way into town we saw a flock of sheep on a hillside beside a church, and Matt came up with a wacky idea that the four of us should herd them and take a small shearing of wool as a unique souvenir from the Meseta.

I keep my eyes closed but offer a salute.

When the boys are finished showering, I haul myself up and go about the daily chores of a pilgrim—laundry, shower, refilling my water bottles. Laundry consists of scrubbing the day's clothes in the large communal sink with the shampoo I also wash my hair with then hanging it to dry wherever I can find a breeze.

When I'm done, Gordon and I leave together to find the boys.

The town is prettier in the waning afternoon light. The sun sets behind a gas station in the distance, and yellow light filters down the street. A woman in a brightly stitched apron waters pink geraniums in a window box outside her leaning mud home, and the swallows now circle in the sky.

"Limping pretty bad," Gordon says with concern.

"We only have three more days to León," I say. "I'll be okay."

Halfway, I think and send a small prayer that my knee holds up to get me to the end.

What happened to Petra is not unusual. Injuries are common and so are a host of other trek-ending ailments and illnesses—stomach issues, tendonitis, heatstroke. There are so many ways in which a pilgrim's dream can end, and it has far less to do with fitness and age than simple, random luck.

We reach the charming yellow brick church and walk around it to get to the grass knoll where earlier we saw the sheep.

"Happy birthday!"

My eyes pop open in surprise.

A dozen people smile at me—Matt, Tuck, Ted, Ned, Ingrid, Bettina, and a handful of pilgrims we've met on the Meseta. They stand around a white sheet laid out on the grass laden with food.

"Wow!" I say.

"Surprised?" Tuck asks.

"Very." I look at Matt, the only one who could possibly have known it was my birthday.

He smirks proudly. He must have remembered it from last year, either from the company monthly newsletter, which lists birthdays, or because John sent a balloon bouquet to the office.

I look away, an unsettling buzz in my veins. Our relationship has changed, and I'm not entirely sure how I feel about it. Constantly now, I need to remind myself of what he did to Karen and how unforgivable it was.

"Let's drink!" Gordon says and pats me hard on the back, encouraging me forward.

There is beer, wine, cheese, salami, crackers, olives, hummus, three different pasta salads, flatbread, tinned fish, and a dozen different cakes and pies. I raise my smoked-salmon-and-cheese cracker to Ted and mouth the words "Thank you," knowing he and Ned were the ones who generously provided the feast.

The two of them, along with Bettina and Ingrid, took a cab here from León, and I can't recall the last time I felt so loved. Canada, Sweden, Scotland, England, Brazil, and Spain are all represented—a great United Nations of pilgrims gathered together to celebrate my birthday. It's part of what is so magical about the Camino, the great coming together of people who otherwise might never meet and the incredible camaraderie that forms along the way.

Ted believes the reason we all get along is because the trail is self-selective. "It takes a certain type of person to embark on such a challenge—people who are open to new experiences and looking to grow and expand beyond who they are."

"It's most definitely universally a good bunch," Gordon agreed after Ted said it.

"If only people who walked the Camino were the ones who ruled the world," Ned contributed. "Think about it. The world would be at peace."

"It's a good idea in theory," Ted said. "The problem is, people who walk the Camino would never want to rule the world."

He's right of course. *Live and let live. Hakuna matata.* Either could be the universal ethos of the Camino and the people who walk it.

"How's the Meseta?" Ted asks, bringing me back to the moment.

"Imagine wheat," Gordon says, "lots of it, endless amounts of it, so much wheat you consider giving up bread and pasta and cereal just so you never have to think about wheat again."

Ted chuckles.

"Then imagine towns like this one, desolate and dusty and smelling of manure."

"You paint quite a picture."

"Now, turn the temperature up past broiling, and have someone stamp on your feet until they're bleeding."

Ted laughs again.

Gordon lifts his beer. "Glorious, mate! Bloody-freaking glorious!"

Matt and Tuck challenge each other to a juggling contest, which Matt loses, though he hung in there for an impressive amount of time. Ingrid breaks an apple in two with her bare hands. Another pilgrim, a man from Italy, performs a few magic tricks. The sun turns orange and then red as it falls toward the horizon.

I will never forget this, I think. *This is one of those moments that will be lodged in my brain forever.*

"Buen Camino!"

I turn at the voice, then blink and blink again, uncertain of my eyes. "John?"

He smiles wide as he walks toward us, and I jump to my feet and run into his arms.

"Hey, babe. Happy birthday."

I bury my face against his large chest, and he wraps his arms around me.

Home! I think as I inhale the smell of his fresh laundered shirt and hug him tighter. Until this moment, I hadn't realized how homesick I've been.

"How?" I say when I pull away, my mind tripping on "this life" and "that life," which have collided so suddenly it causes a dizzying sense of vertigo.

"I didn't want to miss your special day," he says.

"So you flew here?"

He shrugs like it's no big deal, but it is a big deal. It's a very big deal, and I'm overwhelmed by the grandness of it.

Lifting up on my toes, I kiss him. He tastes like him, coffee and peppermint gum, and another surge of love runs through me.

"Introduce me?" he says with a nod over my shoulder.

I flush, suddenly aware everyone is watching.

I make the introductions, and he shakes hands and waves and smiles at each of my Camino buddies in turn. I tense as Matt introduces himself. I've said so many bad things about Matt over the past three years to John, I'm worried he might let it show. But he doesn't. He offers a friendly open smile as they shake hands and says, "Ah, the competition."

Matt shocks me when he answers, "And she's giving me a run for my money."

John moves on to the others, and I am reminded why I love him. There's something so wonderfully open and unguarded about John, his smile genuine and bright as he meets this hodgepodge of strangers and immediately accepts them as friends.

When we've finished most of the food and all of the beer and wine, Matt stands, places his fists on his hips, and declares, "Brothers Templar, who among you is brave enough to join me in the ritual shearing of the sheep!" He raises a tiny pair of grooming scissors like a sword.

Tuck, Gordon, Ted, Ned, and several others leap to their feet.

Desperately I want to join them, but my knee is done for the day.

John looks at me as if asking permission.

"Go forth, brave knight," I say and shoo him toward the others. "Conquer thine sheep and shear your woman some wool!"

He jumps up with the widest smile I've ever seen, and the group sets out for an adventure they never would have had at home.

27

ISABELLE

1997

It is the most beautiful cathedral I've ever seen, the nave a hundred feet tall and surrounded with stained glass. My soul swells as we listen to the choir of singers echoing off the hallowed stone. Peter sits beside me, our hands entwined, and while he doesn't understand the words, I know he is moved as well, his eyes fixed on the altar as the voices swell and recede around us.

After so many days of walking in the quiet of the Meseta, the noisy bustle of León was a shock to the system. Last night was particularly rough. It was the first night Peter and I spent apart since Logroño. The León albergue is part of a convent run by nuns, and the men and women sleep in separate dorms.

In the Meseta, the five of us—me, Peter, Jen, David, and Joe—slept most nights beneath the magnificent stars, forgoing shelter altogether. And last night, I missed Peter so much I ached. Constantly I need to remind myself we've only been together thirteen days. Time a trick in the Meseta, each day is like a month when all you have are your thoughts and the people beside you, and already, Peter is so much a part of me it's hard to recall my life before him.

The singing stops, and with a deep, satisfied sigh, Peter turns and smiles at me, then he pulls out his journal and jots down a note before standing and pulling me to my feet. It has been a glorious day of rest, the two of us free to explore the city with no destination except where our whimsy takes us.

We walk into the square, and my heart leaps when I see the traditionally dressed dancers putting on a performance. Recognizing the jota folk dance, I pull my hand from Peter's and join the back of the line. I stomp and twirl and clap as Peter watches with a wide grin. I play up my swishing and kicks, and when the song ends, twirl my way toward him.

He catches my hand, pirouettes me around, and says, "God, I love you." Then, realizing what he said, his eyes go wide for a second before his brows lift, and he says it again, "I love you. I love you, I love you, I love you."

I lift up on my toes and kiss him, and he pulls me tight, his cast pressed into the small of my back. "Jo també t'estimo," I mumble against his lips. *I love you too.*

He releases me, and hand in hand, we sit on a bench to watch a while longer, our secret between us. I clap and sing along, and Peter writes more notes in his journal.

When the sun sinks below the cathedral's towers, we leave to meet the others at the albergue so we can all go to dinner.

After dinner, I'm going to use Joe's cell phone to call my ma. Peter says cell phones don't work the same way as landlines. The number that will show on the tavern's phone and the phone bill will be from Joe's home state of Wisconsin, not from León, Spain. The technology bewilders me, and I can't get used to the idea of carrying a phone in your pocket.

We reach the narrow alley that leads to the albergue, and I jump on Peter's back, and he carries me a while. Then I hop down and say, "My turn."

He laughs and climbs on, and I stagger a few steps before he falls to the cobblestones. We're still laughing when we walk into the convent holding hands.

"Izzy."

I start at the voice and instinctively yank my hand from Peter's before looking up to see my pa. He stands in the convent's entry beside the Mother Superior. Xavier hovers slightly behind them, his head bent toward the floor. The nun's arms are crossed over her chest, and I know by her haughty expression she's the one who recognized me and called either my pa or my school. I did not consider the idea that the nuns and churches throughout France and Spain would have been notified of my disappearance. Though it makes perfect sense. The network of the Catholic church is the most powerful in the world.

"Bella?" Peter asks, looking from me to my pa and back again. Then, piecing it together, he steps forward with his hand extended. "Sir."

Pa ignores Peter's hand and narrows his eyes.

It's the first time I've seen my pa since Christmas, and I'm slightly stunned by his appearance. His eyes are bruised, his hair long, and his posture stooped.

Peter drops his hand to his side.

Pa's black eyes drill into mine. "Let's go," he says harshly in Catalan.

Peter tenses.

"Peter," I say quickly and shake my head in warning.

Peter has already broken his arm defending me once, and my pa is not a man to be provoked. Still in his prime, not yet forty, he is cattleman strong and would like nothing more than an excuse to defend his property, especially against a gringo from America.

Stepping beside Peter, I say in English. "This is my pa and my brother, Xavier." I switch to Catalan. "Pa, this is Peter Watkins. He has been very kind, and his broken arm is from protecting me." I say it very fast, my eyes on the floor, so Pa knows I am not challenging him.

Pa looks from me to Peter, and I exhale in relief when he extends his hand. "Thank you. I am indebted to you."

Peter shakes his hand while looking at me to translate.

"He appreciates you looking out for me."

"Oh," Peter says. "You're welcome."

Pa turns back to me. "Let's go," he says again and nods toward the door.

"Pa," I say, hoping he will see reason, "it is not a good idea. Senor Sansas thinks you killed the twins." I dare a glance up to see his reaction. It's very subtle, guilt or remorse flickering in his eyes a second before they harden to stone, but it tells me everything. He did not kill Miguel and Manuel, but he is also not entirely innocent in their deaths. "If I go back, Senor Sansas will have his revenge. On me." I nod to my brother. "And on Xav."

His nose flares as he grumbles, "I will protect you."

I start to shake my head, but his harsh words stop me.

"You are not as smart as you think. Senor Sansas also knows you are on the path of Saint James. You are lucky the nun called the school and the school called me first." He nods to the Mother Superior, and smugly she nods back. "This is bigger than you. It is bigger than all of us."

And that's when I see it, the fear in his eyes, a man who isn't scared of anything rattled to his core. And I realize this is no longer about money or his grand dreams of being the powerful lord of Dur, a world-renowned ski resort. Castor and the mining companies have taken over and are running things, and my pa, and possibly Senor Sansas as well, are nothing but pawns in their high-stakes game.

"Bella?" Peter says anxiously.

My pulse races, but with a sweet, reassuring smile and a surprisingly calm voice, I say, "It's okay. I need to go home for a bit to straighten all this out, but it's fine."

"But—"

My gaze locks on his, and silently I plead for him not to go on. This situation is already tenuous, teetering on the brink of detonation, and Peter getting involved will only make it explode.

His Adam's apple bobs as he swallows, but mercifully he respects my wish and doesn't say anything more.

"I need to get my things," I say.

Not trusting me, Pa says, "Xav, go with her."

Xavier follows me down the hall to the women's dorm.

When we reach the door, I say, "Xav, you need to stay here. Only women are allowed inside."

I'm surprised when he says firmly, "No. I need to go with you."

People misperceive my brother. They think he is stupid because he doesn't talk a lot and never did well in school. But what Xavier lacks in book smarts, he more than makes up for in instinct, and like my pa, he senses my plan to flee.

"Xav," I plead, "the only chance we have is if I don't go back."

His eyes hold mine, the deepest endless brown. "Pa will protect us."

It's all I can do not to shake my head.

He opens the door, and I walk into the dorm with him behind me.

Jen looks up from the book she's reading. "How was the cathedral?" she asks, then, seeing my brother, she tilts her head, the purple streak in her bangs draping to the side.

"Fine," I say stiffly and move robotically to my cot to stuff my things into my pack.

"Joan?" she says.

I give the smallest shake of my head, my emotions dangerously close to the surface.

I sling the pack onto my shoulder and walk back out the door with Xavier a foot behind, feeling like I'm leading us to our deaths.

Peter watches as I walk past, and I feel his coiled desire to do something. But there is nothing to be done. They found me. And just like that, it is over, and once again my future is not mine to choose.

Pa and Xavier flank me as we walk from the convent and down the street to Pa's truck. When we reach it, Pa walks to the driver's side, and Xavier grabs my pack from my shoulder and flings it into the bed.

I crane my head back toward the convent. Peter stands on the sidewalk watching, and beyond him is the alley that, moments before, he and I had piggybacked down, laughing.

"Izzy," Pa says.

I turn, and through the open windows of the truck, our eyes, mirrors of the same rebel soul, connect, and I watch as his gaze narrows and his mouth opens to stop me, but already I am whirling and racing down the cobblestones.

A string of Catalan curses and his lumbering footsteps follow, but I run with every ounce of speed I possess, knowing to be caught is to surrender my future and my life. Like a madwoman, I race down alleys and streets, turning this way and that.

I run until I cannot get a breath then stumble to a stop and look around to see I am no longer in the city but on a dirt tractor road surrounded by fields. I stagger sideways into the barley, then collapse to my knees so I am hidden, drop my head, and cry, stunned once again at how quickly my life has come undone.

28

REINA

2024

"Hell of a church," John says, looking up at the soaring facade of the León Cathedral.

"Hell of an understatement," I reply.

The cathedral is magnificent, the grandest yet, and it's impossible to fathom it was built nearly a millennium ago without the aid of lasers, cranes, or power saws. I imagine my mom and dad inside, my dad holding his journal with his cast as he wrote with his right hand.

> I feel the stonemasons' chisels on each enormous block, and imagine the effort of moving and lifting them into place—the dedication, faith, and devoutness it must have taken to create such magnificence and the decades of resolve needed to achieve it.

The handwriting of the second entry looked hurried and sloppy as if he jotted it down quickly while standing:

> She twirls in the shadow of the great cathedral, orange dusk winking in her hair, and I know this is one of those moments, the kind that tattoos your soul and which you never forget.

Beneath it, neater:

> I told her I loved her, and she kissed me then echoed it back, Jo també t'estimo—I love you too. The only Catalan phrase I ever need to know.

His photos matched the words—colored light through spectacular stained glass, and a captured moment of my mother spinning, her hair flying and her hands clapping over her head as she smiled wide with unrestrained joy.

After that, there's nothing more about León—no entries or photos. I looked at the next page, dismayed to find a date but no entry. The page after as well. I didn't look beyond that, determined to stick to my promise of experiencing the journey together.

"Let's go!" I say excitedly, and John almost contains his groan.

Cultural enlightenment is not John's thing. He prefers social enlightenment—hanging out with people, drinking beer, playing cards.

I still can't believe he's here. He said he made the decision the day after I left. He gave nothing away in the single conversation we had on my rest day in Logroño. Mostly he talked about his job. He's an appraiser for the city and is working on the appraisal of an old tenement building in the Bronx that will most likely be torn down by the next owner. He also gave a blow-by-blow description of the dart game he won the previous Friday.

The following day, Ted nearly drowned, and his and Matt's phones were ruined, so my phone became too vital to use on a call back home. And then, on the Meseta . . . well, on the Meseta, I was in a strange, detached place, and my life in New York felt very far away.

The timing of him coming out for my birthday worked out well in terms of logistics. León has an airport, and it is only a short taxi ride to Terradillos.

He has gotten on fabulously with everyone, and I'm proud of how well he's made himself a part of things. He especially gets on with Tuck. Both are soccer fans who can talk endlessly about the sport. Gordon, Ted, and Ned have taken to him as well, the three of them nicknaming him "Big Buddy" in complement to me being their "Little Buddy."

The only person he hasn't gotten to know is Matt. The morning after my birthday celebration, we woke to find Matt gone. He messaged our group, saying he wanted to catch the sunrise in Sahagún, a village full of ancient Romanesque architecture. I was a little hurt that he didn't ask me to join him. He knows I would have woken up early not to miss something like that. Though I suspect he didn't ask because of the comment John made the night before about liking his sleep.

We haven't seen him since. Because of his early start, he decided to do a double leg that day so he could spend an extra day in León.

"Seven euro?" John says, and I look at the sign beside a ticket window at the cathedral entrance. I can expense my ticket, but John would need to pay.

"I guess we don't have to go in," I say, peeking through the doors that lead to the nave and catching a glimpse of the magnificent stained-glass windows at the top that my dad captured so beautifully.

"Agreed," John says, relief in his voice.

He takes my hand and practically pulls me back outside.

The square is very busy, and I notice groups of people in festive, colorful costumes. The women wear wide, flower-embroidered felt skirts, and the men wear black knickers and vests over billowy white shirts with vivid sashes around their waists.

"I think they're going to dance," I say excitedly, thinking of my dad's photo and what he wrote about my mom.

"Yeah. But it looks like it's going to take a while to set up," John says. "The band's still unloading." He nods to a van parked to the side with its doors open.

"Oh," I say, heart deflating.

Noticing, John says, "Maybe we can come back after they get going."

I nod, though I know once John has settled in with the group at the bar, there won't be any leaving. I could send him on without me, but that seems rude considering he flew all this way, and he's leaving tomorrow. Plus, as Ted said, "Experiences are better shared."

"Yeah, okay," I say. "Let's go find the others."

He lights up and kisses my hand. He limps slightly as we walk, and again my heart swells with how great he's been. He has blisters from three days of walking through the scorching Meseta, the blandest landscape of the Camino, and he hardly complained at all.

My feet have healed, but my knee's in bad shape, and I'm glad tomorrow is a rest day. After I see John off, I plan to sit in one place, catch up on my notes, and ice and ice and ice.

We arrive at the bar and find a crowd of friends. Ted, Ned, and Gordon. Ingrid and Bettina. Matt, Tuck, Nicole, and her friend, Cami, who was part of Matt's group when he first arrived. Nicole sits on Matt's lap, and Cami has a leg draped over Tuck's thigh.

Ted, Ned, and Gordon are playing cards with Ingrid and Bettina. There are several pitchers of beer on the table, and I feel John's excitement. He's all about hanging out and socializing. We squeeze a couple of chairs in, and Gordon pours me a beer as Cami says, "Swing," and Tuck says, "Boat."

"Three, two, one," Nicole counts down.

"Hammock," Cami says as Tuck says, "Water."

Matt's eyes catch mine as both of us mouth, "Rope," then roll our eyes because the answer was so obvious.

It takes them six more tries to land on the common answer of "Plant."

"We did it!" Cami squeals. "We are compatible!"

She's cute, a blond wisp of a girl with freckles and a bubbly personality. She's from a small town in Australia, and this morning at breakfast confessed she's not sure why she came on the Camino. "My motive is to find my motive," she said, and Gordon toasted his orange juice to hers and said, "To not knowing why the hell we're doing this."

"Velma and John's turn," Matt says, and my skin prickles, sensing the suggestion is not as innocent as it sounds.

"Yes! Me and Reina!" John says enthusiastically.

He really is one of the cheeriest humans on the planet, the reigning golden retriever of people, his tail wagging whenever he's around friends.

"Let's do this, babe!"

I smile as if excited, though my true feelings are distinctly the opposite, certain we're going to be terrible.

"Three, two, one," Tuck says.

"Owl," I say as John says, "Turnip."

Turnip!

It's okay. I can figure out a way to work with it.

Turnip soup. Purple turnips. Root vegetable. Roots! Owls live in trees, and trees have roots!

"Three, two, one," Tuck says.

"Roots!" I say as John says, "Smart!"

"Smart?" I say, looking at him curiously.

"Dumb as a turnip," he explains. "And owls are smart."

"Oh." I suppose it makes sense in a wonky sort of way.

I look at Matt, expecting him to be smirking mockingly, but his face is cast down and his expression unreadable. Before I can puzzle it out, Tuck is counting down again.

The game goes on, and with each guess, we get further and further apart, John laughing hysterically while I cringe at how bad we're doing. We reach our tenth try, and John holds up his hand for me to high-five.

"Worst!" he declares with pride. "Not compatible at Compatibility at all."

I paste on a smile and slap my hand to his, then risk another glance at Matt to find him looking at me, his dark eyes piercing mine as if he's looking straight into the back of my brain.

"On that note," John says. He stands and turns my chair from the table to face him.

"Reina," he says, "I'm afraid I came here under false pretenses."

He looks at the group to be sure everyone is watching.

"I said I came here for your birthday when I actually came here for another reason entirely."

I look at him curiously.

"It was two years ago today that we first met."

Was it?

It was. We met at the going-away barbeque for a couple who were leaving New York to buy a house in New Jersey. I worked with the woman. John played softball with the man. I was helping set out the food. He was setting up the keg. We both liked the country song playing in the background. He asked if I might want to go to dinner. I said sure.

"It's been the best two years of my life."

My heart triples its pulse as I realize what's happening. John is all about timelines and milestones, and vaguely, in the far recesses of my mind, I recall him saying something about hoping to settle down in two years.

Getting down on one knee, he pulls a blue velvet box from his pocket.

"While we might not be great at the game of Compatibility," he says, "I think we will be amazing at the game of life."

He opens the lid to reveal a tiny round diamond set in a simple gold band.

"Will you marry me?"

Someone gasps. Another claps their hands together.

"Sweet," Nicole says.

"Oh, this is so romantic!" Cami squeals.

Tears rise in my eyes as I continue to stare at the small precious stone. *León*, I think, the city where my parents declared their love. *On the Camino*, as close to my parents as I can be. He flew here to do this. All of it grand and romantic and perfect.

John's face is stretched out in a wide, expectant smile.

Good, I think. He is good—a good, solid man, dependable and kind. A man who will be a wonderful father, a kind husband, and a steady partner in life. I imagine us telling our children about how he proposed, on one knee in front of our Camino friends at a medieval bar in Spain.

"Yes," I say. "Yes, I will marry you."

29

ISABELLE

1997

A frigid mist settled over the field during the night, and I am wet and chilled to the bone. I shiver cross-legged in the barley, trying to figure out what to do. I haven't slept, and between my exhaustion, fear, and heartbreak, I'm finding it impossible to think.

The horizon glows on my left, which means I'm still heading west, though I have no idea if that's the direction I should continue. My heart says yes because I know eventually it could lead to Santiago and to Peter. But it's also the direction my pa and the others will likely be looking for me.

"Hola!"

I startle at the voice and stand quickly so whoever is talking will know I'm not a threat. In Dur, landowners have the right to deal with trespassers however they see fit, including shooting them if that's their prerogative.

The farmer stands on the road in a rain slicker and wide brim hat, his tractor beside him.

"Hola," I say with a wave, and then, in Spanish, I apologize for sleeping in his field. I explain I got lost in the dark and didn't know what else to do.

"The trail is ahead," he says with a smile and points down the road.

"Thank you," I say as I hurry away.

"Buen Camino," he bids to my back, and I lift my hand in a wave.

My breath rattles as I hurry through the drizzle, the start of a cold that formed during the night. My situation is not good. I'm soaked through and shivering. I have no money or food. And I can no longer rely on the Camino to provide shelter or meals.

Peter.

Every other thought is of him and his expression as he watched me from in front of the convent.

It's over, I tell myself for the hundredth time. The whole thing was reckless and horribly irresponsible. From the start, we never had a future, and it was foolish to think otherwise and to let it go so far.

I am being hunted, and if caught, it's likely I will be killed. Allowing Peter and the others into my life was incredibly selfish, and the thought of the danger I put them in twists my insides into a knot. I swipe the tears away and look up through the mist to see a village in the distance. If I'm lucky, there will be a church where I can get warm and rest, and hopefully then I can come up with a plan.

The turrets come into view, and I hurry through the streets toward them and nearly cry with relief when I pull the handle of the large door and discover it unlocked.

The shock of warmth causes an almost violent shudder.

"Billy goat?"

My face snaps to the voice.

"Dan?" I say, blinking in disbelief. "Emily?"

"You're soaked," Dan says as Emily says, "Where's the pack the nun gave you?"

I shake my head, and the small gesture breaks something loose inside me, my body convulsing once before it collapses to the stones in heaving, trembling sobs.

Emily hurries over and leads me to a pew. Dan drapes his Patagonia jacket over my shoulders and sits in the pew in front of us. Emily hands me her water bottle, and I take a sip, then guzzle it greedily.

Feeling bad for taking her water, I force myself to stop.

"No," she says. "Finish it. I have another bottle, and there's a fountain in the square."

I drink the rest, then drop my head and stare at my filthy hands in my lap.

"What happened?" Dan asks.

I sniffle, and my head lolls side to side. I am completely distraught and have no idea where to begin.

"You're okay," he says. "Take your time. God led you to us for a reason, and you're safe now."

And with all my heart, I wish I could believe him.

30

REINA

2024

"I am officially past miserable and firmly in just kill me now," Ned grumbles.

The four of us are all firmly there. Ted, Ned, Gordon, and I got a late start, and it's now pushing a hundred degrees, and the unrelenting Spanish sun is beating down on us without a scrap of shade or whisper of breeze.

The first part of the hike was relatively flat and ugly, a dirt path paralleled by a noisy highway. Then we reached this hill, which at first seemed beautiful—a narrow dirt trail climbing through stunning pastures—until we realized it never ended. For hours, we've been trudging up it, and we're hot, exhausted, thirsty, grouchy, caffeine-depleted, and hungry. The single bar that exists in the micro hamlet of Villares de Órbigo several kilometers back was closed, which means we've been hiking for hours without a break.

My knee is throbbing, and on top of that, Gordon and Ted are in a beef. The Camino is no place for politics, but it came up last night at dinner and quickly heated up as the two realized they are resolutely in different camps on just about everything.

I wish Matt and Tuck were here. They would have lightened the conversation, and I know Matt could smooth things over between Ted and Gordon. But now that we've finished the Meseta, the pair have rejoined their old young-and-beautiful crew, who they met up with in León.

"Hangry," Ned mutters.

I agree. My stomach rumbles angrily, and I wish I could click my heels three times and magically land in Astorga, our destination for today.

As we walk, I keep my eye out for heart stones. My dad wrote that Joe was known as "Cupid of the Camino" because he made a mission out of finding heart stones and bestowing them on other pilgrims.

> According to Joe, expert on all things Camino, if you find a heart stone and offer it as a kindness, the kindness will be repaid.

I feel like I know Joe and Jen, and I think, when this is over, I might try to find them. I'm curious whether they stayed in touch and whether Jen and my Uncle David continued their romance after the Camino. At the very least, I'd like to share my dad's photos with them.

My dad and mom. Uncle David and Jen. Cami and Tuck. Matt and Nicole. The experience definitely brings people together.

And I am engaged.

Each time I think of it, it stuns me anew. Me, a fiancée, a soon-to-be bride. Then a wife. And someday, a mother. It feels so unreal.

While I might have anticipated it, John being as dogmatic as he is about his life plan and the timing of things, I didn't. I fully believed he had come here for my birthday.

Though when I think about it, it also makes perfect sense. He's thirty. I'm twenty-six. We've been together two years. We get along great and never fight. His family likes me. Aunt Robbie adores him. Not every love has to be a grand romance like my parents had. Sometimes it's about being better together than apart, and that's me and John. We are simpatico.

I rub the spot where I wore the ring for a fleeting twelve hours before John put it back in the velvet box, then his pocket, for "safekeeping" so I wouldn't lose it on the Camino.

"I'll start looking into dates and venues," he said in front of the albergue as we waited for the taxi that would take him to the airport.

"Let's wait until I get back," I said.

The idea was still so new I felt like I needed a bit of time to get used to it. "I'll be home in a couple weeks, and we can talk about it then."

"It's just I'm excited," he said, his face lit up.

He's an easy man to read and make happy, his needs simple—friends, beer, food, and me. Possibly in that order.

"I know, but there's no rush. And I need to figure things out with my aunt."

Even simple weddings cost money, and at the moment, any money I have needs to go to helping my aunt get back on her feet.

The taxi pulled up, and John threw his pack in the trunk, then went to climb into the back seat.

"John," I said.

He turned.

"Forget something?"

He cocked his head, adding to the overgrown puppy persona. I arched my eyebrows.

He laughed, then obediently returned and kissed me. "Love you," he said.

"Love you too."

Happily he loped away.

"Is that a mirage?" Ned says, interrupting my reverie.

I look up to see what looks like the edge of a palapa-thatched roof sticking into the trail. As we get closer, I begin to think he might be right and that we are hallucinating. The roof belongs to a small stand painted Kelly green with curly white letters that read, "**La Have de la Esencia es la Presencia.**"

Ted translates, "I think it says, the key to *essence* is *presence*."

I don't care what it says because the cart is stacked with juices and soft drinks, and to its right is possibly the most beautiful sight I've ever set eyes on, an eight-foot-wide round wood table laden with a cornucopia of food.

"Watermelon!" Ned exclaims.

And oranges, bananas, apples, peaches, grapes, salami, cheese, bread, croissants, olives, nuts, granola, jam, honey, cookies, crackers . . .

The Camino provides. Never have those words rung so true. Here, in the middle of a never-ending rise up a mountain in Spain with nothing but sweeping pastures and a speckling of cows, we've happened upon a paradise of food.

We look around for a proprietor to pay or a donation box.

"It's free," a man sitting on a bench says as he takes a swig of a Coke.

"We're not supposed to pay?" Ted asks.

"It's not expected," the man says in English with what sounds like a Spanish accent. "It's called donativo."

His companion says, "It is not required, but it is customary to leave something to buy food for the next passerby. You give what your heart and pocketbook may allow."

It's so Camino-esque I smile, then grab a banana and a blueberry muffin and hobble to the bench. Ted uses an orange press to squeeze himself a cup of fresh orange juice. Ned digs into a giant wedge of watermelon.

None of us talk, all of us lost in the euphoria of the moment.

As I eat, I take in the rest of this wonderful, bizarre place. To my left, a spiraling rock formation swirls on groomed red dirt. To my right is an open adobe shed stocked with shelves of food. And behind me is a rock garden in the design of a five-pointed star, and placed in each point and in the center is a pink rose bush bursting with blossoms.

Beyond the rock garden is an adobe brick wall with a tin-roof overhang and several mattresses beneath it.

"What is this place?" I ask.

"Heaven," Ned says around a mouthful of watermelon, juice dribbling down his chin.

The man who explained what donativo means pulls a five-euro bill from his pocket and drops it beside the orange press. His friend pulls out a handful of coins and does the same. They continue up the trail.

"How'd all this get here?" I ask.

The trail isn't wide enough for a car, and there's no sign of a motorbike or even any sort of electricity, which means the food needs to be brought in fresh each day.

"I imagine it's hiked in from Astorga," Ted says, seemingly as astounded by the idea as I am.

As if our thoughts conjured him, I turn to see a man in the rock garden. Dressed in tan shorts, a worn navy T-shirt, and an old NY Yankees baseball cap, his feet are bare, and he moves gracefully across the stones, plucking away leaves and sticks so the garden is immaculate.

"What can I get m'lady?" Ted asks with a bow.

"Orange juice, please, dear sir. And Brie on a cracker."

Ted turns to do my bidding. All day, he's been very solicitous, worried about my knee. He wanted me to see a doctor in León, but I refused, knowing what a doctor would say. He would tell me my knee's overstrained and that I need to rest, something I can't do. We're two-thirds of the way to Santiago, and I need to finish.

"Are you the owner of this fine establishment?" Ned asks.

I turn to see him talking to the man in the rock garden. The man is a few inches shorter than Ned, making him around six feet, and he looks around the same age.

"Everything you see belongs to God," the man says, "but I am his humble servant."

I smile at the wonderfulness of the statement, the cherry on the proverbial sundae of this mystical, magical moment.

"Well, call yourself what you like, but you, my man, are definitely an angel!" Ned says and claps the man on the shoulder.

The man laughs, and a strange tingle runs down my spine. I try to peer around Ned to see him more clearly, but all I can see is the back of the man's Yankees hat.

"Here you go, my queen, sweet nectar from the trees and cheese from the cows."

"Thanks," I say, blinking several times to clear away the strange buzzing.

Ned returns and sits beside me. He pats my leg affectionately.

Whatever comes of this trip, I've gotten more from it than I ever could have hoped for, Ted and Ned like two adoptive uncles I've gained for life.

"How far are we from Astorga?" I ask.

Ted pulls up the Camino app on his phone that tracks his location.

"Seven kilometers."

"Seven kilometers," Gordon sighs with exhaustion that mirrors my own, the thought of standing and starting again impossible.

"Here, my friend."

The man from the rock garden stands in front of us, and I startle at how silently and suddenly he appeared. In his hand is a tube of sunblock. He holds it toward Gordon.

"You're getting too much sun," he says plainly, his English unaccented, and I look at his bearded face to see that, despite his deep tan, his cheeks are freckled, and I realize he's American.

The bill of his hat shades his eyes, and his dark beard covers most of his face.

"Can I pay you for it?" Gordon offers.

The man waves him off. "Kindness is a gift; that's what makes it kindness."

He turns to the table of food, sweeps the money left by the Spanish pilgrims into a discreet crack in the center, then slices more oranges so they will be ready to be squeezed by the next pilgrims.

"Come on, little buddy," Ned says when I've finished my cracker and orange juice.

He holds out his hand to help me up. I let him pull me to my feet and do my best to conceal the wince as my knee seizes in pain. He looks at me, concerned.

Ted drops a twenty-euro bill on the table, and I pull out a five-euro bill along with the nicest heart stone I found today and set them down as well.

Gordon contributes two euros.

"Buen Camino," we each say to the man, who is now at the stand replenishing the juices and sodas on the counter.

"Have a good life," he says with a smile and wave.

I'm almost past, my hand raised to return the greeting when our eyes meet and my heart stops. The two vivid blue discs widen in matching surprise.

"Reina?"

"Uncle David?"

31

ISABELLE

1997

I hear the sound of a train and hurry into the scrub beside the tracks to wait for it to pass. Today I feel both better and worse than yesterday. Better because I have a plan. Worse because my cold has settled in my chest and causes me to cough constantly.

Thanks to Emily, I now have a sweatshirt and water bottle. And thanks to Dan, I have fifteen thousand pesetas to get me to the coast. Whenever I think about how much I owe the people who have helped me over the past three weeks, I am overwhelmed with gratitude and panicked over how long it will take me to pay them back.

The train rumbles past, and I wait a moment longer, then return to walking beside the tracks. The trek was lovely today, a mostly flat walk through grain fields and a few small suburban towns. I'm somewhere north of the Camino between Astorga and Ponferrada, following the tracks, which eventually will lead me to the coast . . . and Peter.

Emily, Dan, and I talked a long time after I told them my story and how I ended up at the church. Emily went out to get us sandwiches and chips while Dan sat beside me, balled his jacket into a pillow on the pew, and told me to rest. Luckily the church was empty, and I napped almost an hour. As we ate, we talked about what I should do, and I liked how certain Dan was about Peter.

"There is no fear in love," he said plainly. "You say Peter loves you, which means you cannot protect him because it's already happened. The spell has been cast. So now all that's left is to allow him to help."

Emily said, "He's probably worried to death right now."

I nodded. All last night while I sat trembling in the barley field, I kept imagining him and David scouring the streets of León searching for me.

Dan came up with the plan. Walking the Camino is too dangerous, and taking a bus, train, or taxi is equally risky after what Pa said about Senor Sansas also knowing I was on the Camino. He and the mining companies and Castor are surely on the lookout for me everywhere throughout Spain. So Dan suggested I follow the train tracks on foot. He sent Emily to get a map at the station in town.

When she returned, we studied it together. The tracks run somewhat parallel to the Camino but are far enough away that I should be safe. The dangerous spots are where the tracks cross the trail, in the cities of Astorga and Ponferrada. If I can make it past those two points, I should be able to get to the coast where, God willing, in exactly two weeks from yesterday, Peter will be waiting in a town called Finisterre, "end of the earth," where we will meet at the 0,0 kilometer marker for the Camino.

Dan and Emily will find Peter and tell him the plan. Now all I need to do is get there.

32

REINA

2024

I sit in the shade on a stump beside the shed of Uncle David's refuge, unable to believe this is real and that he is here, the uncle I haven't seen in seventeen years, alive and well and living on the Camino in Spain.

Ned, Ted, and Gordon have gone on to Astorga, leaving me to deal with this stunning revelation alone, the discovery so extraordinary that every other minute I'm certain I'm going to wake to realize it's only a dream.

But it's not a dream. I could not make this up.

I watch as he empties the small trash bin into a large garbage bag beside the shed, then replaces the bin beside the table. So much about him is familiar, yet he is a person I no longer know, and watching him, my emotions are all over the place.

My first reaction of shock was quickly followed by a sharp burst of euphoria that he's alive. Yet, now, after an hour of sitting here, watching him, completely healthy and able, his cell phone functional and his mind seemingly intact, my elation has distinctly soured into low-simmering rage. For seventeen years, he's been okay, and he didn't bother to let us know.

He looks over, his eyes catching on mine then blinking several times as if still absorbing the shock as well. He returns to straightening the food and rearranging the table so the offering appears abundant and never-ending. He is very devoted to his work, tending to the food and pilgrims like it's a mission of great importance.

The reward he gets for his efforts is nearly universal reactions of awe and gratitude. Like me, Ted, Ned, and Gordon, the pilgrims who stumble upon this place are amazed. The words *heaven, mirage, utopia, tripping, hallucinating,* and *oasis,* are batted around as they chomp on watermelon, banana bread, crackers, and cheese.

This place is mentioned briefly in the Brierley guidebook, but the description made it sound like it was a religious landmark, a place to receive a blessing. Perhaps Brierley understands that part of its miracle is its element of surprise.

"Have a good life," Uncle David says to a pair of young men who mowed through a ton of food and didn't leave a dime.

"Thanks, man," one of them says.

Uncle David returns to sit on a stump beside me, lowering himself without the use of his hands. I know he is two years younger than my dad, which makes him fifty-four, but his body and nimbleness are that of a much younger man.

"You have questions," he says.

So many, my mind swirls, and I don't know where to begin—why he left, why he didn't let us know he was alive, why he's here. Does he live here? Alone? Has he thought about us? Does he know what Aunt Robbie's been through? Does he have any idea how much his abandonment hurt?

"How did my dad break his arm?" I ask, entirely unsure why that's the question that comes out of my mouth, except possibly that it's been on my mind since Logroño and because the other questions feel too hard.

Uncle David tilts his head as if unsure what I'm asking.

I pull out my phone to show him the picture of my dad with the blue cast, but before I find it, two more pilgrims crest the hill, and Uncle David stands to cut a few wedges of watermelon so the offering will be ready when they arrive.

Before they reach the table, he disappears into the shadows of the rock garden. It's clear he doesn't like to hover over his guests.

The two men, mid-thirtysomethings, both go for the watermelon, which seems to be the universal favorite.

"Praise the Lord!" one of them says as he slumps to the bench.

The second man bellows, "Hallelujah!"

I smile as they dig in, elation passing over their faces as they sink their teeth into the first juicy bite. Things definitely taste better when you're deprived, and I wonder if that's why Uncle David chose this place for his mission, if he knew it was the exact spot pilgrims would be at their most needy.

One of the men notices me and raises a sheepish hand in greeting. Then, seeing the other stumps nearby, he nudges his buddy, and they carry their food over to join me.

"Velma, right?" the first one says.

Ugh! I work to keep my smile in place.

"We met Matteo. He says you're his archnemesis."

"I think he got it backward."

"I don't know. In my experience, it's always the innocent-looking ones that you most need to watch out for."

I laugh.

"Bryan," he says, then thumbs his hand at his buddy. "Mike. San Francisco."

"Reina," I say. "Brooklyn."

"Reina?"

"*My* archnemesis likes to get under my skin by calling me Velma."

"But Velma's a compliment," Mike says.

I look at him like he's nuts. "Have you watched *Scooby-Doo*? Daphne's the hot one."

"I suppose. Technically. But Velma's the one guys are actually into."

"It's the total librarian-turns-out-to-be-a-centerfold thing," Bryan contributes.

"Nerds are sexy," Mike says.

"And Velma's just cooler. She's smart, sarcastic, funny."

"Usually the one to solve the mystery."

I laugh at their back-and-forth and how into it they are, like they've given the subject serious consideration.

"Daphne's the pretty girl who gets chased around and needs to be rescued," Bryan says. "And Velma's the one who comes up with the brilliant scheme to rescue her."

"And she gets to say 'jinkies,'" I contribute, finding the conversation highly entertaining.

"Not to mention the sexiest line of all," Bryan says, "'Mister, you're my mystery, and you know how I love a mystery.'"

"She doesn't really say that?" I say.

"She sure does."

"No comparison," Mike says. "Daphne's the one-night stand. Velma's the keeper."

I'm about to tell them Velma's jailbait, that in the original *Scooby-Doo* series, she's only fifteen, a fact only geeks like me know, when Uncle David interrupts. "How is your journey?"

The men startle at his sudden appearance. I notice he has that effect on people, and I'm not sure if it's because most of the pilgrims are in a mild state of exhausted delirium and therefore less aware of their surroundings, or if he really is a Zen master impossible to detect until the moment he appears. Either way, his stealthiness combined with his piercing blue eyes in this otherworldly place definitely evoke a stunned reaction in almost everyone he greets.

"Rough," Bryan says as Mike says, "Better now," as he raises his watermelon rind in a toast.

Both men stand to shake Uncle David's hand.

"This place is yours?" Mike asks.

Uncle David gives the same answer he gave Ned. "Everything you see belongs to God, but I am his humble servant."

I'm surprised how religious my uncle is. I don't remember him being that way. My family is a mix of faiths. My grandmother was half Jewish, half Catholic. My grandfather was a mix of Protestant, Lutheran, and Baptist. I was raised to respect everyone's beliefs and to decide for myself what I believed, which turned out to be not much in terms of organized religion.

"Is there anything you need?" he asks, a question he asks nearly everyone he greets.

"A new set of knees," Mike says.

"Afraid I can't help with that. But I have ibuprofen."

"Already took my fill. But thank you."

They ask Uncle David to pose with them, and I snap a photo.

"Have a good life," David says and returns to his garden.

Mike and Bryan shrug on their packs with exhausted sighs. Mike drops a twenty-euro bill on the table.

"Take it easy, Velma," Mike says with a two-finger salute.

"Jinkies!" I say back.

When they're out of sight, Uncle David returns and sweeps the bill away. It's astounding how much he's made in the short time I've been here. At least a hundred euros. Almost everyone leaves something, and some, like Ted and Mike, leave far more than the value of what they consumed.

Uncle David cuts more watermelon, then retakes his seat beside me, and I show him the photo of my dad with his blue cast.

I'm surprised when he smiles. "Pete, the bumbling hero."

Then he tells me the most awful story about my dad saving my mom from being assaulted in the albergue in Logroño. It confirms that it was a bruise not a shadow I saw on my mom's face in the photo my dad took of her the following day. She'd been cleaning the albergue to earn money when the man who worked there attacked her. My dad ran in and stopped him before anything happened, and my dad broke his arm in the tussle.

The story is upsetting both because of how awful it makes me feel for my mom and for how poorly it reflects on the Camino. One of the reasons the Camino is so popular is because of how safe it is. More than half the people who walk it are women, and many of them do it alone. The Spanish, for more than a thousand years, have taken great pride in supporting and protecting pilgrims. I've been on the trail three weeks and haven't once felt in danger, and the only crime I've heard of was a pair of hiking poles being taken, and it's possible they were taken by accident.

"And that was when she told you that her name was actually Isabelle?" I ask.

"She only told Peter. To the rest of us she was still Joan or Billy Goat."

"Billy Goat?"

"Your mom hiked very fast, and she could walk forever and never get tired."

"Are you sure I'm her daughter?" I say, extending my left leg with its swollen, bruised knee.

"You are definitely hers," he says, eyes lifting to mine and a shadow of deep sadness passing over his face.

He returns to the phone and scrolls through more of the photos. He laughs and turns the phone to show me a hilarious shot of Joe making his way through a flock of black-faced sheep milling around the trail. His hands cover the crotch of his shorts, and he has a look of pure terror on his face.

"Man, I loved that guy," Uncle David says.

"Did you keep in touch?"

He shakes his head. "The Camino ends. People go their separate ways." He sounds sad as he says it, and silently, I vow not to let that happen with Ted and Ned.

He continues to look through the pictures then stops, and the smile drops from his face. He hands the phone back and walks abruptly to the stand to start moving drinks from the counter into the cabinet below.

I look at my phone to see a photo of Jen shielding her eyes from the sun as she looks up at a nest in the bell tower of a church as a stork flies toward it. I look back at my uncle. The recollection hurt him.

Since I have my phone out, I snap a photo of Uncle David behind the stand. In his T-shirt and Yankees hat, holding a can of Coke in one hand and a Sprite in the other, he looks like an American tending a beverage cart. Only when you look closer and notice the details do you realize that's not it at all—the white Spanish words on the chipped green plywood, the soaring vista beyond, the glinting tin cross around his neck, the lack of power poles, and the matador monkey hanging from the palapa roof.

What I've gleaned from what I've overheard while sitting here is that this place is known as Sanctuary of the Gods. The ramshackle buildings have been here hundreds of years, and Uncle David has been here fourteen of them, spreading his mission of kindness and love. I was right about there being no electricity. There's also no running water, and the only access is by motorbike or foot. Each day, Uncle David walks seven kilometers to Astorga, fills two backpacks with provisions, and walks back.

I look down at the photo and consider sending it to Aunt Robbie and telling her the remarkable news and quickly decide against it. News this big is best shared in person, and I'm not sure how she's going to take it. Uncle David left her holding the bag for everything—dealing with my dad's death, taking care of me, and caring for my grandmother. Maybe it's best not to tell her at all. After all, what good would come from it? He abandoned us. Why reopen old wounds? I feel another surge of anger and tuck the phone back in my pack.

"Rest, dear. I'll get you a drink." I look up to see an older man and woman. Both carry daypacks and look very tired.

The woman slumps to the bench, dazed. She looks to be in her late sixties, her hair silver blond and her face etched with fine lines.

The man looks even older, his skin age-spotted and his posture stooped. He wears a bucket hat in a colorful fish print and looks as exhausted as his wife but continues to press her juice. It's then that I notice the laminated photo dangling from his pack. It's of a blond woman about the age of someone who might be their daughter.

Over the past three weeks, I've met several pilgrims walking in honor of someone they've lost. Some carry ashes they leave along the trail. Others are only here to pray. All are here to mourn and hopefully find a way forward beyond the loss. The memorials along the trail are countless, and each time I pass one, I think of my dad and am reminded of how fickle and arbitrary death is. Some of the markers are for older people, but most are for people my dad's age or younger, lives randomly snuffed out before their time.

The man carries the juice to the woman, then returns to get her a few Chips Ahoy cookies and some grapes. Hand trembling, he sets them on the bench between them.

"Thank you, darling."

Darling. It's such a lovely way of addressing someone you love.

I watch as they share the food, eyes on the pasture across the trail, oblivious to me and everything else around them.

Grief can do that to a person, make you feel like you are in a tunnel.

The food gone, they sit, his hand on hers.

"I'm good," the woman says finally.

The man looks at her with concern, then stands and helps her to her feet.

They do not leave a donation. Hand in hand they walk toward Astorga, their matching laminated photos swinging from their packs. Watching them makes me think of my mom and dad, and I send a wish into the universe for them to have each other for many years to come.

Uncle David doesn't reappear until they're gone. He returns to the stand to finish closing it up for the day. They were the only people he let be and to whom he did not say, "Have a good life." Intuitively, he seems to sense the needs of his visitors, and the couple were clearly in their own private world and wanting to be left alone.

After locking the cabinet, he says, "You need to go or you'll miss the dinner."

His dismissal strikes like a fist.

Realizing it, he adds quickly, "In the morning, I'll meet you at the albergue, and we'll walk and continue our conversation."

"What about this place?"

He shrugs. "The trail was here long before I was and will be here long after I'm gone."

I stay sitting.

"I promise," he says, then holds up three fingers. "Scout's honor."

It's such a hokey American thing to do.

"Believe it or not, I was a Boy Scout. So was your dad."

I knew that about my dad. I didn't know it about Uncle David. He lifts my pack and holds it out to me. "I can't believe you're walking with this old thing. You know your dad bought it off an army vet who was our neighbor. I think he paid five dollars."

"I think he got ripped off," I say, causing him to laugh and making him look so much like my dad I startle, and my heart pounds out of rhythm.

I wince as I push to my feet, my left knee protesting violently.

"Tomorrow," I say as I swing the pack onto my shoulders and level my eyes on his. "Scout's honor."

He holds up the Scout's oath again.

I limp off, my left leg swinging like a club in front of me, and my mind in a strange state, like I've walked through a looking glass and entered an alternate reality, nothing as it was, though everything is almost exactly the same. I look at the golden pasture on my left, bathed in the waning light, and feel the illusion of my dad beside me.

I walk this hot, dusty trail with purpose, the future unfurled like a yellow brick road leading me to my destiny. Steadily, I walk toward it, yesterday a reminder to never give up hope. In my darkest hour, Dan and Emily arrived and delivered a miracle. As Carl Jung says, "Man cannot stand a meaningless life." And I have my meaning. Bella.

Something changed between León and Astorga, and tomorrow I will finally get some answers.

33

ISABELLE

1997

My nerves buzz as I walk toward the city of Ponferrada, the second place where the tracks cross the Camino. I made it past Astorga under the cover of night, using the stars to guide me and by walking through the neighboring fields. I had hoped to do the same in Ponferrada, but there was a reason the Knights Templar, protectors of pilgrims, chose the city as their stronghold. With uncrossable rivers and mountains on either side, there's no way around it. If there are two places Senor Sansas's men are sure to be waiting, it's the single route into the city and the single route out.

A cough rattles my lungs, and I stagger slightly with the dizziness it causes. To my left, a hundred meters or so from the tracks, I see stone ruins among the scrub and decide to rest there until it's dark and my chances are better.

Most of the structure has collapsed, but part of a curving stairway as well as a few remnants of wall and the bases of the turrets remain. I settle on the bottom step, and as I pull my water bottle from the shopping bag I carry, I imagine I'm a princess waiting for my prince—Peter, of course.

I'm about to take a sip when high-pitched peeping stops me. I look toward a bramble of leafy vines in front of one of the crumbled walls, hear the sound again, and move closer to investigate.

"Oh," I say when I see the four tiny kittens and a mother cat on her side, hidden in a hollow beside the wall, then "Oh no," when I realize the mother isn't moving.

"It's okay," I say to the squealing litter.

One of the kittens is solid stormy gray, the other three are mottled black and white.

I reach in and set my hand on the mother's fur to discover the body is cold.

Dur has plenty of cats, and I know kittens need to eat often.

"You're okay," I repeat, eyes welling with tears as the tiny creatures continue to mew.

I look from them to Ponferrada in the distance, and my chest tightens as I consider the choice before me—leave the kittens to die or risk going into the city now when it is light.

One of the kittens, the gray one, nuzzles my hand. His nose feels dangerously dry. He looks at me with yellow-green eyes, and my heart tightens.

"Hang in there," I say. "I'm going to help you."

I return to the steps, stuff the food from the shopping bag into the pockets of Emily's sweatshirt, and return to the kittens. One by one, I place them squirming and crying in the bag.

"I know you're scared," I say, "So am I. But God is watching and has a plan." The words are as much for myself as the kittens.

The bag in one hand and my water bottle in the other, I walk along the river beneath the trees to stay out of sight.

Like Andorra, Spain looks after stray animals. If I can make it into the city, I know the kittens will be taken care of.

I stop at the edge of the woods. A hundred yards in front of me is the highway overpass that crosses the river and leads into the city. Fifty meters left of it is a medieval footbridge used by the Camino pilgrims.

I scan the trail that leads to the footbridge, hoping I might join a group and possibly blend in, but as far back as I can see, there is no one.

I gauge how much time it would take to reach the footbridge and cross it. Running full-out, my guess is it will take at least five minutes. I imagine a series of walkie-talkies conveying the message that I've been spotted, and an army of pursuers converging and waiting for me as I stupidly run toward them.

A car drives onto the overpass, followed by a truck. I watch the vehicles bump from the smooth asphalt onto the rough cobblestones of the city. Their speed slows momentarily as the gears shift to lumber up the steep hill that leads into the town, and the sliver of an idea forms.

"Okay," I say to the kittens as I glance back at the road to see another vehicle in the distance, a van, approaching. "Ready? Here we go."

With a deep, ragged breath, I tighten my grip on the bag and sprint for the overpass. My congested lungs struggle to get air, and I pray I have the endurance to do this.

I see the two men before I've made it halfway across—one young, one old. They were watching the footbridge but now race to intercept me at the road. The young one stops suddenly and turns back for the footbridge. Smartly, he's decided to race across it and onto the overpass to stop me from doubling back.

The old one stands at the end, arms spread wide as if waiting to catch me.

I slow to a walk, ears straining. I hear the sound of the tires behind me and focus on how fast they are traveling. I will only get one shot at this. When the van is nearly upon me, I break into a full-out sprint, racing straight at the man like I'm going to bowl him over.

He braces himself, legs wide and chest puffed out.

I'm ten meters away when the van passes. Quick as a rattler, I dart sideways behind it and race off the overpass, leaving the man stuck on the other side until the van is able to shift gears and rumble up the hill.

My relief lasts less than a second. The younger man's footsteps echo behind me.

I turn at the first intersection, then turn again and again and again. I weave through alleys and down streets in a dizzying pattern, lungs wheezing and legs on fire.

I risk a glance behind me and don't see the man but don't dare stop. In front of me I see a sign for a hospital, **HOSPITAL DE LA REINA**. I race down the drive toward a group of three women in scrubs standing outside the entrance, smoking.

I run up breathless. "Kittens," I gasp in Spanish, "I found these kittens."

I hand the bag to the woman closest and race away, darting around the building and back into the winding streets. Half a block later, I duck into the doorway of a house with a **For Sale** sign. Spots dance in my eyes, and I bend over, hands on my knees. I try to get air, but it's like trying to suck honey through a straw. No oxygen is getting in. I lean sideways and vomit on the sidewalk, then stagger and grab the wall for support. Half a second later, my legs go weak, and I slump to the ground like a rag doll.

"Are you okay?"

I look up to see a teenage boy with a soccer ball.

I try to say yes but have no breath and only manage a gasp.

"Ma!" the boy yells up toward an open window one story up.

A woman pokes her head out.

"Come down. A girl needs help."

I want to protest but can't. Something is wrong. It feels like an elephant is sitting on my chest.

The woman appears. "Oh," she says. "Pedro, call for an ambulance."

I shake my head hard before mustering enough breath to lie. "If I go to the hospital, my boyfriend will find me."

I watch as she takes in the fading bruise on my face before giving a curt nod of understanding.

"Pedro, help her inside."

Peter.

And once again, I feel God's hand.

34

REINA

2024

"Come on, Velma. Don't be a killjoy."

"No," I say and attempt to quicken my pace, but my swollen knee makes it impossible, and Matt easily keeps up.

"Play with someone else," I say. "There are lots of other pilgrims to choose from." I nod to the band of misfits traveling with us today—Ned, Ted, Gordon, Tuck, Nicole, Cami, Bryan, Mike, and . . . Uncle David.

As promised, Uncle David was waiting outside the albergue this morning. What I hadn't expected was for him to have his pack and walking stick.

"There's too much for us to cover in one morning," he said.

"What about Sanctuary of the Gods?"

"It will still be there when I return." He nodded to my left leg. "Plus you need my help."

"I'm okay."

"No. You're not."

Ted, who was sitting on the wall waiting for Ned, weighed in. "No, she's not."

"I'll carry your pack," Uncle David said.

"You have your own pack."

"I'll carry both."

I looked at him like he was nuts.

He mirrored my expression, which made Ted laugh. "For fourteen years, I've carried two packs from Astorga to Santuario de los Dioses loaded with watermelons, oranges, sodas, waters, and a whole lot more. Trust me, this will feel like a vacation."

He gestured for me to hand him my pack, but I kept it firmly on my back.

"But then I'm not *doing* the Camino."

"Not *doing* it?" he said, head cocking to the side.

"Not carrying my worldly possessions."

He scoffed. "You really think lugging twenty pounds of modern crap on your back is what God had in mind when he offered forgiveness for those who follow the footsteps of Saint James?" Before I could answer, he was pulling the pack from my shoulders. His eyes caught for a second on my dad's Camino shell before he shrugged it onto his chest and said, "Let's go."

He set out at a brisk clip, and I was thankful I didn't have my pack because otherwise I'd never have kept up.

"I'll start at the beginning and tell you everything I know," he said.

"I want to know everything," I said, "but if we only have a day, maybe you should start with the Camino."

"A day?" he said, turning his blue gaze on me. "I told you; you need my help. I am walking with you."

"Wait. You mean the Camino? The whole Camino?"

"Well, not the whole Camino. But from here to as long as it takes. Yes."

I was stunned, and my heart pounded strangely.

We've now been hiking together two days and have had so little time alone together, we've only made it through my dad's grade school years.

"Someone count us in," Matt says, relentless as ever.

I glare, and he laughs.

"Three, two, one," Tuck calls out.

"Cookies!" Matt cries out as begrudgingly I say, "Sweater."

Matt smiles smugly, and I roll my eyes, the answer so obvious it's not even a game.

"Three, two, one," Tuck says again.

"Christmas," Matt and I say together.

Matt holds up his hand to high-five. I ignore it.

"Happy?" I say.

"Very."

Ugh! I know the only reason he wanted to play was to show off. Cami and Tuck are nearly as bad at the game as John and I were. Ted and Ned can't finish a game because they end up bickering too much over the other's answers. Mike and Bryan are meh. Gordon always ends up quitting out of frustration because he can't come up with a word. Nicole refuses to play. And Uncle David has no interest in competition of any kind.

Our band of pilgrims has taken to my uncle like cats to cream. All of them had the pleasure of meeting him at his mystical Sanctuary of the Gods, and they are in awe at the idea of him hiking with us.

"Look, there it is," Ted says.

I look up to see the Cruz de Ferro, the famous iron cross, a hundred meters ahead. The cross is the highest point of the Camino, over 1,500 meters above sea level. It is a profound point of the journey and, for many, the culmination of their reason for being here.

All of us stop out of respect for a woman standing at its base. Her hand rests on the wooden post, which looks like a telephone pole. At its top is a small cross. The woman looks to either be crying or praying. Either way, we don't want to disturb her. She stands on an enormous mound of stones, physical testimony to how many pilgrims have walked this path and laid down their offerings at the base in the form of a stone brought from home. The tradition is to toss the stone over your shoulder with your back to the cross to symbolize leaving your burdens behind and the start of a renewed life. Uncle David explained that according to the Bible, the way to salvation is to take the things plaguing or weighing you down and to turn them over to Jesus.

"It's when you stop trying to fight or conquer them yourself that you find peace. You grip a stone tight and let it absorb the sorrow and grief you want to unload, then leave it at his feet. Stones can take it. It's why they're so hard."

Seeing the small mountain makes me feel as I often have on this journey, small yet relevant. This place was here before I arrived and will live on long after I've passed, but, without me and those who came before and those who will come after, it wouldn't exist—each stone a wish, a prayer, a thank-you of the pilgrim who left it.

"Did my parents leave stones?" I ask Uncle David.

"Your mother wasn't with us for this part of the journey," he says, shocking me.

"She wasn't?" I say, wondering how that's possible. Only two days ago, my dad wrote that his purpose was Bella.

"After León I never saw her again."

"Not even after I was born?"

"I only came home after I learned of her death and found out that you and your dad were living in New York. The two of you were my reason for coming back."

Before I can ask more questions, Ted announces, "Here we go. A few more steps, and we'll be at the pinnacle of the Camino."

All of us fall silent, reverent of this moment and the twenty-six incredible days it took to get here.

Tuck, Nicole, and Cami reach the mound first. Cami lays a pink ribbon near the base. It's for her mother at home, battling breast cancer.

Tuck and Nicole each take a selfie with the cross behind them.

Mike and Bryan stand for a moment with their hand on the wood post, their heads bent in prayer. Mike lost his wife, Margie, a year ago. Margie was Bryan's sister. She had always dreamed of doing the Camino, so they are doing it in her honor. When they finish, they each toss a stone over their shoulder.

I wish I had brought a stone . . . two stones. One for my dad and another for my mom.

Matt walks around the circle of rocks, checks the direction of the sun, then pulls a rock from the pocket of his shorts, kisses it, and places it carefully on the dirt at the edge. He takes a photo of it, then backs away to take another with the cross in the background. He smiles and walks away, making me curious.

"Ready?" Ted says to Ned.

"No," Ned answers.

Gordon shakes his head, finding the drama of Ned's big moment ridiculous. He marches after the others.

Ned pulls the package of OREOs he bought at our last stop from his pocket and looks at it forlornly. He brings the blue package to his lips. "Goodbye, dear friend," he says and lays the package on the stones.

Among his offering are other offerings just as mundane—cigarette packs, a mini vodka bottle, a cut-up credit card. There are ribbons, photos, a plastic necklace, a rubber dog bone that says *Bonz*.

Ted claps Ned on the shoulder, and I hug him around his wide waist.

Uncle David crosses himself in honor of the monumental moment, and the four of us continue toward the trail. Before we reach it, I detour to look at the stone Matt left. It's oval and painted like a ladybug. Across its red and black-spotted back in yellow childlike letters is painted the name *Fiona*, the *N* backward.

I reach the others just as a thunderclap bursts overhead, and it starts to drizzle. We stop to pull on our rain gear.

I cover myself with the clear plastic poncho I bought in St. Jean Pied de Port. Uncle David puts a trash bag over each pack, rips holes for the straps, then puts another over himself with a hole for his face.

"What the hell?"

I look in front of me to see Matt crouched on the trail, a rock in his hand that he pulled from the rain-cover compartment of his pack.

I hold in a laugh, unable to believe he's been carrying the rocks I stuffed in his pack in Navarrete, over two weeks ago, all this time.

His face snaps to mine.

"You!"

I think of denying it but can't, laughter bubbling over. The others join in, cracking up as he pulls rock after rock from the compartment and the rain pelts down on him.

"This means war!"

35

ISABELLE

1997

"How are you feeling?"

"Better," I say, pushing up on my elbows from the couch I've been resting on for nearly two days. The apartment is tiny, cramped, and tidy, with a simple cross over the archway to the kitchen and a painting of the Madonna beside the front door.

Though my chest still hurts, the pain is less sharp, and air flows easily in and out of my lungs. Pedro's mom, Eliana, who is a nurse, explained I likely had a pneumothorax, a partially collapsed lung. She thinks my bad cold combined with my race through the streets brought it on. Often if there's only a small tear, the lung will repair itself, which thankfully mine appears to have done. And now I am only tired . . . and worried.

My recovery has taken two precious days, which means I have only seven days left to reach Finisterre to meet Peter.

Eliana kneels beside me and sets the back of her hand on my forehead. "You're still warm. You need to rest." Seeing my fallen expression, she adds, "It's not a choice. Your body needs to heal. As I said, you are welcome to stay as long as you need." She smiles warmly and stands. "I will make us some soup."

She reminds me of my aunt, the one who served in the army, pretty but worn down by life. Her thick black hair is threaded with silver, and lines etch the corners of her eyes. Her husband died when Pedro and his sister were very young, leaving her to raise them alone. I see in her face how hard her life has been and feel guilty for the additional burden I've brought uninvited to her doorstep.

Before she reaches the kitchen, I ask, "Auntie, may I use your phone?" Auntie is the affectionate term Andorrans and Spaniards alike use for female adults who are close.

She turns back, a question on her face.

"I want to call my ma to let her know I'm okay. I will pay you for the cost."

She waves me off. "Mothers help each other. Someday, when you are a mother, you will help the child of another."

I nod and hope someday I get the chance to do just that—Peter and I the parents of a brood of children and our place in the world secure enough to offer kindness to others.

She brings me the handset and returns to the kitchen.

With a deep breath, I dial.

The phone on the other end rings six times.

"Ya," my ma says, and with that single utterance, I lose it, tears spilling from my eyes as sobs rack my body and cause a coughing jag that brings Eliana rushing back into the room.

I suck in a wheezing breath to calm myself and nod that I'm okay as my ma on the other side of the line says, "Marie, I'm taking this upstairs. It's about the olive delivery. Hang up when I holler."

The noise of the tavern in the background echoes through the handset—voices, music, the clanging of plates. I look at the clock on the mantel. It's near one, the end of the lunch rush.

"Marie, hang up," Ma yells.

I hear a click, and suddenly the line is much quieter.

"Izzy?"

I whimper.

"Oh, Iz." I hear her tears as well.

"I'm okay," I lie.

"You're not. Where are you—no. Don't tell me. Are you sick?"

"I am, but I'm getting better. I've met some very nice people who have helped me." I look at Eliana in the kitchen, her wide back to me as she stirs the soup.

"I've been so worried." Her words hiccup. "It's all so awful. Tell me what I can do."

"Nothing," I say, which is the truth. Pa rules our house, controls the money, and is the one who put us in this mess. "I just wanted to let you know I'm okay."

We both pause to rein in our emotions.

Finally she says, "Don't come home. Do you hear me?" She sounds angrier than I've ever heard her. Normally, she is easygoing as water down a stream. It's how she's been able to live so long with my pa. "There is nothing but danger for you here."

"Are Ana and Xavier okay?"

"I sent Ana to stay with Rosaria, and Xavier is still with your pa, looking for you."

Rosaria is an aunt who lives in Barcelona.

"Oh, Ma—"

She cuts me off. "Izzy, the only person you need to worry about is yourself. I need you to promise me that."

"Okay," I sniffle so as not to upset her more, though I don't know how I can do that. How do I not think about the people I love? How do I not worry and want to protect them?

"Whatever is to come," she says, her voice softening, "I am with you. Each night, look up at the stars, and I will do the same, and on Sagitta's arrow, we will send each other our love."

My ma has always loved the constellations.

I try to contain a sob, and it causes another coughing jag.

"Izzy?" Ma says with alarm.

"I'm okay." I take a trembling breath and force the rattle to still.

"Sempre seràs la meva obra mestra," she says. *You will always be my masterpiece.*

36

REINA

2024

I walk lost in my thoughts, my knee and heart aching in equal measure. I wanted so badly to know the truth, but with each revelation Uncle David offers, I am gutted.

The higher I rise, the cooler it gets, and the sweat beneath my layers turns cold and causes me to shiver. We're on our way to the mystical Galician hamlet of O Cebreiro, a leg of the journey that promises to be one of the most strenuous and rewarding. I walk in and out of thick woods of pine and walnut, the trail so high the clouds float below and the hilltops beyond pierce the cover like ethereal floating islands, all of it like I am walking in a dream.

Our group started together, but the trail is narrow and the ascent so steep we're now spread apart, no one in sight. Uncle David is somewhere far ahead, his pace unmatchable. Though I'm sure Matt and Tuck are doing their best to keep up. Somewhere behind me are Ted, Ned, and Gordon. And sprinkled between are Mike, Bryan, Cami, and Nicole.

This is the steepest, longest ascent of the journey, an unrelenting seven miles. I carry only a water bottle and can barely pull myself forward. It feels as if I've climbed a thousand flights of stairs and still have a thousand more to go. I keep my head down and focus on the step before me, counting as I go. When I reach a hundred, I stop to catch my breath.

. . . ninety-nine . . . a hundred.

I bend over, hands on my hips, and suck the thin mountain air into my lungs. When I finish wheezing, I open the water bottle and take a sip, doing my best not to think about yesterday and my upsetting conversation with Uncle David.

Yesterday afternoon, after reaching our destination of Molinaseca, we finally had time alone to talk.

The village is one of the prettiest of the journey. You walk across a great medieval bridge known as Bridge of the Pilgrims to reach it, and beyond the town, far in the distance, a stunning majestic church nestles into a backdrop of lush green rolling hills. Many of the houses and buildings are adorned with coats of arms, and the entire place conjures up images of brave knights on horses and princesses in castles.

After lunch with the group, Uncle David and I walked to the river. I sat beneath a tree and pulled off my shoes so I could soak my feet in the water. The downhill trek had done a number on my feet, and I had a host of fresh blisters, and my toenails were bruised.

"Those are bad shoes," Uncle David said, taking in my wounds.

I nodded. They were. But we were only nine days from finishing, and I felt a sentimental attachment to the boots. Several pilgrims call me "Doc" because of them. "Hey, Doc." "What's up, Doc?"

The river was wide and lazy, and Uncle David stripped down to his shorts and waded in to his chest, then dove into the current. He popped up a hundred yards upstream and shook the water from his hair like a dog, a wide smile on his face, and looking at him, I wondered, not for the first time, if maybe he has it right and the rest of us are idiots. His life is so simple, and he seems so utterly content. He does what he likes, when he likes, however he likes, without the least bit of concern about success or appearances.

Yet it's not as if his life is frivolous or without meaning. For fourteen years, faithfully he has carried out God's will as a messenger of love and kindness. And while I understand part of the reason he does it is out of guilt, misplaced self-blame over my dad's death, the penance has turned into a calling, and his mission is as gratifying and fulfilling as any purpose I know.

He started Sanctuary of the Gods on the third anniversary of the accident. He explained he was walking the trail, something he'd been doing continually since he'd made his way to Spain a few months after leaving the hospital. He would walk from Roncesvalles to Santiago then turn around and walk back. On that fateful day, he stopped to rest in the adobe building that still stands there today and lay down to take a nap.

When he woke, several pilgrims were sitting in the shade of the chestnut tree. It was an exceptionally hot day, and they were out of water. Uncle David passed around his canteen and shared a bag of almonds with them. They were incredibly grateful, and when they left, he said, "Have a good life," and that was it. That afternoon, he walked to Astorga, bought as much food as he could carry, and walked back. The next day he did it again, and he has been doing it ever since for fourteen years.

In the offseason, from November through March, he wanders. He's been all over Europe, Asia, and most of Africa. He says there's a whole community of drifters, perpetual pilgrims who eke out livings one way or another as they walk across continents, traveling until they reach the end of a trail then turning down another to walk some more.

It's hard to imagine living that way, so capriciously and without roots. Yet I also think the wanderers might be on to something. Uncle David is relaxed, carefree, and unencumbered in a way I've never known.

For as long as I can remember, since grade school, I have competed, scrabbled, and scraped to secure a foothold in the world. I've studied, taken tests, and worked relentlessly to inch myself forward. And for what? I'm a copyeditor for a nearly defunct magazine publisher, drowning in school debt, and living in a windowless sublet in Harlem.

David waded out of the water and joined me on the bank. He sat in the dappled sunlight beneath the tree, his elbows on his knees.

Eyes on the water, he said plainly, "I'm sorry I left you."

The words caught me off guard, and I made a small sound like the air had been knocked from my lungs.

"It's my second-greatest regret," he said.

He didn't need to explain the first. We both knew it had to do with the accident.

"Aunt Robbie did a good job looking after me," I managed.

He looked sidelong at me. "She did. But that doesn't make what I did any less of a mistake." He looked down at the dirt, then back up at me. "I didn't think you needed . . . wanted . . . me. It was a confusing time." He sighed out heavily. "Then days turned into months and months into years, and I didn't feel like I had a place or a right to be in your life anymore."

I didn't know what to say to that, so I said nothing and looked at my feet in the water.

"It's taken me a long time to make peace with my mistakes," he went on, "and part of that has been owning up to them. I left because I couldn't stay, and I stayed away because, it turns out, I was a fool, but I want you to know, I wish I'd done better."

It made me wonder how different my life might have been had he been a part of it and how much easier things would have been for Aunt Robbie. I thought of my grandmother and how bitter and sad she was at the end. Would having had Uncle David around have changed that?

"When your dad died, I couldn't take it. Not metaphorically, but actually. He was my compass, the only thing that ever kept me flying straight. All my life, I'd been a screwup—in school, with my dad, at work. Too much energy and not enough direction. But Pete never saw me that way. It was his idea for us to do the Camino, and I think the reason he wanted to do it was for me. It was like he knew, even back then, that I'd find my place here. It was the first time I didn't feel"—he stopped for a second as if trying to find the word—"wrong."

I felt a deep pang of love at that moment, thinking of the twenty-three-year-old David in the photos and his coiled, almost palpable energy, a loaded spring ready to explode.

"The day I left the hospital, I didn't intend to leave forever." He took a deep, trembling breath. "But I started drinking. And didn't stop. Not for three years."

Three years. The day he stopped to rest at Sanctuary of the Gods.

"I'm sorry," he repeated.

"Thank you," I said, the only thing I could think to say, my voice tight with emotion.

"I hope you know I won't ever leave you again." He turned so his blue eyes pierced mine. "Whatever you need, I am here for you."

The tears I'd been trying to contain leaked.

"You're so much like your mom," he said.

"When I cry, you mean?" I sniffled and wiped at my face with the back of my hand.

"No. The way you try so hard not to. She was like that as well. She felt things deeply but didn't want people feeling sorry for her, so she kept her emotions inside."

It was a nice thing for him to say, though I wasn't sure I believed him. From what I could tell I wasn't much like my brave, billy goat mom at all.

"Do you know why she was here?" I asked. "On the Camino?"

I'd been wondering about this since I discovered my dad had given her the hiking boots. She had lied about who she was and evidently was too poor to afford decent shoes. In the photos, she looks young, barely older than a teenager, and my dad's journal offers no clues as to what inspired her to take a pilgrimage across Spain.

"I do," Uncle David said, "but I didn't learn the truth until after her death, after I came home to New York to be with you and your dad."

"Where were you before that?" I asked.

"Walking," he said. "I did the Portugal route, then wandered through Morocco, Algeria, Tunisia, and finally Italy." His voice was wistful, the memories of that time good.

"How'd you survive?"

"I worked odd jobs. I picked grapes. I waited tables. I worked at the hostels." He shrugged. "It suited me, and there was nothing for me in New York. Your dad was living here in Europe with you and your mom. I didn't get on with my dad or Robbie. I didn't want to build houses. I liked roaming and not being tied down."

He blew out a breath.

"But then your mom died, and your dad moved home, and suddenly I had a reason to go back. Your dad needed me. In the span of a single, horrible day, he'd gone from the happiest man on earth to a grief-stricken single dad, barely able to function and scared out of his mind that someone would discover your secret."

"My secret?" I asked.

He nodded, then went on to tell me the most unbelievable story, a tale so fantastic I would have thought he was making it up, except I knew Uncle David didn't lie.

When he finished, sensing my skepticism, he said, "The town is called Dur. Look it up. There was even a movie made about the scandal. It's called something like *Murder in the Pyrenees* or *Death in the Pyrenees*. It's in French, so I never watched it, but the story is based on the feud over the mountain."

"A mountain in Andorra?"

He nodded.

"Which means, you're saying my mom was Andorran, not Portuguese?"

"Yep."

Of all the things he'd told me, this was possibly the most stunning. My whole life I've prided myself on being Portuguese, believing it was an essential part of who I am. I'm obsessed with Portuguese food. In high school, I had a mad crush on Shawn Mendes, mostly because he's half Portuguese. In college, I joined the Portuguese club. I always check the box that says nonwhite Hispanic.

Are Andorrans Hispanic? I know nothing about Andorra. I barely know it's a country and couldn't tell you where it is on a map.

"Why didn't you or my dad tell me?" I said, upset that such an important thing as where I come from would be kept from me.

"To protect you."

"From the Andorran mob?" I nearly scoffed.

"Yes," he said plainly. "To protect you from the people who were trying to find your mom."

It was the part of the story that sounded most outrageous, the idea that a bunch of murderous thugs were pursuing a seventeen-year-old girl because of a vote over a ski resort.

"Your mom and dad were scared. In the event of her death, her share of the mountain passed down to you."

"So you're saying I own part of a mountain?" I grinned. "Which means I could be rich."

He didn't join in my humor. "Legally it's possible, though I doubt it. Your dad did everything he could to keep anyone who might be looking for your mom from knowing about you."

"Oh," I said as a thought occurred to me. "Which is the reason he didn't go back?"

"Yes," Uncle David said. "He was frantic, knowing that the landlord, who was the one who found your mom after she died, had called an ambulance and that your mom had been taken to the hospital. It meant there would be a paper trail. Up to that point, your mom and dad had been so careful. A midwife delivered you. Your mom worked for a friend who paid her under the table. They never officially married. For five years, they'd lived off the grid and out of sight. No one knew where they were. Not even us."

"You didn't know they were in Portugal?"

He shook his head. "We knew they were living somewhere in Europe, but your dad made a point of never flying in or out of the same airport when he came home. That's how careful he was. He knew your mom's father knew about him because of what happened in León, and he was worried the father was keeping tabs on him. Each time he brought you home for a visit, he was taking an enormous risk."

"That's crazy," I said, reminded once again of how much my dad must have loved my mom to do all that.

"After your mom died, he was certain their cover had been blown, so he paid the landlord to clean out the apartment and throw away everything. For years, he was worried someone would discover the truth and come after you."

"Is that how she died?" I asked. "They found her?" Implausible as the story was, I was starting to believe it.

Uncle David shook his head. "No. Your mom died of something called a pulmonary embolism, which the doctor said was likely caused by leftover scar tissue in her lungs from a case of pneumonia she had when she was younger, combined with being pregnant."

"My mom was pregnant when she died?"

Uncle David sighed heavily. "You were going to have a brother."

A brother. I felt it, the hard ache of loss for the thing that could have been. Me, my dad, my mom, and a little brother living happily in Portugal. My mom cooking. My dad taking photos. It hurt, like someone dangling a dream before my eyes a second before snatching it away.

For a moment we were silent, Uncle David looking at the water while I sat beside him, my mind whirring with the phantasm of what almost was.

Finally, he said, "Did you know it was your mom who led me to my destiny?"

I blinked several times to bring myself back to the moment.

"She was very devout. It drove me crazy how she wanted to stop in every cathedral and go to every mass."

I sensed that from my dad's photos, so many of them of my mom in a cathedral.

"In the Burgos Cathedral, she pointed to a painting of a king holding a harp and told me he was my namesake, King David."

Uncle David puffed out his chest and pulled his shoulders back like he was royalty, but I didn't smile. The afternoon was simply too burdened.

"It was funny because of how much the guy looked like me." He winked. "Though not as good looking, of course."

"Of course," I said and forced a tight grin.

"Your mom went on to say that God chose David to be king because he believed David shared his heart and could therefore minister his will."

"Tall order," I said.

"It was. And the day I stopped at Santuario de los Dioses to rest, your mom came to me in my dreams, and that's how I knew tending to God's will was what I was meant to do."

His reasoning doesn't make a lot of sense. Had his name been Lucas or John, I'm sure he would have found just as valid a reason for doing what he does. But perhaps all of us are looking for justification for the choices we make.

"Maybe she knew someday it would lead you back to me," he said.

He stood, dusted off his shorts, grabbed both packs, and trudged up the bank.

I sat for a long time thinking about everything he'd said. It felt so unfair—my mom dying of a blood clot, my dad dying because a bird flew into the engine of his plane, Uncle David unable to cope and abandoning his family and his life.

I shivered and, realizing I was cold, pulled on my Doc Martens and started back for the albergue. On the way, I passed the town's cathedral and decided to go in.

I arrived as mass was starting and sat in the back. The words were foreign, but the devoutness of the worshippers moved me. I closed my eyes and again imagined what my life might have been like had my mom lived—a mom, a dad, and a brother beside me as the four of us sang hymns, responded to a sermon in Portuguese, and prayed.

That was when I felt it, familiar warmth on my spine that I'd always associated with my dad, but that I knew in that moment was my mom, and I understood, when I was little, she did this with me, took me with her to worship. It was startling, a single sharp memory of my mom and another gift of the Camino.

. . . *ninety-nine . . . one hundred.*

I bend over and suck air into my lungs.

While I definitely did not inherit my mother's "billy goat" genes, today her spirit glowed bright inside me, and when I finish the Camino, I'm going to find out more.

37

ISABELLE

1997

"Thank you," I say to Eliana. We sit parked outside the train station of O Barco de Valdeorras, a village forty kilometers from Ponferrada, in a tiny car she borrowed from a friend.

"I don't like it," she says in the tut-tut motherly way she has. "You still have a fever."

"I'll be fine. The train is coming, and my ma is meeting me in Santiago."

She reaches out and touches my cheek, and I cover her hand with mine. "Thank you, Auntie. I will write when I am settled."

"I'm glad God put you in our path."

"Me too." I climb out and walk into the depot, though I have no intention of buying a ticket. Even being at this train station, though it is far from the Camino, makes me nervous. My race through the streets three days ago made it clear my pursuers have not given up.

I wait until Eliana's car disappears down the road, then return outside and walk into the town to buy food and to find a pay phone. I couldn't make this call in front of Eliana. No one can know about it.

I find a small market where I buy peanut butter, crackers, almonds, and raisins to last me the six days I have left to make it to Finisterre. I will need to hike nearly forty kilometers a day, which is a lot but not impossible. And the reward will be worth it—six days of effort for a future of happiness.

I find a pay phone outside the store and lay out a handful of coins.

"Sixty pesetas," the recording says.

I drop the coins in the slot.

The line buzzes twice before Senora Sansas answers exactly as my ma did yesterday. "Ya?"

"Senora, it's Izzy. Izzy Vidal."

Silence.

Senora Sansas is a plain woman in appearance and personality. Her greatest achievement is the ten healthy children she bore. I imagine her small eyes darting around her kitchen.

"I need to talk with Senor Sansas."

More silence.

"Senora?"

"Ya," she repeats. "He's not here." Then dumbly she adds, "He is in Spain looking for you."

"Yes," I say. "Which is why I'm calling. Do you know where I can reach him?"

Though I cannot see her, I know she is thinking, trying to puzzle out whether this is some sort of trick.

"He's looking for me," I say, giving her a nudge. "He'll be glad to hear from me."

"Yes," she says. "Okay. One minute."

I hear her set down the handset.

"Please deposit sixty pesetas," the machine says.

I deposit more precious coins in the slot.

She comes back on the line and gives me the name and number of a hotel in Santiago.

I thank her and hang up, then deposit more coins and dial. I ask the receptionist for Senor Sansas's room, and again listen as the phone rings. It's not yet seven in the morning, and I pray he is still in his room.

He answers with a grunt.

"Senor Sansas?"

He gives another grumble.

"It's Izzy."

"Izzy?" I hear the surprise in his voice.

"Yes, sir," I say, feeling odd using the respectful term considering he's trying to track me down and kill me. But I've known him all my life, and it's how I've always referred to him.

"There are a lot of people looking for you," he says.

"Yes, sir. Which is why I'm calling."

"You want to turn yourself in?"

"No. But I do want to talk about my options."

He is quiet, and I take it as a good sign.

"I don't care about the ski resort," I say.

"This stopped being only about the ski resort when my boys were killed," he says, his voice low and rumbly.

My throat tightens with my emotions as I say, "I was so sorry to hear about their deaths."

"Your condolence will not bring them back. Nothing will."

I nod and remain silent, allowing him his anger and grief.

"Your pa is responsible," he goes on. "He knew they were in danger, and he could have warned them, or he could have warned me so I could have protected them until their birthdays passed and this whole thing was over. But he didn't. He chose instead to let them die, and in doing so, sealed not only their fates but your own. He is the one, not me, who put the bull's-eye on your back."

His rage sizzles, and I squeeze my eyes tight against it, the whole thing horrible. There was a time, not so long ago, when our families were friends, when my pa and Senor Sansas would have fought side by side to protect either one's children.

"I understand your anger," I say. "But just like this war had nothing to do with Miguel and Manuel, it also has nothing to do with me or my brother and sister."

"I wish for your sake that was true. But that's not how it is."

I was careful with my statement, and he was just as careful with his response. He is telling me he intends to exact his full pound of flesh, two lives for two lives—mine and, after I am caught, either Xavier or Ana.

"Please," I say, all my composure of the moment before erased by my fear for my brother and sister. "Xavier and Ana are only children."

"So were Miguel and Manuel," he says flatly.

I take a deep, slow breath and play the only card I have left. "If you don't find me, in less than a month, I will be able to cast my vote."

"That's a big if, but is that why you're calling, to suggest that your vote is up for negotiation and that, if I continue to spare your brother and sister, you would be willing to vote our way?"

A chill shudders my spine with the words "continue to spare your brother and sister," and the insinuation that the only reason Xavier and Ana are still alive is because he hasn't caught me yet and was waiting for exactly this moment before he decides how to deal with them.

"I wish it were that simple," I say, "and would happily make that trade, but unfortunately I can't do that."

"Sure you can. You said you were calling to discuss your options. That's your option. Vote for the mining rights, and I will declare my boys' deaths an accident, and Xavier and Ana can go back to their lives without threat of retaliation."

I notice he does not include me in the bargain, signaling he is still intent on getting his revenge.

"You are not the only one I'm worried about," I say. "If I vote your way, my family will face an equal threat of retribution from the other side."

"This conversation is growing tiresome. You said you called to discuss your options, yet so far, you are offering me nothing."

Closing my eyes, I take a deep, slow breath and then propose the idea I've rehearsed in my head since the day I fled from Pau. "Give me your word that you won't hurt my brother, sister, or ma, and I promise never to return to Dur and never to cast my vote."

He's quiet for so long I need to deposit another sixty pesetas.

"And if I don't agree?"

"If you don't agree then, when I turn eighteen, I will vote for the ski resort, and you will lose. You will exact your vengeance on my family, staining your hands with the blood of innocent children, and the feud will escalate, and more people, possibly people you love, will be hurt, and it will continue like that until all of Dur and everything you care about and everything I care about is destroyed."

My frustration and fear and anger boil over, this conversation and everything that's happened so awful and unnecessary.

"What I'm offering is a compromise," I go on. "You don't win, but neither does my pa." I add the Andorran phrase, "És millor mig pa que no pas pa." *Half a loaf is better than no bread at all.*

"You are assuming I will not find you and claim my full loaf," he says.

"You have not found me yet."

"I'm a patient man."

"I made it past Ponferrada. Now I can go anywhere."

"Even if I agree, the men I'm working with won't stop looking for you. Neither will Castor and his men. You hold the key to a fortune both sides have invested a lot of time and money in. They will do whatever it takes to find you and take that power from you."

"I understand that. But they don't have a personal vendetta against my family."

"And what about my boys?"

"My parents will no longer have me in their lives. That's something."

I hope he recognizes the full weight of what I am offering, that I am giving up ever seeing my home and family again, and that for the rest of my life I will be relegated to a life in the shadows, where constantly I am looking over my shoulder, worried about being discovered.

"You won't come back," he says, "and you won't cast your vote if I promise not to hurt Xavier and Ana?"

He is cunning, the slight rewording almost slipping past.

"And my ma," I clarify.

It was my pa who taught me that vengeance is all about inflicting pain, and that it's far more devastating to have a loved one destroyed than to be destroyed yourself. Senor Sansas wants my pa to feel the same anguish he felt when his sons were killed. He wants him to suffer, and banishing me and killing my ma would do that.

"I want your word that Xavier, Ana, and my ma won't be hurt," I say carefully, my heart twisting with the words, the silent omission of my pa exactly what it suggests. I will not retaliate by voting for the ski resort if my pa is harmed.

It's clear Senor Sansas is not willing to walk away without compensation for his sons, so to save the others, I am offering a sickening solution. My hope is that my pa was right when, at the convent, he said he could protect what was his, and pray that includes himself.

For a long time, Senor Sansas is quiet, the line buzzing between us as he considers the offer and silently calculates the odds of catching me against the chances of me continuing to evade him and, when I turn eighteen, casting my vote against him.

Finally he says, "I underestimated you, Izzy."

It's possibly the greatest, most awful compliment I've ever received.

"I give you my word," he says and hangs up.

I slump to the ground and drop my head to the knees at the exact moment a thunderclap splits the sky, and it begins to pour.

38

REINA

2024

O Cebreiro is glorious. It makes me think of *Lord of the Rings* and hobbits. The small village sits on a mountaintop, surrounded by panoramic eye-popping green valleys. Originally Celtic, it is the heart of Galicia. A smattering of oval-shaped thatched houses and shops called pallozas line ancient meandering cobblestone walks, and to add to the magic, the residents speak Gallego, a form of Spanish that sounds medieval as the place itself.

I walk through the town, chilled and damp but happy, feeling like Bilbo Baggins embarking on a grand adventure.

"Excuse me," I say to an old man sitting beneath the eave of the souvenir shop.

The closer we get to Santiago, the kitschier the trail becomes. Since leaving León, each village has offered an array of trinkets and souvenirs for the trail—Saint James magnets, Buen Camino shot glasses, plastic Camino shell key rings, and yellow-arrow T-shirts.

I explain to the man that I'm trying to find the hermitage. Uncle David told me O Cebreiro was one of the most memorable places for him and my dad. They had learned from a villager of an ancient hermitage in the woods supposedly used by the Knights Templar, then spent the night there pretending they were knights on a quest.

My dad's entry read:

> Today we were brothers of the Knights Templar, and we carried our drink and fare to an ancient hermitage known only to those in the Order. And tonight, I go to sleep with dreams of guarding gold from the mines of Las Médulas and defending fair maidens (one fair maiden in particular) in my head.

I needed to look Las Médulas up on the internet. It's a historical gold-mining site near Ponferrada that has existed since the first century and was written about by Pliny the Elder, which was probably why my dad knew about it. My dad was a huge fan of the ancient philosophers, and Pliny the Elder was one of his favorites.

Unfortunately, Uncle David couldn't remember where the hermitage was. He said he'd simply followed my dad. Its location is a closely guarded secret, and so far, the villagers I've asked have pretended not to know what I'm talking about.

The old man says something in Gallego. The language has Latin roots, and the single word I catch is, "promesa." I have no idea if it translates to *promise*, but I answer with the Knights Templar pledge that my dad wrote down in his journal.

"Non nobis Domine non nobis sed Nomini Tuo da gloriam."

Not to us, O Lord, not to us, but to your name from glory.

The old man's cheeks crease in a smile, and he nods to the church across from us then points to the arrow that is part of the cross over the bell tower.

"Gracias," I say, my heart leaping with delight that I figured it out, and again thoughts of Bilbo Baggins fill my head, thinking this is exactly how he must have felt when he solved the riddle to escape Gollum's cave.

I wish Uncle David were here to share the experience. But he ran into an old friend at the bar when we arrived, and the two left to have dinner with another mutual friend. He said he'd leave my pack at the albergue and rejoin me the day after tomorrow in Sarria.

Ted and Ned had checked into their hotel "pooped and ready to be pampered," as Ned put it.

Halfway up the trail today, they booked massages for tonight. Camino massages are a thing, and there are signs advertising them everywhere.

I considered inviting Matt or Tuck, but when I walked from the albergue, they were contentedly eating, drinking, and playing cards with Nicole and Cami. Plus, if I find the hermitage, it will give me something special for the story Matt won't have.

In my string bag, I've packed a wedge of cheese, half a loaf of bread, grapes, nuts, and olives, along with a bottle of wine—the "fare and drink of a knight."

I reach the church and set myself in the proper direction. The arrow points to a forest of dense pine woods at the bottom of a steep slope. It looks like the perfect place for a secret order of ancient knights to hide out, and I head toward it.

The slope is steep and the grass slippery, and several times I need to scuttle down on my butt. I wish I would have thought to bring my rain poncho and flannel shirt, my sweatshirt no match for the misting frigid rain. The good news is, because of the cold, my knee is only half as swollen as it usually is at the end of the day and only hurts half as much.

I reach the woods and smile when I look back and see how far I've walked. It will be a chore to get back, but I'm about to be inducted as a brother of the Knights Templar in an ancient hermitage hidden in a cloak of a dark wood at the foothill of an ancient hobbit village, so I'd say it will be worth it.

The rain lightens when I enter the dense trees, and it becomes eerily dark. I pull out my phone to light the way. The trees hang with moss, and birds caw and trill in the leaves. It's mystical, magical, thrilling, and a little scary.

I try to maintain my direction, though it's difficult now that I'm in the woods and the church is out of sight. I see a large boulder that looks promising and walk toward it, ducking beneath a pine bough at the exact moment I hear the buzz.

I reverse direction and cover my head and neck with my elbows as I race back the way I came, making it three steps before I feel the sting through my jeans.

I stop and look down, panic turning my brain white.

Dropping to the ground, I shimmy my jeans down to look at the spot I was stung. I shine my phone to see if there's a stinger. I don't see one, but already my skin is turning red and starting to swell.

Stupid. Stupid, stupid, stupid.

I left my EpiPen in my pack with Uncle David. The entire time I've walked the Camino, I haven't seen a single bee.

I feel the toxin spreading and fumble for my phone to turn on my cell service.

No service.

My throat begins to swell, and my numb fingers struggle to pull up my jeans. I lie on the damp ground and tilt my head back, hoping to expand the airway as I pray it doesn't close completely. The trees above me sway, and tears leak from my eyes. I can't believe this is how my story will end, cold and alone, when I've only just realized how much there is that I still want to do.

～

I don't know how long I've been here, wheezing through the pin-size tunnel that remains open in my throat, when I hear my name through the trees.

I open my eyes and try to answer, but it's impossible, the effort causing a terrifying pause in my breath. Fresh tears form and freeze on my cheeks as I pray whoever is looking for me doesn't give up.

I am here! I cry in my head. *Please, please. I am here!*

The flood of emotions causes sickness to rise dangerously, and with tremendous effort, I heave myself onto my side so the vomit won't choke me.

"Oh! Crap!" I hear someone say.

From the side of my vision, a shadow holding a phone with its flashlight on runs toward me.

"I've got you."

Matt.

He lifts me from under my arms and turns me so my head dangles over the ground and the vomit spews to the dirt.

"Bee sting," I try to explain, but my tongue is too swollen, and what comes out is a gurgle. I choke back another spasm of nausea as he drags me a few feet from the puke and lays me on the ground. Greedily I suck air through my nose to pull it into my lungs.

He pulls off his jacket and drapes it over me.

"I'm going to get help."

My right hand, the only limb functioning at all, shoots out and snags hold of his pants.

"No!" I cry, certain if he leaves, I will die.

"But—"

"No!" I repeat, and snot and hot tears cause another violent, choking jag.

"Okay," he says, eyes darting around, clearly terrified as well.

His hair is wet and drips in his eyes. It's grown long over the past month, and he hasn't shaved in weeks and now has a half-inch black beard.

His teeth chatter as he says, "I passed the ruins of the hermitage a few meters back. It's still intact. It will at least get us out of the rain."

I'm so tired I don't answer; the jacket holds the warmth of his body, and my eyes start to close.

"No! Don't sleep! You can't sleep!" He kneels beside me, pulls off the jacket, and roughly rubs my arms and legs. "Stay awake!"

"Okay," I gurgle.

Awkwardly, he scoops me off the ground, staggers to his feet, then blindly trips with me through the woods.

He stoops through a door of what must be the hermitage.

The space is dry and the darkness absolute. Matt sets me on the stone floor and turns on his phone's flashlight. He shines it around. The space is the size of a classroom with two columned arches that divide it. Across from the door are the remains of what appears to be an altar.

Matt drag-carries me to a wall and props me against it. I slump like a rag doll, and again my eyes begin to close.

"No!" he snaps, then jolts me awake by jerking me forward.

He climbs behind me so his legs straddle mine, then yanks me back so my back is against his chest. He maneuvers his jacket over me and threads his arms backward through the sleeves, a clever solution that allows both of us to share the jacket's warmth.

"Don't sleep," he orders.

To emphasize the point, he jostles me. It's very annoying, and I elbow him in the gut.

He laughs through chattering teeth. "That's it. Get pissed off. That should keep you awake."

Every minute or so, he does something else to irritate me and keep me from drifting off. He tells lame jokes. He flicks my swollen cheek with his finger. He chafes the back of my neck with his scruffy beard. He calls me "Velma" and hums the *Scooby-Doo* theme song.

"You know," I slur through my fat tongue. "Velma's a compliment."

"*I* know that," he says. "Velma is my sister's favorite superhero."

Velma, a superhero? I instantly like his sister for thinking of a nerdy teenage detective in a seventies cartoon as a superhero.

"How old's your sister?"

"Thirty-two."

The answer surprises me. I was imagining a little girl. Matt is twenty-eight, which means his sister is older.

"What's her name?"

"Fiona."

I think of the ladybug stone he left at the iron cross with the bright-yellow letters.

"That's pretty," I say, getting a clearer picture of who his sister might be.

"Don't tell her that." He chuckles, his chest moving with his laughter against my back. "She prefers fierce, fiery, or feisty. Any of the *f* adjectives. Her favorite is Fiona the Fabulous."

I smile again, imagining a woman who looks like Matt, with the same dark hair and deep dimples, declaring she is Fiona the Fabulous.

"And she's a *Scooby-Doo* fan?" I ask.

"Yep. *Scooby-Doo*, *The Flintstones*, Road Runner, Bugs Bunny. The classics."

"It sounds like your sister has outstanding taste."

"She does. After all, I am her favorite brother."

"Does she have another brother?" My words are less garbled, and I realize the swelling in my face and throat has gone down, and I can breathe more easily.

"She doesn't. But that's not the point."

I laugh again, freer now, knowing I'm not going to die.

"How'd you find me?" I ask.

"I looked at your dad's journal."

"You what?" I snap.

"And you're glad I did, right?" he says, flopping his jacketed arms up and down.

Realizing he's right, begrudgingly, I say, "Thank you," then, with no warning at all, start to cry.

Perhaps it's relief, or maybe just the drain of adrenaline, but out of nowhere, tears stream from my eyes and mucus leaks from my nose. I try to sniffle it back, not wanting to slobber on his jacket and because I can't wipe it away with my arms pinned and still mostly useless.

Matt reaches his right jacketed arm up and windshield-wipes my face, a giant inelegant sweep back and forth, then up and down, doing it again and again until, somehow, instead of crying, I am laughing.

His chest jostles against me with his matching giggles.

Then, even though I've stopped crying, he does it again, and I elbow him in the ribs.

"Ouch," he says. "Nice to see you're getting your punch back."

He drops his arms back around my waist so his hands are resting on that awful, wonderful spot just below my belly button. I try not to think about it, or that his warm breath is tickling the back of my neck, or that his large chest is pressed tight against my back, or that his right leg is nuzzled against my knee. I've thought about shifting it, but haven't, and now feel like I can't without it looking like I'm making a point.

"I'm hungry," he says abruptly.

"There's food in my bag."

"Great," he says and shoves me forward so he can climb out from behind me. "I'll be right back." He turns on his flashlight and heads out of the hermitage, and the cave turns dark, and I am cold and miss his warmth.

He returns, bag in hand.

"Brrr," he says and shoves me forward again so he can climb back to his spot and reinsert his arms in the sleeves of his jacket. The wet dampness of his chest touches my back, and through the cotton of his T-shirt I feel his racing heart.

"Okay, what do we have?" he says as he pries open the string bag and pulls out the feast. When he gets to the bottle of wine, he says, "Yes."

He unscrews the top, takes a swig, then holds it to my lips, and I drool as I drink but manage to swallow about half.

He eats. We drink. We chat.

Since my tongue is still impaired, he does the lion's share of the talking. He tells me about Fiona. Her mental age is six, and she lives in a community in upstate New York called Lambs Farm, but that he calls Bacon Farm because it costs so much. It's just the two of them since their mom died seven years ago.

"So you pay for it?" I ask, astounded, knowing what journalists make, which is about twice what copyeditors make but still not a lot.

"She's happy there," he says in way of an answer, and I feel the uptick of his heart against my back and suddenly understand a little better his ruthless ambition. Becoming a journalist wasn't only about him. He needs to take care of his sister. It doesn't excuse what he did to Karen, but it does explain it.

"So how are the wedding plans going?" he asks, changing topics.

"Fine," I lie. "Any more wine?"

He dribbles the last sip into my mouth, and I swallow. I'm a featherweight when it comes to alcohol and am in my happy place, loopy and a little dazed. It helps with the extraordinary discomfort of the itchiness of the hives, which extend from my thigh up and down the entire left side of my body.

"John wants to have it at Muldoon's," I say, heat rising in my cheeks, both with embarrassment and irritation.

John's text arrived this morning.

> I talked with Meghan the manager at Muldoon's and she said we could rent the place for the wedding if we guarantee enough people. We just need to do it on a Monday after summer and before the holidays. So October.

I thought we had agreed to wait until I got home to figure things out and that we'd take it slow. October is three months away. And he wants to do it at Muldoon's, a pub he goes to every week for happy hour, which is possibly the last place on earth I want to get married. I closed the message without responding, and all day I've told myself it doesn't matter. The wedding is a single day; a marriage is a lifetime. If it makes him happy, why not get married at Muldoon's?

But each time I think about it, I get annoyed. And then I get annoyed with myself for getting annoyed.

John's a great guy, and I'm lucky to have him. He loves me and wants to marry me, and we're going to have a good life. A great life. Yes, I will have to put up with a few quirks, like his inflexibility when it comes to his routines, but every relationship has its compromises. And spontaneity isn't all it's cracked up to be. After all, look at me. Thanks to my whimsy, I almost died and am now on the brink of hypothermia and stuck in a medieval hermitage with my archnemesis.

"Muldoon's, the pub?" Matt says, and though I can't see his face, I imagine his smirk. "Are you going to walk down the aisle to bagpipes?"

I think of elbowing him again but don't, my playfulness deflated.

"Cheer up, buttercup. I hear the fish-and-chips at that place are great."

I huff-laugh. "We could give our guests a choice, fish-and-chips or corned beef and cabbage."

"And you could have a green beer fountain, darts, riverdancing."

"The color scheme's a no-brainer."

"What girl doesn't love hunter green and brass?"

Laughing about it helps. And maybe, if I embrace it, it will be fun.

"Shhh," Matt says, his warm breath blowing on my ear. "I think we're being watched."

His beard nods against my ear toward the altar, and in the pale morning light I see a sculpture of a saint, his hands pressed together prayer fashion on his chest.

"Do you think that's Saint James?" I ask.

"Possibly. The church was built in 836, so I'd guess the hermitage was built around the same time, and Saint James was all the rage back then."

Again and again Matt astounds me with how much he knows about the Camino. He really researched the assignment before coming here, which is both impressive and intimidating. I have a lot of catching up to do.

"Looking pretty good for being almost twelve hundred years old."

"That's funny, he doesn't look a day over a thousand to me," I say in my best Shaggy impersonation. *He doesn't look a day over two thousand to me* is one of Shaggy's most famous catchphrases.

"You do like *Scooby-Doo*!" Matt exclaims.

"Everyone likes *Scooby-Doo*," I say at the exact moment someone outside the hermitage hollers, "Velma! Matt!"

"Here!" Matt shouts back then crawls out from behind me and props me against the wall. "Stay!" he says as if I have a choice.

"Brother Templar!" he roars as he ducks out the door.

"Matteo!" Tuck responds.

"You have arrived, brave brother, in the nick of time to assist me in rescuing a lame horse not worth the price of its saddle but who we might save as a good deed and for the pity of it?"

I roll my eyes.

In a last-ditch effort to preserve the little dignity I have left, I attempt to stand, but my limbs still don't work, and all I manage to do is topple sideways, flailing like a thrashing fish as I fall at the exact moment Matt and Tuck step inside.

39

ISABELLE

1997

The rain has been heavy and persistent for a day and a half, and I am soaked and struggling. Since Eliana dropped me at the train station, I've barely slept, my cough has gotten worse, and there have been moments I've been delirious with exhaustion.

In front of me, a city appears. I've grown used to the miracle—walking for hours through endless fields or scrub, and then suddenly there are buildings.

The city marker says Monforte de Lemos. It's a hill town, and I see what looks like a monastery at the top. Though I'm weary to my bones, I trudge toward it, my soul needier at the moment than my body.

Since my conversation with Senor Sansas, past, present, and future have weighed heavily on my mind. No sin is without penance, and no mercy is without sacrifice, and only now am I realizing the true cost of the bargain I made for my family's safety.

With my promise to never return to Dur, I've forfeited any chance I had for reclaiming the person I was and my identity. Wherever I end up, I won't have citizenship or any chance for claiming it, which means I will never be able to emigrate to the United States with Peter.

And now I'm left with the reality of my situation. The only way Peter and I can be together is if I were to ask him to give up everything for me—his job, his home, a future of living near his family—and I'm not sure I can do that.

I pull open the heavy wood door to the church, and the musty warmth of the sanctuary causes a shudder. The interior is grand with soaring ceilings, a gilded altar, and enormous ornate paintings lining the walls. I sit on the second pew from the back. Hundreds of red votive candles burn around me, and the scent of candle wax permeates the air.

A few rows in front of me, an elderly woman recites the rosary, and her melodic singsong voice lulls me into a trance. Desperately I want to sleep, but I have less than four days to get to the coast if I'm going to meet Peter, and there are still a daunting two hundred kilometers to go. The rain and my sickness have slowed me down, and I'm starting to think I might not make it. Though I am also wondering if I should, my desire warring with my conscience.

Despite what Dan said about Peter already being involved because he is in love, I'm no longer certain that is the only factor to consider. His family needs him. David needs him. I'm not sure I can ask him to give up everything to be with me.

I bow my head, fold my hands, and pray for God's guidance.

I wait and feel nothing, my mind hollow and empty, like my soul has been coughed from my body from my cold.

The old woman stands, and as she passes, her rheumy eyes find mine. She smiles, revealing a remnant of youth in her face, and for a fleeting instant, I am reminded of my ma.

I blink the mirage away and return to my prayer. But when I nearly nod off for the third time, I snap myself awake and force myself to my feet and back out the door.

The rain has stopped, a small mercy.

I start down the hill toward the town. The road leads past the church's graveyard, and as I pass, a gust of wind stirs the foliage around the graves. My eyes catch on a small cyclone of orange and yellow leaves in front of a headstone a few meters in, and I read the words engraved on it:

1814
I was once what you are now.
You will one day be what I am now.

I stop and read it again before looking upward. The sun beams warm on my face.
Thank you.
It's not what I expected or even what I was considering, but that's how I know it's real. One of Gemma's favorite sayings is, "We only have this one life; better make it count."
I'm in trouble, and I need to call my friend.

40

REINA

2024

I am in the hospital in the city of Lugo, waiting to be released. After Matt and Tuck embarrassingly drag-carried me up the hill back to O Cebreiro, a local hotelkeeper drove me and my backpack to the nearest hospital.

Matt offered to come with me, but I felt I'd already put him through enough. Plus, one of us needed to cover the two legs of the trail I would be missing.

Constantly, I think about what he did. Not only that he saved me, but that he thought to do so in the first place, noticing I wasn't in the albergue and caring enough to look for me. It was no small thing. And for the past day, I've been grappling with this side of him I never saw and wondering how a person who would do such a thing could be the same person who so callously steamrollered over an old woman who had fallen on hard times.

"How are you doing?" the nurse asks as she walks in the room.

"Good. Raring to go!"

She laughs and hands me my discharge papers with a stern "Stay away from bees."

I give a mock salute and pull on my pack.

The doctors and nurses have been wonderful. It's clear how much they care about the well-being of pilgrims and consider it a time-honored, sacred responsibility. In the day I've been here, I've seen half a dozen others brought in for everything from heatstroke to alcohol poisoning, and the staff treated each with compassion, patience, and kindness.

Though I was out of danger, the doctor gave me an antihistamine to reduce the inflammation around the sting and to help with the itch. I think it might have also been spiked with something to help me relax because I fell into the deepest sleep of my life and slept nearly eighteen hours.

When I woke, my nurse asked if I wanted her to "fix" my blisters. Expertly she drained, cleaned, and bandaged them, and now I hardly feel them at all. Then, as a bonus, a new doctor came in and asked if I wanted him to drain my knee. He explained I had an effusion, which means fluid had collected in the joint.

The procedure was simple, and miraculously, my left knee is now the same size as the right and bends and acts like a knee! It's as if I've received a Camino tune-up and am all set for the last five days of the trail.

Five days! Each time I think about it, it doesn't feel real. Though I've only been doing this for less than a month, there are moments it feels like I've never been anywhere else.

I walk from the hospital, unable to believe how much better I feel, rejuvenated. The doctor explained my bright mood and energy spurt might be in part from the sting. Bee venom, he said, is a cure for all sorts of things including inflammation, stress, asthma, and exhaustion—a magic elixir of sorts, so long as you aren't allergic and it doesn't kill you.

I lift my face to the sun to feel its warmth, thankful in a way I can't remember. Had I not been wearing jeans, had the sting been closer to my heart, had Matt not come looking for me, I wouldn't be here. It's remarkable, and I hope this feeling of gratitude never leaves.

The taxi drops me in the city of Sarria beside the river, and I follow my phone's directions toward a pizza restaurant Uncle David mentioned.

On the bridge that leads to the riverwalk of stores and cafés, I stop to take in the pretty, festive scene along the grassy bank. It makes me think of the painting *A Sunday Afternoon* by Georges Seurat. Couples stroll hand in hand, kids eat ice cream, a mother chases a toddler squealing with glee, a large floppy dog trots alongside a jogger.

My phone rings, and I look down to see that it's John. I consider not picking up, my mood so blissfully serene and peaceful, but knowing I should probably tell him what happened, I answer.

"Hey," he says chipperly. "You're not going to believe the week I had."

I continue to look at the joyous scene, knowing whatever he's going to tell me can't possibly compare with what I've been through. In no rush, I let him talk. He tells me the latest on the appraisal of the tenement building and then about the outrageous cost of replacing the tires on his truck.

Down by the river, a couple sits reading. The man's legs are on either side of the woman's, and she is using his knees as armrests. It makes me think of Matt and our night in the hermitage, my back against his chest and his legs straddling mine. The woman's book looks serious, the cover red and plain. The man's book is colorful and looks like a comedy.

"Did you hear me?"

I blink. "Sorry, the connection's not great," I lie.

"I said Muldoon's wants us to guarantee at least two hundred guests or they won't shut the place down for the wedding."

Two hundred guests!

"I don't think it's a problem," he goes on before I can respond. "My family alone is like eighty people. And we have our friends. But I don't think we should offer an open bar. My family would drink us into bankruptcy." He chuckles. "People will need to pay for their own drinks."

The man shifts so he is beside the woman, and he lies back on the grass. The woman sets down her book, turns sideways, and rests her head on the pillow of his stomach. I like watching the way they move, the secret dance between them.

"We'll need to spring for the food, but I'm thinking just appetizers. My brother can officiate . . ."

I'm on a bridge in Spain on a stunning summer day, and as easily as it is happening, it could also not be happening. I could just as easily not be here. I could be dead and not be watching a lovely couple resting on the bank. I could not be doing anything ever again.

"We could also get married in the morning, and avoid the food thing altogether . . ."

"No," I say, unaware I was going to say it until the word was out of my mouth.

"No? You're right. Morning's probably not a good idea—"

"No," I say again, eyes still on the couple.

"No about my brother officiating?"

I turn my attention fully to the conversation. "No to all of it," I say, surprised how certain I am when the decision only just came to me. My heart pounds, but not with fear. "I'm sorry, John. I made a mistake. I don't want to get married."

Silence.

I imagine him in his apartment, his feet on the scarred coffee table his sister gave him, the television across from him showing a basketball game or some other sport.

"Why?" he says finally.

I shake my head, not sure of the reason, only certain beyond a shadow of a doubt it's the right choice.

"I'm not even sure I'm coming back to New York," I say.

"But you have to. What about your job?"

"I'm thinking about going to Andorra."

"Andorra? The country? Why?" His voice has grown tight, and I feel his anger growing.

"To see my family."

He doesn't ask what that means. Instead he says, "But you said yes?"

I close my eyes, sad but also incredibly relieved, like I've been pushed out of the way a moment before getting hit by a bus.

"I did," I say, "and I'm sorry, but things have changed."

"Is this about Matt?"

The question catches me off guard, and I answer too quickly, "No!"

"You know he has a thing for you."

I let the comment go. The last thing Matt said as I got in the cab to the hospital was, "Don't worry about the team, I'll give them the *buzz* and let them know you *stung* things up." He laughed at his own joke, which I knew he'd been saving up for some time.

I rolled my eyes and tried to slam the door on his leg.

"It's not about Matt," I say. "It's about me. There are some things I need to figure out."

"So you just need time?" His tone softens, and it causes an intense ache in my heart. I care deeply about John, and I know how unfair this is. He had our lives planned out, and I told him I wanted the same things as him. He didn't do anything wrong, and there's nothing he can do to fix it.

"I'm sorry," I say. "I thought it was what I wanted, but it's not."

"I can't believe you're doing this."

I squeeze my eyes tight. Neither can I. But as my aunt has always said, you can't live your life based on someone else's happiness. When it comes down to it, John and I are two people who happened to meet one night at a party and who have allowed inertia to carry us along since. We're not soulmates. We might not even be that compatible at all.

He grumbles something almost unintelligible before hanging up, and it's only after the line goes dead that I realize what he said. "Damn Camino."

The target of his anger is justified. After all, had I not taken this journey, it's likely I'd have married him. I probably never would have questioned it, and our life together would have continued in its imperfect-yet-entirely-acceptable way. It's even possible that, had I not been stung by the bee, things might not have changed. But today, the future is not what it was, and as I continue to the pizza restaurant, my feeling is undeniably one of relief.

I take a table beside the window, swooning at the delicious smell of charred pizza crust and sizzling tomato sauce wafting in the air. The server arrives, and I order a Margherita pizza along with the lemon soda I've become addicted to over the past month. When he leaves, I pull out my dad's journal, open to his entry for Sarria, and laugh.

> Before criticizing another person, it is wise to walk a mile in his shoes. That way, if he doesn't like the criticism, you're a mile away and wearing his shoes.

41

ISABELLE

1997

My leg jiggles, and my eyes dart to the clock every other minute. It's 12:03 p.m., and the train is supposed to arrive at 12:05. My lungs hurt, but mostly it's my heart that aches.

After passing the graveyard yesterday, I knew I had my answer. Each of us only has this one life. And Peter deserves a chance at the best life possible. I cannot ask him to give up his world to be with me, and I will not knowingly put him in danger. True love means putting the other person first. It's what he would do . . . has done . . . for me. Though I also understand, even had I not made the choice, I believe the choice would have been made for me. I'm simply too sick. God putting his thumb on the scale to ensure I made the right decision and set Peter free.

The sound of the train lifts my head, and I watch as it wheezes to a stop. I scan the struggle of departing passengers.

Gemma is on one of the forward carriages, and when she sees me, her eyes bulge, and I imagine by her expression that I must look quite horrid.

She hurries over, drops her suitcase, and throws her arms around me.

"Oh, Iz."

I bury my face in her dark curls and breathe in the sweet scent of jasmine and mint gum that I will always associate with school, slumber parties, and friendship, and my eyes close in comfort and relief.

She pulls away and bats me on the shoulder. "That's for not calling." She bats me again. "That's for worrying me half to death." She bats me one more time. "That's for going on the Camino without me when we promised we'd do it together."

"I'm sorry. I'm sorry. I'm sorry."

"You're forgiven," she says then runs her eyes over me head to toe. "You look awful, which for you is quite an accomplishment."

I drop my eyes and confess, "I'm sick, Gemma. And scared."

42

REINA

2024

"Velma?" Tuck says.

Seven of us crowd around two tables on a patio in the hillside village of Portomarín waiting for our albergue to open. Four of us—me, Tuck, Gordon, and Matt—are playing poker.

"One euro," I say, pushing a coin into the pot. I hold a pair of nines in my hand.

Matt matches the bet. Tuck and Gordon are out.

At the table beside us, Ted, Ned, and Uncle David watch as they chat about existentialism and whether it's possible for the concept to coexist with God. Uncle David believes it can. Ted is fairly certain the ideas are in conflict. Ned vacillates from one view to the other depending on who's talking. Over the past week, the two brothers and my uncle have grown close. They're around the same age and surprisingly share a lot of the same views.

Ted and Ned drink wine. Uncle David drinks a lemon soda. Uncle David no longer drinks. He also doesn't eat meat. He is so different from the man I knew when I was a child. I remember him as a wild, crazy uncle whose energy never stopped, who gave me piggyback rides, tickled me until I literally cried "Uncle!" and spun me around until I was so dizzy I couldn't stand up.

At moments I see glimpses of that man, his endurance astounding and his easy laughter the same. But more and more, each day, I notice something else, echoes of my dad—in his posture, his walk, the wink of his dimples when he smiles. And each time I catch sight of one of those things, it's as if part of my dad survived and still lives on. It both rips my heart open and unburdens it, my understanding of his death different and far more manageable than when I was eight.

"How many?" Tuck asks.

"Three," I say, causing Matt to smirk.

I roll my eyes. *Yes, I have a pair.*

Tuck shells out three cards, and I place them in my hand and pretend to look at them while actually studying Matt to see what he's going to do.

Over the past month, I've figured out his tells. If he likes something, the muscle below his left eye tightens. If he really likes something, it twitches. If he doesn't like something, his lower jaw sets slightly off center. And if he's worked up or angry, his right nostril narrows.

"One," Matt says, his face neutral, which means he holds a potentially good hand, the start of a straight or a flush, but he needs to draw the right card.

He takes the card and tucks it in on the right side of his hand with a brow lift as if admiring it as his jaw shifts ever so slightly. And I give a silent cheer, then look at my own hand. It still holds only the lonely pair of nines.

"It's to you, Velma," Tuck says.

"Five," I say, sliding the coins into the pot, careful not to overplay it.

"I see your five," Matt says a bit too enthusiastically. "And raise you ten." He plucks the coins from his pile and sprinkles them noisily into the pot.

I work hard to keep my face neutral and calmly place a stack of five two-euro coins beside the pile, then just as Tuck opens his mouth to tell us to reveal our hands, I say, "I see your ten and raise you ten."

Ted, Ned, and Uncle David stop talking, the game suddenly interesting. Our normal bets hover around the five-to-ten-euro range.

I hold Matt's eyes, challenging him. *Fold or pay up.*

His right nostril narrows a half second before his cheek twitches, and he says, "Too rich for my blood."

He places his cards face down on the table, and I whoop and rake the pot toward me.

Uncle David pats me on the back. "A chip off the old block, a born swindler and shark."

And there it is, another unexpected slash to my heart, sharp and bright. *A chip off the old block.* It's something my dad used to say.

"Hola, amigos!"

I look up from stacking the coins into piles to see Cami and Nicole. Both wear pretty Spanish sundresses and strappy sandals. They didn't walk with us today. Nicole said she had a blister. Cami volunteered to join her for a day of shopping in Sarria, happy to have an excuse not to walk.

Gordon told me he thinks the real reason Nicole opted for a day off was because of the fight she and Matt had in O Cebreiro. I felt bad when I discovered their spat was because of me. The night I got stung by the bee, Nicole didn't want Matt to leave the albergue to look for me. She said I'd probably left with Uncle David. It made sense since I hadn't shown up at dinner, and I don't blame her for thinking it, though I'm awful glad Matt didn't agree.

They squabbled, but Gordon said the real row happened the next morning. After sending me off in the taxi, Matt went to the albergue to get his things. Nicole was there waiting, and he snapped at her that, the next time he says he's going to look for a friend, he's not stopping to debate about it.

Nicole, understandably, didn't take it well. She had waited up all night for him and had been legitimately worried. She was the one who woke Tuck and asked him to go out and look for Matt.

They hiked separately to Sarria, and this morning she made the excuse about the blister.

But it seems whatever beef they had is now over. Matt scoots his chair out, and Nicole takes her place on his lap. She wraps her arm around his neck, and he wraps his around her waist.

I focus on stacking my coins, intently straightening them and trying not to notice as she snuggles against him and whispers something in his ear.

It makes no sense that I should be upset seeing them together. They've been together since the beginning of the Camino, and it's not like anything happened between me and Matt in the hermitage. The closeness we shared was out of necessity. I know that. And the feelings it's stirred up are childish and, quite frankly, ridiculous. I don't even like Matt. He hurt Karen. He's a jerk. And a player. He goes through girlfriends like socks.

And he doesn't like me. Despite the stupid, jealous comment John made about Matt being into me, the truth is, I'm a lame horse not worth the price of my saddle. Meanwhile, Nicole is a thoroughbred who looks like a million bucks.

I'm confusing gratitude for what he did with attraction. Hopefully these feelings will go away quickly, and we can get back to the bickering, safe relationship we had.

"Are you feeling better?" Cami asks me. She sits beside Tuck, caressing his neck with her nails.

While she says her motive for coming on the Camino was to find her motive, her motive seems pretty obvious to the rest of us. She came here to find her other half and thinks she might have found it in Tuck. But Tuck is twenty-two, and in four days, he returns to Cambridge. I imagine he'll relegate Cami to a hot little sidenote he brags about when he regales his college buddies with his Camino adventures.

I feel bad for her. While she and I are not exactly friends, over the past few weeks, a mutual fondness has developed. She's sweet and does small kindnesses for people, like turning their laundry on the line so it will dry quicker and buying mints for all of us when she went to the store.

"I am," I say. "Other than my thigh itching, I'm fine."

"What did John say when you told him? He must have been so worried."

I nod noncommittally and fiddle with the coins some more. The only person I've told about the breakup is Uncle David. Everyone was so excited when John and I got engaged that part of me doesn't want to tell them. We only have a few days left of the Camino. I might just keep it to myself.

"Is it true you're getting married at a pub?" Gordon asks, the words slightly slurred. He lifts his almost-empty beer. "If so, count me in."

I give a wan smile and feel Matt watching from across the table.

Uncle David, perhaps sensing my discomfort, interrupts. "Did you know Portomarín is one of the most remarkable towns on the Camino?"

Thankfully everyone turns his way.

"How so?" Ted asks.

"In the sixties, the decision was made to dam the river to create a reservoir."

On the way into the town we crossed a magnificent bridge over a stunning lake that had been created by the dam.

"But damming the river would have meant the village, which was built on its banks, would have been lost."

"Ah, a true conundrum," Ted says.

"Exactly," Uncle David says. "The village was established in the Middle Ages, and they couldn't just let it be washed away. So they came up with a plan to move it."

"The village?" Ned asks.

"Yep. Brick by brick they relocated it to higher ground." He waves his hands at the ancient buildings around us. "And ever since that remarkable feat, the town has come to symbolize resilience and renewal. And each summer, when the reservoir's water level recedes, there's a festival where people come from all over to see the remnants of the old village emerge and to get a haunting glimpse of the past."

"Astounding," Ted says. "Like the city of Atlantis."

"Exactly. It's beautiful to witness."

"Humans really are something."

"Some humans more than others," Ned says with a nod to Gordon, who is now snoring on top of his arms on the table.

Tuck plucks a daisy from the planter beside him and tucks it behind Gordon's ear. Gordon doesn't move.

"Looks like someone's Camino-tose," Matt says.

Camino-tose. The word causes a prickling in my brain.

Matt is always doing that, making up punny words, like he did when he put me in the taxi. *I'll give them the buzz and let them know you stung things up.*

"Cat-a-tonic" was the title of the article Matt stole from Karen, a clever play on the soothing effect of cats and very similar to Camino-tose.

Karen was never punny. Her humor was highbrow and dry.

"Reina, you okay?" Uncle David asks.

"Huh?" I say. "Yeah. Fine." I blink several times then stand. "The albergue's probably open." I leave my poker winnings on the table. "This round's on me." I smirk. "Actually, on Matt."

"To Matt sucking at poker," Tuck says, raising his beer. The group toasts.

Uncle David leaves with me. Very sweetly and quite annoyingly, since my mishap with the bee, he's been nervous as a mother hen and hasn't let me out of his sight. We now have four EpiPens between us—one in each of our packs, one in his pocket, and one he insists I keep in mine. "At all times." "No matter what." "No exceptions."

A group of high-school-age kids limp past. They slump with exhaustion and grumble about their blisters, their sunburn, and their soreness. I smile, remembering the first night in Roncesvalles and how wrecked Ted, Ned, and I felt. It seems like a lifetime ago, the three of us now such hardened veterans that today's hike was barely notable at all.

To receive a Compostela, the certificate of completion for the Camino, pilgrims only need to walk the final hundred kilometers of the trail. Which is why this morning in Sarria, busloads of tourists, students, and church groups rolled in to walk the final five days, hug Saint James, and get their certificate so they can claim they "did the Camino."

"I think I have blisters on top of my blisters," one girl says, and I admire her wide smile as she says it.

Uncle David and I sign in at the albergue and claim our beds. The dorm is a single massive room with the bunks packed so tight there's barely two feet between them. Using items from my pack, I claim seven beds around us for our friends.

Uncle David heads off to shower, and I sit on my bunk and log into the albergue's Wi-Fi. I pull up the *Cat Story* archives and reread the "Cat-a-tonic" article, then work backward to read every article by Karen going back two years.

It turns out to be ten months longer than necessary.

How did I not see it? It's so obvious.

"Everything okay?" Uncle David asks. His hair is wet, and he's shirtless.

"I messed up," I say.

"About John?"

"No. I misjudged someone. Badly."

Matt didn't steal Karen's story. He'd been writing her articles for her for over a year, from the time she started insisting Matt be her copyeditor. The writing goes from dry and disorganized to witty, insightful, and tight, with quips and anecdotes Karen never would have come up with. He was covering for her. She was struggling, and he recognized it and stepped in so she wouldn't lose her job. Brenda must have figured it out and was likely the one who changed the byline, giving Matt the credit he deserved.

"Screwing up is part of being human," Uncle David says and lifts his right hand. "I should know. I'm former world champion."

I almost smile but can't quite manage it. For two years, I've railed against Matt and made it my mission to let everyone know what he did to Karen. And Matt never said a word, letting people believe the worst about him to protect Karen even after she died.

Uncle David's hypnotic eyes hold mine. "'Every morning we are born again, and it's what we do today that matters most.' It's a Buddhist quote, and I use it to help me forgive my mistakes and move on from them. Maybe it will help you as well."

43

ISABELLE

1997

Someone touches me on the shoulder, and my eyes fly open. For a moment, I am trapped between past and present. I'm on the floor of the albergue's bathroom in Logroño, the wood beamed ceiling above me and the sting of the hosteler's hand hot on my cheek. In the next second, the ceiling is white, and the surface below me is soft.

"Joan."

My eyes dart to the voice to find the kind, bespectacled eyes of the doctor who is treating me. I suck in a ragged breath and remind myself I am safe.

"You're in the hospital," the doctor says. "In Porto."

I blink his face into focus.

"It's not uncommon for a fever to bring nightmares."

I look past him to Gemma, and my chest unclenches.

"You gave us quite a scare," the doctor goes on. "The pneumonia was advanced, but the antibiotics seem to be working."

My memory of what happened after Gemma arrived at the train station is spotty. I remember a lot of hurrying around when I got to the hospital. I remember an IV being stuck in my arm and an oxygen mask being put on my face, then nothing.

We're in Porto because Gemma's uncle is a director at this hospital, and he gave Gemma his word that my identity would be protected. I'm registered under the name Joan Silva. Gemma hired a private car to pick us up in Monforte de Lemos to drive us here.

"You're a lucky young woman," the doctor says.

I look at my hands on top of the white sheet. I don't feel lucky. I feel the opposite. I made a deal with the devil, and for that I am paying the price. No home. No identity. And no chance at the future I dreamed of with Peter.

"It will take a bit for your lungs to heal, but you are young and healthy, so I expect you will make a full recovery."

"Thank you," I manage, my voice a rasp and the effort of talking a strain.

He touches my shoulder again gently. "Rest. I'll be back to check on you in a bit."

When the door clicks closed, I turn to Gemma. "What day is it?"

I think I've been here two days, but it's possible it's been longer.

"Thursday," Gemma says, causing tears to spike in my eyes.

Gemma hands me a tissue. "Today was the day you were supposed to meet him?"

I nod. I imagine him standing at the 0,0 km marker, pacing, and I hope he doesn't wait too long.

"Sorry," I say, feeling bad that she is here in a hospital, babysitting me, when she is supposed to be spending the summer in Milan with her mom.

"Well, you should be," she says with mock indignation. "I thought it was understood that I'm supposed to be the one with all the heartbreak and drama in her life."

I try for a smile but can't quite manage it.

"Wow, not even a smirk. Peter must be a heck of a guy."

He is. He's unlike any man I've ever met, and I know I'll never meet anyone like him again.

"Hang in there," Gemma says, "these things have a way of working themselves out."

She's wrong, but I don't have the strength to argue. Despite the doctor's reassuring words that the drugs are working and I'm getting better, I feel like a motorbike without an engine, with so little energy it's all I can do to breathe.

44

REINA

2024

"Well, I'm pretty sure this place ranks as my least favorite," Gordon grumbles.

We're sitting outside the albergue in the town of O Pedrouzo, a dump of a place one day's hike from Santiago. All of us are grouchy, worn down from the journey and done with this final overcrowded slog from Sarria to Santiago, which is overrun with Compostela hikers.

For four days, we've hiked mostly on paved roads and trails, surrounded by hordes of selfie-snapping, hip-hop-blasting chatterboxes. It has made it impossible to get in our normal rhythm, and today, I counted the minutes until the hike would be done.

We arrived at the albergue a little after one to find a mass of anxious pilgrims waiting to claim the limited beds. Not wanting to risk not getting a spot ourselves, the seven of us stayed as well and have been stuck baking in the sun for nearly an hour.

Ted and Ned messaged, warning us not to leave our post. Their hotel is booked, and the registrar told them every other hotel from here to Santiago is likely booked as well. With so many pilgrims on the trail, there simply aren't enough beds.

I lean back against my pack and idly scroll through my dad's photos for the day.

I stop on a shot he labeled "The Four Amigos." It's a photo of Jen, Joe, Uncle David, and my dad in front of a bar. I marvel at how different they look from when they started. The purple streak in Jen's hair has faded to lavender, and she's ruddy cheeked and beaming. She looks lighter in every way. Joe looks like a grizzly gold miner from the turn of the century, his sandy hair grown out and wild, and the walking stick he carries is as gnarled and gray as Gandalf's staff. He looks like the hero in his own great novel. Uncle David smiles mischievously at the camera with a toothless grin that makes him look like he just got away with something and looks wholly in his element, as if, even back then, he was destined to never leave the trail. My dad stands beside him, smiling, but the smile doesn't quite reach his eyes.

"This is one thing I'm *not* going to miss about the Camino," Cami says. "I can't wait to sleep in my own bed. Alone."

Tuck nudges her shoulder. "Oh, come on, babe. Are you telling me you don't enjoy sleeping surrounded by the fresh stench of a bunch of strangers who have just hiked dozens of kilometers in hundred-degree heat?"

"I love the smell of BO in the morning," Matt says, doing a pretty decent impersonation of Robert Duvall in *Apocalypse Now*.

"What I'm going to miss," Nicole says, "are the noises. The snoring, farts, mumbling, night terrors, and seventeen bathroom runs people make in the middle of the night."

"I can't believe this is our last night," Gordon says, and I think he really is going to miss all those things.

The silence returns, each of us lost in our private thoughts. It's hard to imagine that tomorrow we'll reach Santiago and the journey will be over. I feel like I'm not ready . . . not prepared . . . to go home. Since I stood on that bridge and told John I wasn't going to marry him, the future has been so uncertain.

What's next?

The question haunts. After tomorrow, there won't be any more yellow arrows to guide me or curfews to obey or certainty of what the next day holds—walking, laundry, beer and cards, dinner, sleep. The Camino is so simple. Difficult but easy. Each day starts with promise and ends with satisfaction and a deep sense of fulfillment. I'm going to miss this shared, simple life, and the thought of leaving and going back to the hustle and bustle of New York City fills me with a certain sense of dread.

I like the person I've become out here—easygoing, confident, at moments even bold—able to stand in front of a mountain, know it's mine to climb, and certain I can do it. And while this newfound confidence feels unshakable, I worry that it's not, and that I'll return home and lose this wondrous new sense of myself and revert to the old, lesser me.

Feeling sentimental, I say, "Let's take a photo. Our last night."

Everyone struggles to their feet, and I give my phone to a girl beside me. The seven of us wrap our arms around each other.

The Seven Amigos, I think as she snaps the shot, already missing these incredible people even as I hold them.

It's remarkable how close we've become in such a short time, especially when you consider that, in our everyday lives, there's very little chance any of us would have met or have chosen to become friends if we had.

"Did you call Robbie?" Uncle David asks, interrupting my thoughts.

"Not yet," I say as I sit back on the ground and lean again against my pack.

He frowns in the annoyingly paternal way he's adopted, which makes me feel like I'm back in high school.

Channeling my fifteen-year-old snarky self, I roll my eyes. "I will."

"You need to call her," he persists.

I ignore him.

"Reina."

I glare. *Yes, I know I need to call her. But do I have to do it right this minute?*

His piercing blue eyes hold mine.

"Fine. I'll do it when we get inside."

"Good," he says. "Knowing my sister, she's already bought her dress, picked out her wedding gift, and is working on the playlist for the reception. You need to tell her it's off before she starts sewing your veil."

"Off?" Cami says. She sits across from us, her head on Tuck's shoulder. "What's off? The wedding?"

My skin warms, and I feel everyone looking at me, the thirty strangers around us as well.

Fortunately, before I can answer, the door to the albergue opens.

The gaggle of us stand and heave on our packs. The weight always feels so much heavier after having set it down. I grab the walking stick Uncle David found for me on the trail to Sarria and turn to see Matt looking at me in a strange way, his expression unreadable except the slight twitch beneath his left eye.

"Matteo, I need my passport," Nicole says, causing him to snap out of it. Quickly he pivots to rummage in the front pouch of Nicole's pack for her Camino passport for the hosteler to stamp.

"Thanks, babe," she says and pecks him on the lips.

I blink several times and shake away the odd vertigo that has me off-balance.

Gordon steps up beside me. "Sorry to hear about you and John. I really liked that guy."

I nod. I really liked him as well.

Then Gordon surprises me. "But take it from me, who you choose to travel the journey with in this life is the most important decision you're ever going to make, and you're smart to take a minute if you're not sure."

He pats me on the shoulder and continues to the desk. A cautionary tale, his marriage of over thirty years was miserable and left him alone in his fifties and full of regret.

I register and walk into the large, plain, and overcrowded dorm. Despite leaving in the dark this morning to get here early, the seven of us are relegated to top bunks. I take the one across from Uncle David. I lug my pack up and flop on the mattress with my arm over my eyes.

Two bunks away, someone is already snoring. Another talks on his phone loudly in a language I don't understand.

"Let's go, Matteo," Tuck says, and I look beneath my arm to see Matt, who is on the bunk beside me, stop writing and toss his journal toward his pillow before climbing down to join his friend.

"You coming, Velma?" Tuck asks.

"In a bit. I want to shower and wash my clothes. I don't want to stink too bad when I hug Saint James."

"I'm sure he's smelled worse," Tuck says, "but suit yourself."

One of the Camino traditions when you reach Santiago is to embrace the statue of the saint in the cathedral. It's a gesture of gratitude for safe passage on the Camino and allows you an opportunity to offer a prayer of thanks for the people who helped along the Way.

A toilet flushes. The man still snores. The other man still shouts into his phone. Someone in the showers sings Italian opera in a stunning contralto voice that ricochets off the stone walls.

After tomorrow, all this will be nothing but a memory.

Sleep impossible, I pivot to sit up with my legs over the side of my bunk. Uncle David sits cross-legged with his back against the wall reading a book called *Pigman*. It turns out he and I have the same taste in books, and he promised to give it to me when he's finished. I think again how astounding it is that we found each other and the remarkable randomness of it. Had Matt not had his passport stolen. Had I not been working late and happened to see the email to Brenda. Had I not worked up the courage to ask to go in Matt's place. None of this would have happened. And I cannot help but wonder about the miracle of it all.

All the roads in life, one way or another, lead you to what was predetermined—a purpose, a thing, a someone.

I know when my dad wrote those words he was thinking about my mom, feeling exactly as I do now, wondering about the happenstance that brought her into his life.

I glance at Matt's bunk, at the moleskin journal, the same brand and style of journal my dad used. It is open, the ribbon marking the page he'd been writing on.

I think of the twitch I saw beneath his eye, and the way he looked at me the moment after he heard the wedding was off.

Did I imagine it?

Maybe it was nothing.

Maybe he was happy for some other reason.

I glance at the open journal. The scrawl on the open page is only a few lines long, and it's slanted and quickly written, not bullet pointed like his notes typically are for the team. Stream of consciousness writing. Like my dad's entries are when he was hurriedly capturing a thought.

You know he has a thing for you. John's voice echoes in my head.

I lean sideways but cannot read what's on the page. So I get on my knees to look closer.

"What the hell are you doing?"

My face snaps sideways to see Matt beside the bunk looking at me, his jaw tight and his eyes hard.

I look at the journal a few inches from my face then back at him and open my mouth to say something, but nothing comes out.

He snatches the journal away.

"Matt . . ."

"Screw you," he spits.

Then stupidly, skin flaming, I say, "You looked at my dad's journal."

His eyes flash. "To find you! I looked in your dad's journal to find you! I never would have stolen your work."

"I wasn't—"

"Don't!"

Journal in hand, he grabs his pack from his bunk and marches to the other side of the room.

"Hey, mate," he says to a man reading the Brierley guidebook. "I'll trade bunks with you."

The guy doesn't hesitate. His bunk is next to the bathrooms.

Matt throws his pack on the mattress and, journal in hand, walks from the room.

The line I read before Matt caught me was:

> In this moment, I am more whole than I've ever been and more content than I can remember, my destiny revealed fittingly on the setting eve of the Way, and now all that's left is to tell her.

And just like that, I had ruined it.

45

ISABELLE

1997

I sit on the back porch of the inn where I now have a job in the café and a room thanks to Gemma's uncle. I've been here three weeks, and Gemma left a week ago.

It's a beautiful night, still and warm, and I look at the starlit sky as I eat my dinner and think of my ma. *Each night, look up at the stars, and I will do the same, and on Sagitta's arrow we will send each other our love.* I don't see the constellation, but I know it points north so that is the way I look.

The food is bland and overcooked—roasted chicken, potatoes, and green beans. Soon I will ask Carolina, the owner of the inn, if I can move from being a server to working in the kitchen so I can cook and share my ma's recipes.

I force the food into my mouth. Gemma made me swear on the soul of John Lennon, our most sacred oath, that I would eat after she left. I've lost so much weight I need to tie a string around the waist of my jeans to keep them from sliding down, and each time Gemma calls, which is nearly every day, she asks for an accounting of what I've eaten.

It's a true blessing to recognize the treasures in your life while you have them, and over the past month, I've come to realize Gemma is pure gold. Someday I hope to repay her, not only in kindness, but for all the money she spent to help me—the car to the hospital, my medical bills, the long-distance phone calls.

Two days ago, I mailed Dan a check for the fifteen thousand pesetas he lent me along with Emily's sweatshirt. I included a long letter of gratitude as well as a small wedding gift, a hand-smithed silver ring box engraved with a cross and roses that I knew Emily would like.

Paying back Gemma and Peter will take much longer. Each time I consider it, I get overwhelmed and need to remind myself that, with a step at a time, you can climb mountains.

I press the heels of my hands to my eyes and try to readjust my thoughts. Thoughts of Peter still bring me to my knees. I know I need to figure out a way to move past it, but at the moment, with my constant loneliness, I am finding it impossible.

I hear Carolina humming in the kitchen and try to imagine I am home and it's my ma behind the door, preparing the food for tomorrow. This place isn't so different from Dur, a small village a dozen miles from Porto, the villagers familiar with one another, and the café a place to gather each day and gossip.

"Joan."

I drop my hands from my face and turn to see Carolina in the doorway, her arms crossed over her ample chest as she looks at me with concern. She's a large woman in every way, including her kindness.

"There's someone here to see you." Her voice holds a tease, and her painted eyebrows arch playfully.

I tilt my head. Other than her, I don't know anyone well.

"Alberto," she says as if revealing a prize.

Thanks to Gemma, Carolina knows about Peter and that I am heartbroken, and gently she's been trying to encourage me past it. Alberto is a young man who has come in for lunch nearly every day since I started working here. He apprentices as a stonemason under his uncle, and they're working on restoring a twelfth-century hotel a few blocks away. He is near my age and typical looking with thick black hair, a pleasant wide face, and dark unremarkable eyes.

"He brought flowers," Carolina says. "Sunflowers from his mother's garden."

The thought causes me to think of Peter and the flowers he so carefully photographed on the trail, and my heart slams closed like a fist.

"Come, child," Carolina says. "Não é porque o passarinho está na gaiola que o impede de cantar." The literal translation is, *Just because the bird is in a cage, doesn't mean it doesn't sing*, which means, even if your circumstances are not what you hoped, you can learn to be content with what you have. "At least say hello."

I force myself to my feet, and she takes my plate from my hands. "Good girl." She reaches out and tugs the hem of my T-shirt to straighten it, then brushes a loose strand of hair from my face.

With a silent steeling breath, I paint on a smile and walk through the kitchen to greet a boy who will never be the man I love but might be more than I have any right to hope for.

46

REINA

2024

"You're not out with the others?" Uncle David asks, joining me at the picnic table in the courtyard of the albergue. He holds a rectangular box and an envelope and sets them on the table beside him.

I've been here nearly an hour contemplating the ruin of my life and where I go from here. In front of me is a graffiti-laden concrete block wall, and in angry red letters, scrawled across its length, **WHY DOES LIFE ONLY MAKE SENSE IN RETROSPECT?** Looking at it makes me wonder about who wrote it and if, when they scrawled the words, they were as lost and confused.

"Matt hates me," I mumble as I rest my head on Uncle David's shoulder, and he wraps his arm around me. He had been reading on his bunk across from me when Matt caught me looking at the journal.

"He's upset. That's all."

There's no condemnation in the tone, and I love him for it.

"It's the Camino," Uncle David says. "She can be cruel, especially when you're about to leave her, and she can make you do things you otherwise wouldn't do."

I wish I could blame it on that, some Camino voodoo that possessed me, but there's no defense for what I did. Knowingly and deliberately, I looked at Matt's private thoughts, and there's no one to blame but myself.

"I don't know what to do," I say.

"About Matt?" Uncle David asks.

"About the rest of my life."

Before coming on this trip, my life was humming along, not perfectly, but reasonably enough. I had a decent job. I was working toward a promotion. I had a boyfriend, my aunt, friends. I cooked. I went to Pilates. I had a routine and, if asked, would have said I was content. And now, in the span of only a few short weeks, the idea of returning home to that life makes my head feel as if it's going to explode. The Camino is supposed to give you clarity. But for me, it's done the opposite, and never have I been so confused.

"Hang in there, Rainbow," Uncle David says. "Things have a way of working themselves out."

I almost smile at the pet name, surprised and pleased he remembers it. He used to call me "Rainbow" both because of my name and because I loved to dress in colorful mismatching clothes and, not having a mom to tell me otherwise, was allowed to choose my outfits as I pleased.

For a long time, we sit quietly as the sun puts on its magnificent evening performance, the fading light painting the dusty courtyard in delicate blues and pinks.

"It's strange how we think of the sun as sinking," Uncle David says, "when we are the ones perpetually turning from light to shadow and back again."

"That's something my dad would have said."

He huff-laughs. "That's probably where I got it."

"You're a lot like him."

"I was thinking the same thing about you. How much you're like him and your mom, a startling combination of both of them."

I accept the compliment, though I don't believe it. If there's one thing I've learned on this trip, it's that I'm nothing like my parents. My dad was brave and noble as a knight, and my mom bold and fearless as Joan of Arc. And neither seemed to doubt themselves at all.

My dad never would have looked at Matt's journal. My mom would have plainly told a man she cared about how she felt.

In this moment, I am more whole than I've ever been and more content than I can remember, my destiny revealed fittingly on the setting eve of the Way, and now all that's left is to tell her.

I'm not even certain the entry was about me. I'm basing it on half a second of our eyes connecting and a cheek twitch. It's possible he was writing it about Nicole, though even as I think it, I know that's not the case. But that still doesn't mean it was about me. It could have been about anything. Maybe he's decided to change career paths and needs to tell Brenda he's leaving. Or maybe he's decided he wants Fiona to live with him, and he needs to talk to her about it.

"Did you know I didn't go home after the Camino," Uncle David says, interrupting my mental spiraling.

"Aunt Robbie said you stayed in Spain," I say, working to keep my voice neutral.

Aunt Robbie refers to Uncle David's decision not to return after he did the Camino as his "first abandonment." She said he was supposed to come back and help their dad with his construction business but instead chose to continue traipsing around Europe.

"The day I was supposed to go home, I couldn't," Uncle David says, eyes on the orange halo above the wall. "Walking did something to me, broke something loose, and I needed to keep going to figure it out."

A month ago, I wouldn't have understood, but now I do. Time alone with yourself is a powerful thing, and some need more time than others to get acquainted with the person they've uncovered.

"Plus, I was in love with Jen, but she wasn't in love with me."

"You were?" I say, surprised. In the photos, they looked like they were just having fun, and there was such an obvious age gap between them.

"The heart wants what the heart wants," Uncle David says wistfully. "She was everything, even though I knew it would never work. I had nothing to offer and would have made a terrible husband."

He stretches out his legs, one and then the other.

"I'd never felt that way before, feelings too big for my body, like my heart was going to explode out of my chest."

I think of John and how I never felt that way about him.

"I needed to work through that and figure out the man I wanted to be. I didn't have a plan except to keep walking. I went south because there was no more room to walk west."

I smile imagining it, the young David in the photos trekking endlessly through Europe and North Africa like a nomad.

"Do you know what your dad said the day we parted ways?"

I shake my head against his shoulder.

"He said, 'You do you, and don't worry about what anyone else thinks.'"

It sounds like something my dad would have said.

"He was giving me permission to stay and wasn't judging me for it. It was huge, and I don't know, if he hadn't done that, if I ever would have figured out my life." He gives my shoulder an encouraging squeeze. "I guess what I'm trying to say is, there's no right path; there's only the path you're on and the single step in front of you."

The angry red letters disagree. *Why does life only make sense in retrospect?* Looking back on things, it's so obvious all the right and wrong steps you've taken, like looking at an open journal that doesn't belong to you.

"And whatever path you choose," Uncle David goes on, "I'm here for you." He pulls his arm away. "But before you go, I have something for you."

He picks up the envelope. "For Robbie."

I take it, but he doesn't let go. "Did you call her?"

"Not yet," I say with an eye roll. "I will."

He smiles and releases it. "You're going to miss my nagging."

I knock his shoulder because I am. I'm going to miss every single bit of this, including his overprotectiveness and pestering.

"There's a check in there for enough money to take care of the house and any bills she has from taking care of Mom."

I look at him curiously, and he shrugs.

"Sanctuary of the Gods provides well, and my expenses are minimal." He drops his eyes. "Had I known she was struggling, I would have helped sooner."

I know he would have.

"You're helping now," I say, thinking of the Buddhist quote he offered earlier. *Every morning we are born again, and it's what we do today that matters most.*

"There's a letter as well. I hope it helps explain things and that maybe, someday, she might forgive me."

I hope so as well. They could each use the other in their lives.

"Now for you," he says. He lifts the box beside him and hands it to me.

I'm stunned by its weight.

"You hiked with this?" I say. It weighs at least ten pounds.

"Don't open it until you've finished," he says, ignoring my amazement.

He carried his pack and my pack, and one of the packs contained this brick.

"I'm sorry I can't carry it for you to Santiago, but I have my reasons."

Uncle David told me this morning that he will be heading back to Sanctuary of the Gods tomorrow when we reach the final hill that leads into Santiago. He said the city holds ghosts he'd rather not revisit. I think now that those ghosts likely have to do with having his heart broken.

"So you never contacted Jen again?" I ask.

He smirks sheepishly. "No, but I did find her on Facebook."

"Cyberstalker!" I accuse mockingly.

"Guilty," he says. "She has a kid."

"She does?" I know from my dad's journals how much she wanted that.

"A son. He's a little younger than you. The stork found her."

His grin is wistful, and I get the sense he dreamed at one time of he and Jen getting married and having a child together.

"She retired from teaching a few years ago. She still lives in Nebraska. She and Joe stayed friends, and she and her son used to visit him each summer in Wisconsin. Joe passed last year. Cancer."

Two of the four amigos gone. Life fickle and marching on.

I look at the box on my lap, curious.

"Not until you're done," Uncle David admonishes. "When you have your Compostela and are in your hotel on the final night."

"Fine," I pout and set the box aside.

"Would you like to hear one final story?" he asks.

I return my head to his shoulder, and he rewraps his arm around me.

"The morning of the last day, the four of us—Jen, Joe, me, and your dad—decided to go to the cathedral to hug Saint James. Your dad and I weren't into it. The day before, we'd gone to mass and had seen the pilgrims behind the altar reaching up and hugging the statue. It looked touristy and cheesy. But Jen insisted. She said we had a lot to be grateful for, and we should honor the tradition. So we waited in line and hugged the guy. The experience was as uninspiring as I imagined, but what happened after made me wonder if there might not be some magic to it after all."

My pulse ticks up. Like my dad, Uncle David is a wonderful storyteller.

"As we walked beneath the tunnel that leads from the cathedral, we passed an old woman begging for change. Typical of your dad, he stopped and fished a few coins from his pocket. As he dropped them in her cup, she grabbed hold of his wrist."

Uncle David pauses for effect.

"No one else was in the tunnel. It was just us. And there was this feeling, odd, like we knew something was happening that was more than it seemed, one of those strange moments that changes things."

A tingle shudders my spine, a sense of déjà vu, knowing I've had that feeling, something mundane that for whatever reason you recognize isn't ordinary at all.

"The woman said something in Spanish, then released her grip and stepped back into the shadows."

"What did she say?" I ask when his dramatic pause grows annoying.

"Jen was the only one who spoke Spanish, and she took a second, as if considering the words before repeating them, and then she told us, 'I think she said, "Don't think. Wish. And the future will be what you dream."'"

I sigh heavily, let down by the story. The woman probably doled out fortune cookie wisdom to anyone who dropped coins in her cup.

"We stepped from the tunnel," Uncle David goes on, "and looked at each other, all of us thinking the same thing, but none of us saying it until Joe blurted, 'Am I crazy, or did that woman totally remind you of Joan?'"

"My mom?" I ask, lifting my head from his shoulder to look at him.

Uncle David nods. "He wasn't crazy. Sure as I'm sitting here, that old woman was the embodiment of your mom, and she was in that tunnel to give your dad a message."

I work to conceal my skepticism. Uncle David is a man of faith and looks for miracles and meanings in just about everything.

"It was before your dad and I went to Finisterre, and she didn't show up. And it turned out it was the same day she almost died from pneumonia."

"And you think it was her spirit on the mortal edge talking through a woman begging in the streets?"

"I think it was God, but we all have our perspectives," Uncle David says. "Regardless, the thing is, had the woman not been there, I don't think things would have turned out the way they did. Your dad genuinely believed the message was from your mom, and it gave him faith. He never gave up looking for her, and I swear it was like he manifested finding her into existence."

"But you told me it was my mom who eventually got in touch with my dad."

"Yes. But only because your dad wished it."

"Fine," I say, allowing him his enchantment.

"All I'm saying is, you set out to walk the Camino with your dad, so maybe you should continue to follow in his path."

"What do you mean?"

"I mean, maybe it's time to start listening to your heart instead of your head and to allow it to show you the way."

47

ISABELLE

1998

"Joan, I'll take a refill."

I carry the coffeepot to where a customer named Franco sits at the counter. He's a fixture at the café from noon to closing time, holding court with the other regulars who come in to drink coffee and share the latest gossip.

Each day I'm amazed how similar this place is to Dur. The people speak Portuguese, not Catalan, and their faces are darker and heavier featured, but every morning, the men sit at Carolina's counter and drink coffee, then later in the day, beer and wine, while the women stay home cooking, cleaning, and tending to the children. Even the pea caps the men wear are similar, and each time I see Franco or any of the other middle-aged men, I think of my pa, and my heart clenches closed like a fist.

It's been three weeks since Gemma called with the news of his death. The story made the international news, which was how she learned about it. The article she sent me, clipped from *The Paris Press*, was short, an eighth of a page.

It was titled "Murder in the Pyrenees."

Dur, Andorra. A local conflict regarding ownership of the mountain range of the rural Andorran village Dur seems to have led to the murder of one of the principal players. Earlier this week, the body of Ruben Vidal was found by two hikers on an ancient smuggling route that travels over the range into France. It appeared he was bludgeoned to death and had been dead several weeks before the discovery of his remains. Vidal was a cattleman intent on turning Dur into a touristic ski resort, an idea many of his neighbors opposed. It is uncertain what will happen to the mountain now that the man spearheading the effort is deceased.

Vidal's death casts a long shadow on the provincial little hamlet that has survived for more than a millennium in relative isolation. With no local law, the national police of Andorra have been called in to investigate the death, and though they have a long list of suspects, they had not made any arrests as of the writing of this article.

Two photos accompanied the story: One of the town with the mountains in the background, and the other of my pa standing unsmiling in front of his cattle. I keep the article in my room, and each night, I pull it out, look at the photo, and cry.

"Alberto!" Carolina exclaims, and I turn from the coffee maker to see the young man I've been dating for the past six months.

His face lights up as it always does when he sees me, and it warms my heart. I've been lonely since I moved here. While this place is similar to Dur, it is not my home, and I am not a part of it the way I was in Dur.

"Hello, Auntie," Alberto says to Carolina.

He is kind and respectful, and I know my ma would approve. My pa would have as well. Alberto is hardworking, traditional, and Catholic, the sort of man they expected me to marry.

Alberto is dressed in a white dress shirt and fresh-pressed trousers.

I step from behind the counter to greet him with a hug, wondering what prompted him to shave and look so nice.

"Minha linda," he says when I release him. *My beautiful.*

He backs up a step, and I look at him curiously.

His dark eyes hold mine, and he says, "Since the first day you came to our town, I knew I wanted to make you my wife."

My eyes widen, and my heart pounds as I realize what's happening and why he's dressed in his Sunday best.

"You are the most beautiful woman I've ever met."

He drops to one knee and unfurls his right hand to reveal a simple gold band.

"Joan Marie Silva, will you marry me?"

Carolina claps, and Franco whoops.

Peter!

I feel a dizzying lightheadedness and need to blink several times to still it.

Peter is not here. God willing, he is thousands of miles away, living a life that has nothing to do with me.

Alberto is here, and he is kind and decent and asking me to be his wife, which feels like more than I deserve.

"Yes," I say. "Yes, I will marry you."

48

REINA

2024

"Let's get drunk!" Tuck says as a fellow pilgrim takes a final photo of the eight of us—me, Ted, Ned, Gordon, Matt, Tuck, Cami, and Nicole—grinning with our Compostelas, certificates of completion, in front of the fountain in the courtyard of the pilgrim's office. The official distance written on our certificates is 775 km, which is approximately 482 miles.

"Hear, hear!" Gordon bellows, but his words lack their usual boisterousness.

I'm discovering that's the thing about knowing you're doing something for the last time—it often takes the joy right out of it. All day I've felt it, an underlying lament in every act, from tying on my Doc Martens to ordering my café con leche. Commingled with the immense pride of knowing I achieved something amazing is my agitated anticipation of the nostalgia I know is to come.

"Drinks are on me!" Ted says and claps Ned on the back.

He is enormously proud of his brother. Ned lost twenty-two pounds. Which isn't the forty pounds he set out to lose, but it turns out that wasn't the point. Ned achieved something far more valuable.

He rediscovered his inner warrior. He walked nearly five hundred miles, carrying a backpack, and literally scaled mountains.

He and I share a special bond in that way, each of us knowing how unlikely it was we would make it when we started. It's almost hard to recall the girl I was that first day; I feel so different, and so much has changed.

None of us seem to have had the experience we expected. Regardless of the ambition that puts you on the path, the Camino doesn't bend to a pilgrim's will, and the growth experienced by each who walks it is unpredictable. The purpose of a pilgrimage is to allow time and space away from the familiar, so old ideas and beliefs can fall away and new higher perspectives can arise, and the profoundness of the effect varies. Tuck seems mostly unchanged, while I believe Ned and Gordon are permanently altered and will never be the same.

Uncle David left us this morning as promised at Monte do Gozo, the final peak before Santiago where pilgrims get their first glimpse of the cathedral. The tradition is to cry out in rapture at finally seeing the end of the path, and the nine of us put on an impressive howling.

When we finished, he said goodbye. "The Camino is only the beginning," he said. "You are pilgrims now, wanderers. Farewell and welcome." He hugged each of us, smiled the creased, weathered smile we'd all grown to love, and blue eyes sparking, offered his signature "Have a good life," then set out to return to Sanctuary of the Gods.

The rest of us continued the final slog into the city, a seemingly endless march through the congested streets of Santiago to the cathedral.

We had an emotional moment when we arrived. Ted and Ned stood with their arms around each other's shoulders, looking up at the gaudy masterpiece and grinning. Nicole surprisingly cried. Cami consoled her. Gordon looked melancholy and a bit forlorn. Matt and Tuck hammed it up for a dozen goofy photos.

I wasn't sure how I felt. *Unfinished* is the word that comes to mind, the same emotion I'd struggled with the night before in the courtyard with Uncle David, feeling like I wasn't done.

The city was very crowded, and the plaza around the cathedral more so. Hordes of travel groups, students, and tourists swarmed and waited in line, hoping to get a spot for the noon mass. Obligingly, after taking a few moments to appreciate our accomplishment, we joined them. I don't remember much about the service except that it gave me time to get used to the idea that I'd done it, had reached my goal, and made it to the end.

After, we walked to the pilgrim office for our Compostelas.

"Ultreia!" Tuck whoops to some passing pilgrims and punches the air.

The group of four men look at him strangely but then raise their fists in solidarity. "Buen Camino!" one of them says.

Tuck has his non-fist-punching arm slung over Cami's shoulder and is grinning so wide I think his cheeks must hurt. Cami, on the other hand, looks bereft. It's clear Tuck hasn't made any overture for them to continue their relationship after today, and Cami will go back to her lonely life in Australia and her dead-end job as a grocery clerk.

Nicole is the opposite. Excited the trip is over, a dozen times she's mentioned Barcelona and how she can't wait to get back to "civilization." She and Matt seem to have already made their Camino split and walked today as friends.

Matt.

Matt has avoided me all day. Twice I tried to catch up with him on the trail to apologize, but both times he sped up, making it clear he wasn't interested in talking.

"Doc!" someone says.

I lift my head to see Mike and Bryan sitting in front of a café with enormous steins in front of them. I kick out my Doc Martens, the embroidered once-bright flowers now muted beige and brown, and the boys lift their beers in a toast.

"We did it!" Bryan says.

"We did."

"Buen Camino!"

"Buen Camino," I answer back, the words tight.

Ted, knowing me, takes my left hand, and Ned takes my right. Somewhere in the distance, bagpipes play a melancholy rendition of "Amazing Grace," and around us, restaurants and bars teem with reveling, weary pilgrims. I tuck the moment away—me, Ted, and Ned walking down a street in Santiago in the late afternoon on the final day of the most amazing adventure of my life.

49

ISABELLE

1998

"I know," I say as I scruff the old cat behind his ear, a spot he's particularly fond of. "It's time."

His purr motor-revs, and he rubs his face against my leg. I call him "Joe," though he's feral and therefore free to be who he wants. Blind in one eye and with a permanently bent tail, he is the motliest creature I've ever laid eyes on. We met several months ago and became fast friends. Each day, during siesta, I carry my lunch to this spot beside the river, and he finds me. We share my food, and he repays me with his quiet, easy company. Sometimes I talk to him, conversing in French, Spanish, English, or German so I won't forget what I worked so hard to learn, or lose another part of myself.

Alberto likes that I speak so many languages and calls me "minha coruja," which means "my owl." We've been engaged a month, and I told him we can marry after a year has passed from my pa's death, a proper period of mourning.

He doesn't know my story. He thinks I'm from France, and that I came here to live near the ocean to recover from a bad bout of pneumonia. He thinks my pa died of a heart attack and that he was my only family. He thinks I'm someone I'm not, which is okay. I barely remember the person I used to be.

I know Alberto is disappointed I've asked him to wait so long, but the truth is, though I said yes, I'm not ready. The pretext of needing to wait because of my pa is an excuse. Hopefully in ten months, my heart will be healed, and I can be the bride and wife he deserves. Each day I grow stronger in body and spirit, and today I'm taking a big step toward letting go of the past, which hopefully will allow me to move forward.

"Okay, buddy," I say to Joe. "Let's do this."

With a sigh, I pull the card I bought the day after Alberto proposed from my canvas bag. On the front is a drawing of dark-green leaves and purple flowers outlined in gold. The inside is blank.

Joe eyes it with his single yellow eye, the glint of gold interesting him.

I pull out a pen and toy with him, waving it back and forth as he swats at it. Eventually he gets bored and saunters off to lie in a patch of sun.

"Fine," I say. "Be that way."

With no more excuses, I open the card and start to write.

> Dear Peter,
> You are the writer not me, but I will do my best to explain what happened and put into words the feelings in my heart.
>
> I do not blame you if you hate me. You owe me nothing, not even the minutes it takes to read this. Deciding not to meet you in Finisterre was the hardest choice I ever had to make. Over the course of the days I was apart from you and trying to reach you, I was reminded that family is everything. I will never be able to live in your world, and I cannot ask you to sacrifice the beautiful life you have in New York to live in mine. So I had to let you go.

I owe you so much more than the sum I am repaying you. I would not have survived without you. You were my greatest adventure and my greatest love and you will live in my heart forever.

Always,
Bella

I wipe the tears away with the back of my hand, and Joe jumps on my lap and nuzzles the hand with the pen.

I work around him to put the money, fifty thousand pesetas, in the envelope with the card. I address it to his father's construction company in Ithaca, New York, and leave the return address blank.

"Ultreia," I say to Joe. *Onward.*

50
REINA

2024

Frustrated, I throw back the covers and begin to pace. It's my final night in Santiago, and, as a parting gift, Ted generously bought me a room at the Hostal de los Reyes Católicos, one of the oldest hotels in Spain. The Catholic monarchs founded it in 1499 as an albergue for pilgrims who had completed the long journey of the Way of Saint James. Ted said he hoped it would inspire me for the win.

We had a sob-fest when we said goodbye after dinner. He and Ned were catching a late train to Bilbao, where they'll spend a week before heading back to Alberta.

"Write your heart out, little buddy," Ned blubbered as he hugged me.

My tears soaked through his Camino de Santiago T-shirt, which he proudly boasted he'd bought off the shelf, size extra-large.

He swayed back and forth and said into my hair, "As Winnie the Pooh says, 'How lucky I am to have something that makes saying goodbye so hard.'"

The quote made me cry harder. Christopher Robin was a kindred spirit through my sibling-less childhood, and I've read each of A. A. Milne's Pooh Bear tales several times.

Even Ted, a man not prone to sentimentality, misted up when he said, "I've still got my money on the dark horse."

I did my best not to slobber on his cashmere sweater as I fell into his arms.

Now they're gone, along with Gordon, Tuck, Cami, Nicole, and Matt.

I look at the open box on the bed—a challenge and a taunt. The note on top of the goading gift that Uncle David gave me read:

> Sometimes the only way forward is to take a step back.

Beneath the sheet of lined yellow paper was a treasure trove of notes and photos for *Wisdom of the Way*. There was a spiral-bound notebook with meticulous notes written by my mom. Seeing the tight, precise handwriting, something I've never seen before, made my heart beat strangely, the phantasm of her incredibly strong. Another smaller notebook was filled front to back with facts and history about the Camino. Inside the cover was Joe's name and a phone number. There were also hundreds of photos from multiple cameras and at least a hundred scraps of paper with random notes that Uncle David has contributed over his fourteen years of living on the trail.

It's clear he gave me the box with the hope that I will finish what he, my dad, my mom, and the others started. He wants me to write *Wisdom of the Way*.

Which is why I am finding it impossible to sleep. The crossroads of my life is in front of me. I am planted squarely at the proverbial fork in the road that will determine everything that comes after, and I have no idea which direction I want to go.

I pace harder, walking from the bathroom to the window then back again.

The air conditioner clicks on, startling me. I'm no longer accustomed to such things—air-conditioning, television, endless hot water for showering. It's going to take some time to reacclimate. The room is quiet, cool, and clean, and I'm entirely out of sorts.

I've finished my article. It just needs one final edit, and I need to decide which photos to include. The story is good, probably the best thing I've ever written. It's relatable, funny, and heartfelt—a profound journey of emotion and humility as I followed in my parents' footsteps and discovered them and myself along the way.

My flight isn't until tomorrow afternoon, which means I have plenty of time to give it a final polish before posting it to the portal. Matt was booked on an earlier flight, so his story's already there, posted under the title, "Journey of a Lifetime."

I haven't looked at it. After what happened last night, I want to avoid any appearance of impropriety. I would never take another journalist's work. That wasn't the reason I looked at Matt's journal. But of course Matt doesn't know that, and each time I recall that awful moment of him glaring at me as I knelt over his words, my heart seizes, and I wish I could turn back time and undo it.

All day he made a point of avoiding me, and when our group split up after drinks, he gave a heartfelt goodbye to everyone but me.

I look again at the box and think of Uncle David's words when he gave it to me. *All I'm saying is, you set out to walk the Camino with your dad, so maybe you should continue to follow in his path. I mean, maybe it's time to start listening to your heart instead of your head and to allow it to show you the way.*

My heart. That's the problem. Where it's pulling me is where I'm terrified to go.

Back and forth I pace, until finally, unable to take it, I stomp to the desk, open the laptop I rented from the hotel, and pull up the portal.

I click on Matt's story and start to read.

"Journey of a Lifetime," by Matt Calhoun.

Once upon a time I walked across Spain . . .

I fall into his words and the stunning account he's written of the past thirty-three days, his story so different from my own, it's as if we were on two different trips entirely.

While my story is mostly about how the Camino affected me—my emotions, my personal growth, my reconciliation with my past, and my relationships—Matt's is all about the adventure. He writes about the cities and villages, painting them so vividly with his words it's as if you are there, at the bars, eating the food, experiencing the nightlife, cathedrals, landmarks, festivals, and people.

He talks about the day-to-day, from the mundane to the extraordinary, describing everything from the songs and games we sang and played on the trail to our albergue dinners and card games at the pubs. He describes the remarkable sheep-shearing adventure and the wine we drank from our Camino shells from the wine fountain outside Estella. He gives practical advice on what to pack, tips on trekking, and how to deal with blisters and sore knees. Masterfully, in less than a dozen pages, he takes the reader on a five-hundred-mile journey that makes you feel both a part of it and apart from it, leaving you both satisfied and yearning.

It flows effortlessly, yet parts are profound.

There's something uniquely moving about walking the Camino, humbling and illuminating. Hours of walking in nature does something to a person. Your mind turns off, and your feet march on, and in the vast emptiness, the essence of what it is to be human is revealed.

Other parts are hilarious. A third of the way through is a photo of Matt squatting on the trail as he carves the final stroke of a message in the mud that reads:

F@&# MARTIN SHEEN!

He's grinning wide, his rain slicker dripping water.

I remember seeing the message and laughing. Martin Sheen and the movie *The Way*, written by Sheen's son Emilio Estevez, are the reason many people embark on the Camino. I had no idea Matt was the one who left the soul-lifting missive on that dreary, rain-soaked day.

The ending causes my eyes to go misty for how perfectly he captures the essence of what we experienced.

> Never have I witnessed such beauty—God-made or man-made—rivers, pastures, flowers, trees, mountains, cathedrals, monasteries, and bridges. But more than the physical seen by my eyes was that which was felt by my heart—the kindness, generosity, fellowship, and grace I encountered along the way. Hearts opening and breaking in the cocoon of acceptance and compassion the Camino provides as we traveled the trail as individuals, but together. The reasons for doing the Camino are as varied as the people endeavoring to walk it, yet among us resonated a single common goal, to expand beyond ourselves and hopefully become more than what we were. Free from judgment and pretense, responsibilities and concerns, each footfall was a step toward letting go of the familiar and moving on toward the possibility of something new. "Who am I?" confronts you each day as your body is pushed to its limits, and then, more importantly, "Who do I want to be?" Painful at times, old beliefs not easily surrendered, the walk is a pause, a rare and precious chance to reset or possibly change direction altogether.
>
> I cannot promise this will be your experience. Each Camino is its own, and while others may walk with you, no one can walk it for you. It begins with a single

step toward a goal that at first feels insurmountable until you learn the only impossible journey is the one you never begin.

Buen Camino!

My dad used to say, "A good story is a dream shared by the author and the reader." Matt achieved it in spades, and I am humbled by his talent.

Turning from the screen, I look out the window at the dark spires of the Saint James Cathedral silhouetted against the bruised night sky. *Who am I? Who do I want to be?*

The answer rises clear in my mind, and I turn back to the computer to do what I do best.

It takes five hours, and I'm bleary eyed when I finish and proud. My contributions are mostly structural and grammatical, though in the margins I've included dozens of suggestions for Matt to consider. I also include a link to my photos.

My email reads:

Dear Brenda,

The story was always Matt's, and he did an amazing job. His article conveys both the practical and the profound, and it is beautifully written. My only criticism is that, after readers read it, the Camino is going to be flooded with new pilgrims.

Thank you for having faith in me as a pinch hitter. As Matt wrote: "I set out on this adventure to discover Spain; what I discovered instead was myself." I feel I've only just started that journey, which is why, with this final copyedit, I am tendering my resignation so I might continue that quest.

Thank you for everything.

Best, Reina

My cursor hovers over the folded airplane symbol. The message is addressed to Brenda, and Matt is cc'd.

I stare at his name until it buzzes.

Taking my thumb from the touch pad, I return my fingers to the keyboard and type:

PS After O Cebreiro, none of it was about the story.

Before I lose my nerve, I hit send.

51

ISABELLE

1998

"Joan, can you take over the grill? I want to have a smoke."

I stop wiping the counter and nod to Jesus, the cook, through the pass-through window.

Franco perks up. "Joan, if you're cooking, I'll have your ma's special."

Since I got engaged, Carolina has agreed to let me sometimes work in the kitchen. She says it makes sense since soon I will be pregnant, and when I get "fat," it will be a better place for me. The wedding is still nine months off, but she's excited. The whole town is, and everyone pesters me for making them wait so long.

"If you're making your ma's trinxat, make it two orders," another customer says. Her name is Helga, and she runs the market down the street.

Trinxat is one of my ma's signature dishes. It's a simple cabbage, potato, bacon hash, but my ma uses pancetta instead of bacon and adds thyme and garlic to make it more flavorful. I add my own touch by using one of Carolina's cookie cutters, a large flower, to make it pretty.

As I gather the ingredients, my heart lightens. Cooking makes me happy, especially when I cook my ma's food.

I set the cabbage, potatoes, and pancetta on the counter and pull out the cutting board.

"Bella."

The name freezes me and causes me to drop the potato in my hand. And though I've yearned to hear his voice for nearly a year, I don't believe it's real until he says my name again.

"Bella."

I turn slowly to see him in the doorway to the kitchen, so different from the last time I saw him. His hair is short and his face clean shaven. He is thicker than he was, and the traces of boy have been erased. He wears a light-blue short-sleeved, button-down shirt, black jeans, and tan Nike sneakers.

I watch as he takes me in as well, and I imagine I am different too. My hair is no longer to my waist. A month ago I cut it to shoulder length. And I've regained the weight I lost on the trail and now have back my curves. I wear a simple flowered dress, the kind young women often wear in Portugal.

His eyes move from the top of my head to my feet before returning to settle on my face.

"You found me," I say, my voice tight with emotion.

"I never would have stopped looking. You are my heart."

52

REINA

2024

"Hold up," I wheeze.

Aunt Ana looks back and frowns. Despite my aunt being fifteen years older than me, these mountains don't seem to affect her. I'm in the best shape of my life, having finished the Camino only a week ago, but the thin air and steep incline of Smuggler's Pass are killing me.

"Your pa's gringo blood is showing," she says with a snort of superiority.

Her grasp of English is rudimentary, but she knows enough to insult me regularly, and in the six days I've been here, I've grown to adore her.

She is nothing like I expected. My research on Dur made me think I was traveling to a provincial hamlet a lot like the medieval villages on the Camino, and that my family would be simple folk living a rural, outmoded existence.

Instead, what I found was a thriving tourist town both old and new at once, and an aunt who is as savvy a businesswoman as I've ever met. Though they look nothing alike, she reminds me a little of Brenda, a call-it-like-she-sees-it, no-nonsense woman.

Twenty years ago, when she was only twenty-two, Aunt Ana was elected the first mayor of Dur, a position created after Senor Sansas passed away. After he died, the families who owned the mountain went to court to have the ballot measure that had caused all the division between the villagers nullified. The judge ordered that the town instate a local government, and since my aunt had initiated the action, he suggested she be the one put in charge.

"We're losing the sun," she says, hand flicking impatiently toward the pastel sky.

I haul myself forward, cussing and smiling at once as I follow her up the path, her amber hair winking in the fading light. The first time I saw her, I was so stunned I couldn't speak. She looks so much like my mom.

She was clearly flabbergasted as well.

"It's clear you're not making up that you're Izzy's," she said, hazel eyes wide. She shook her head once as if to clear it. "How?" she mumbled, but before I could answer she shook her head again and said, "Makes no difference. You're home now."

She took my pack from my shoulder, slammed it at the man beside her who turned out to be my uncle, and pulled me into the tavern by the hand to introduce me around.

Uncle Xavier doesn't look like his sisters. First off, he's big, at least six-two and built like a box. He has dark hair, and a shadow of dark, thick beard covers his face from midmorning on. He also doesn't share my aunt's wit or sass. Candid and boyish, he is sweet and, unlike Aunt Ana, would never insult anyone. He runs the auto-repair shop and, according to my aunt, "fixes anything that needs fixing."

Because he doesn't speak English, mostly we take walks and play cards. He's married to a woman named Lia, who surprisingly is one of the Sansas daughters. They have two children—a boy named Manuel and a daughter named Isabelle.

Ana also has kids, three boys and two girls.

Which means I've gone from having no cousins to having a bushel.

I also have a grandmother, and of all the gifts I've discovered this past week, I believe she is the most precious. Everyone, even her customers, call her Mi Jefa, the boss, and though we don't speak the same language, each night we sit behind the inn together to look at the stars. Often she takes my hand, and I've come to realize sometimes words aren't needed.

The feud long over, the town is reconciled and peaceful. And prosperous. Aunt Ana worked with the founding families to come up with a plan that benefited everyone. They agreed to lease the mineral rights of a remote section of the mountain to an iron mining company and to use the proceeds to fund the town's development. They've restored the cathedral and castle, and expanded and repaved the roads. Beyond the village, a community of two hundred homes was built along with a school, city hall, small hospital, store, and gas station. Dur now has over two thousand residents, and thanks to the mineral rights profits, there are no local taxes, and everyone has free Wi-Fi and cell service.

Dur has also slowly developed into a thriving tourist destination. People from all over Europe visit to hike Smuggler's Pass, eat my grandmother's food, and ski Vidal Run, a treacherous ski run named after my grandfather and built in honor of his dream. The rickety two-seat chairlift carries any intrepid daredevil brave or stupid enough to ride to the top of a rocky peak. It's up to them to get themselves down. There is no lift operator, and the slope is never groomed. It's littered with rocks and trees and is open year-round, even though, during the peak of summer, the snow is spotty at best. It's quite a draw, and thousands visit each year just to test their nerve. One person has died, and countless others have been injured.

When Aunt Ana showed it to me, she shrugged and said, "Idiots."

I imagine she is a lot like my grandfather. His prized cattle are how my family makes most of their living, and she is the one in charge of that business as well.

"About time," she says as I haul myself over the final crest to find her sitting on a boulder on a plateau that overlooks such a grand expanse that I'm certain we've reached the edge of the earth. A mattress of clouds floats below us, and distant peaks poke through like islands.

"This is amazing," I say breathlessly.

She nods. "The trail continues there, and it's a few more hours' hike to the capital, or if you stay north, it's another day's hike to France."

Aunt Ana hands me a waxed-paper-wrapped sandwich.

I carry it to a boulder a few feet from hers, and my eyes close in bliss as I sink my teeth into the first delicious bite. Tomatoes, cheese, arugula, and some sort of amazing sauce on a fresh baked baguette. Dur brings a whole new level of meaning to the concept of farm-to-table. The tomatoes and arugula were grown in the garden behind the inn. The cheese was made from milk from the family's sheep. The bread is from wheat grown in the fields across the river and ground at the mill down the road. And I'm pretty sure it's the most delicious sandwich I've ever eaten.

As I eat, nature works her silent wonder, putting on a magnificent show of shadow and light as the colors continue to change with the minutes and the sun takes its daily bow.

I pull out my phone and aim it at Aunt Ana. "Smile," I taunt, knowing she hates being told what to do and is stingy with her grins.

She sneers, and I snap the photo.

"Come on," I say. "One smile. Is that really so hard?"

"Yes," she harrumphs, but then begrudgingly offers a smirk.

And in that moment, the setting sun glinting off her burnished hair and the vista of peaks behind her, she looks so much like my mom that for a second my heart stops. I look down at my phone to the captured shot and run my fingers over it. It's the photo I will send Aunt Robbie, Uncle David, Ted, Ned, Liam, and Jake when I get back to the village.

"Time to go," Aunt Ana says and stands.

I shove the last bite of sandwich in my mouth and hurry after her down the trail, trying to keep up, but finding it impossible. I think she knows it and is doing it on purpose. When we get back to the tavern, she will make endless fun of how slow I was.

As I slip and slide down the narrow, serpentine path, I wonder if I tripped and broke my neck if she would come back for me.

Halfway down, my aunt now out of sight, I stop to catch my breath and to take in the view. The village from here looks straight out of a storybook—quaint stone houses with flower boxes bursting with geraniums, cobblestone streets, a meandering river with two arched bridges, a stained-glass cathedral, and a four-turret medieval castle.

A car slows at the foot of the bridge that leads into the village, and I smile as a woman leans out the passenger-side window to take a photo of the sign that greets each visitor:

THE OWNERS OF DUR MOUNTAIN ARE NOT RESPONSIBLE FOR ANY PHYSICAL OR MATERIAL DAMAGE THAT OCCURS ONCE YOU ENTER THE TOWN.

That's it. One sign with a single universal warning that you proceed at your own risk and that you are responsible for your choices. At its heart, Dur is the same lawless, independent place it's always been.

The car passes the cathedral and then the graveyard where my mom is buried beside my grandfather. My mom's childhood friend Gemma, on learning of my mom's death, went to Portugal and brought her home. Perhaps someday I will try to find Gemma to fill in more of the missing pieces. But for now that quest will need to wait because, after this visit, I have another more pressing mission. *Wisdom of the Way*.

The first call I made after canceling my flight home and booking a new flight to Andorra was to Ted. I told him about *Wisdom of the Way* and that I was thinking of pursuing it.

His response was, "So a guide of all the intangibles? The mystical, magical, and mysterious?"

"Exactly. The stuff you don't get from the Brierley guidebook."

"And you want to make it an app so it tracks the user in real time."

"Exactly. Point your phone at whatever you're curious about—"

"A cow, a tree, a monument, a building," he said, his enthusiasm growing.

"And it gives you information—"

"Or a quip or an anecdote."

"Or a story or possibly even a song."

"I love it!" he said. "And pilgrims on the trail can contribute and offer updates to keep it current."

"A link in the menu that says *community*," I said.

"Or *trail crew*."

"Ooh. I like that."

"We're in," he said. By we, he meant him and Ned.

Ted's geek squad is developing the tech. Ned is figuring out the business side of things. And I'm in charge of the content. The task is enormous, but a step at a time I will figure out a way to get it done. My goal is to have a framework in place by next summer, which is when I intend to return to the Camino to hike it again so I can fill in the blanks.

I reach the inn as the last light of day kisses the horizon, and my stomach rumbles as the delicious smells of my grandmother's cooking waft through the open door and drift past my nose. The nearly full dining room is bustling, but as soon as I enter, the noise stops and every head turns to look at me.

I wonder what's going on, but only for a second.

Across the room, from a stool at the bar, he stands.

"Matt?" I say, blinking several times.

His hair is short, and he is clean shaven.

"Still rocking the Docs," he says with a nod at my shoes.

I nod numbly, my throat gone dry.

I've thought about him so often, since the moment I hit send on my computer, it's as if I conjured him from my mind. The only response to my email was from Brenda. She thanked me for my work on the article and wished me luck in my future endeavors.

"What are you doing here?" I manage, the room silent and everyone watching.

"I brought you a prepress copy of the issue," he says, closing the distance between us and holding out a copy of the newly formatted *Journey*. The cover features a stunning photo I took on my hike up to O Cebreiro, two pilgrims with their packs silhouetted on the trail with the floating mountains beyond them. "I thought you'd want to see it and figured they don't probably sell *Journey* in Andorra." His lips twitch with a grin.

I take the magazine and open it to the earmarked page.

"Journey of a Lifetime." By Matt Calhoun and Reina Watkins.

I lift my face back to his. His clear amber gaze holds mine, and the skin below his left eye twitches.

"After O Cebreiro," he says, his voice tight, "none of it was about the story."

"I'm so sorry I—" I start, but he stops me.

Stepping forward, he lifts my chin with his fingers, then bends and brushes a kiss across my lips, so gentle it's light as a butterfly's wings.

"You can do better than that!" my aunt roars.

He laughs and, to the delight of our viewing audience, wraps his arms around my waist and pulls me into a kiss worthy of V-J Day and the cover of *Life* magazine.

The crowd roars their approval.

When he releases me, he punches the air. "Yes! Shaggy finally gets the girl!"

AUTHOR'S NOTE

Dear Reader,

I had never heard of the Camino de Santiago until my daughter told me about it when she was nineteen. She said she wanted to go to Europe with her best friend to backpack over the Pyrenees and across Spain to the far reaches of the Iberian Peninsula.

The idea was outrageous until I started to read about it and discovered the Camino's long history and came to understand it was more than a backpacking adventure. The ritual of following the path of Saint James was over a thousand years old, and the experience deeply affected many who walked it.

My daughter was no exception. She came back changed. The thirty-three-day adventure turned out to be a profound coming-of-age passage for her into adulthood. She discovered how capable she was and figured out her calling. She met people from all over the world, and it widened her perspective, and ultimately transformed her destiny.

For years after, she told me I should do it. And each time I responded with "Yeah, yeah. Someday." The truth is, I had no real intention of following through. Unlike my daughter, I wasn't looking for self-discovery or enlightenment, and the idea of traipsing across a country with a backpack and sleeping in hostels surrounded by strangers didn't appeal.

Then life threw me a curveball. My husband had a health scare, and it rocked my world. I was in his hospital room a few days after we dodged a proverbial life-altering bullet, and for whatever reason, I thought about the Camino and how for years I'd been saying "someday" I would do it. Sitting there, I realized plainly that none of us really knows how many somedays we have left.

I started making plans that day.

Terrified of embarking on the journey alone, I bribed my daughter, her boyfriend, and my son to join me for the first seven days by offering to foot the bill. It was a wonderful, torturous week. I don't know if I've ever been in so much pain or pushed myself so hard, and I don't know if I've ever loved my kids so much. They were incredibly encouraging and supportive, and I knew the tables were turning. My kids were now the ones looking out for me instead of the other way around.

My daughter's two pieces of advice as they were leaving were "Don't get lost" and "Make friends."

Like a life ring, I clung to those words. I sought out yellow arrows, checking and double-checking constantly that I was on the path. And I forced myself to meet people. Each day, I would talk to anyone who spoke English. Sometimes we walked together. Other times we shared a meal.

Which is how this story came about. When I started the journey, I had no intention of writing a story about it. The Camino is actually a pretty mundane thing to try to write about. You walk. You sleep. You wake up and do it again. But storytelling is more about characters than setting, and there was no way to meet that many people and hear that many personal accounts and not wind up with a head full of ideas.

The first inspiration struck twenty-four days into the journey. I was hiking with John from Indiana and Gordon from Scotland up a grueling leg of trail. We were tired and grouchy and hadn't passed a café for hours when La Casa de los Dioses (the House of the Gods) appeared in front of us like a mirage. It was very much like how I describe Sanctuary of the Gods, and Uncle David is based on the real-life proprietor, David Vidal (Instagram @peregrinodelavida33). When I asked the real David if the property was his, he responded, "Everything you see belongs to

God," and when he noticed Gordon was sunburned, he gave him a tube of sun lotion. And when we left, he bid us goodbye with his signature, "Have a good life." So while Uncle David is a work of fiction, he shares the same generous, kind spirit as the real David Vidal.

The nugget of the idea for the story came a full week later. David had been swimming in my head, but he was only a character, a human embodiment of the Camino that I knew would someday make it into some future work. Then, as the saying goes, "The Camino provides."

I was a few days from Santiago, in a crappy town, after a miserable, lonely day of hiking. I went to a small pizza restaurant for dinner and sat down alone, but within a few minutes, a pair of Americans sat down at the table beside me. Rick and Eliana, father and daughter, were from Ohio. Rick had hiked the Camino as a young man. Eliana was eighteen and was headed off to college at the end of summer. They were doing the Camino together so Eliana could experience the trip that had meant so much to her dad.

Rick pulled out his phone and showed me a photo of himself with three buddies on the trail from twenty-five years before. The muscled, grinning man was unrecognizable from the slouched, overweight man at the table beside me, and he knew it. His voice grew thick as he pointed to each of his friends and then himself, and I felt his anguish. Eliana did as well and set her hand on his arm, and in that small gesture was everything. Eliana wasn't doing the walk for herself; she was doing it for him. Her dad had lost his way, and she was hoping returning to the trail might help him find it.

I don't know if it did. I caught a glimpse of Rick the next day, struggling up a hill. I passed with an encouraging, "Buen Camino," and that was the last I saw of him. I'm sure Eliana was way out in front of us. She was long-legged, and Rick had proudly nicknamed her "Billy Goat" for how quickly she walked.

Reina and Isabelle were inspired in part by Eliana, and Peter and Ned were inspired in part by Rick. And over a delicious dinner of pizza and wine, the idea of writing a story about two Caminos walked a generation apart was born.

I started working on the idea before I left Santiago. As always, I began with a deep dive into the topic I was writing about. And one of the first things I stumbled upon was an article titled "Murder in the Pyrenees."

It was a story from the nineties about a feud between thirteen founding families of a small village near the Spain–Andorra border. The dispute was over a developer's proposal to turn "their mountain" into a ski resort. It resulted in the murder of two men, and the ski resort was never built. Dur and the feud between Isabelle's dad and Senor Sansas are based on that story.

I loved the idea of the Camino offering refuge for someone with nothing. I wanted the tenet "The Camino provides" to be part of the story.

Writing about the Camino helped me transition back into my life. I came home in an odd state—let down, like a balloon deflated. Things felt oddly meaningless. I purged my closet. I purged my friends. I lost at games I used to care about winning. I drove slower. I walked faster. I struggled to engage. I struggled to explain the experience. I started humming.

I wear a leather bracelet with a ceramic scallop shell bead on my left wrist, which I bought on the trail and look at often as a reminder of those thirty-five strange, wondrous, exhausting, glorious days. I'm no great athlete. I have thin skin that blisters easily. My legs are shorter than most. Yet one foot in front of the other, I climbed mountains and walked across a country. I learned how little I need and how much I have. How frail I am and how strong. I discovered things about myself I never knew. I gave myself grace, forgave myself for regrets of the past, and released grudges I didn't even realize I was holding. I discovered the lowest lows are often followed by the highest highs. I met people I otherwise never would have met. I was uncomfortable. I got lost. Eventually I found my way.

Day after day, I was stunned by the extraordinary. And the mundane. I sat beneath a shower of shooting stars. A music student from Juilliard stopped on the trail to sing me an aria. I watched an old woman in a handstitched apron pull onions from her garden. I witnessed a cow in a pasture giving birth. I was astounded. I was often bored to tears.

It was everything, and it was nothing. It took forever. It feels like a blink. Time goes on.

The Camino is a contradiction, a complicated melody known only to the person who experiences it.

For those who have walked it, I hope this story brought back some beautiful memories. For those who haven't, I hope it gives you a glimpse of the promise it holds.

Buen Camino,
Suzanne

PS This is a work of fiction. To move the story where it needed to go, I put in the scene about the hosteler attacking Isabelle, but I want to make it clear that crime on the Camino is extraordinarily rare. The Camino is safer than almost any Western city, even those with extremely low crime rates. While I was on the Camino, I never felt unsafe. There were always people around, and everyone was friendly, helpful, and respectful. I was never uncomfortable, and no one ever did anything that was even slightly inappropriate. There were at least as many women on the trail as men, and many, like me, were traveling alone. I hope that scene does not discourage anyone from taking this remarkable journey.

ACKNOWLEDGMENTS

The Camino is a shared experience. Though I traveled most of it alone, I was never without company. So I would like to thank all those I walked with and who inspired me to write this story: Joe, Halle, Ian, Jen, Erika, Dan, Emily, Brian, Francesca, John, Gordon, Rick, Eliana, Tina, H, Gar, Holly, Kahlie, Anita, Nicole, Mary, Bob, Matteo, Sadie Ellen, Louise, Brooke, Kyhran, and the dozens of others I met along the way.

As always, thank you to my daughter for being my first reader and to my son and husband for their continued encouragement and support.

This book would not have been possible without my agent, Gordon Warnock, and my two editors, Chantelle Osman and Laura Van der Veer. I also want to thank Jodi Warshaw for her insightful input that elevated the story to the next level, Andy Hodges and Katherine Kirk for their meticulous copyediting and proofreading, Mary Ruth Govindavari for her thoughtful review of the cultural and sensitivity topics in the story, and the entire Lake Union team, who continue to astound me with their professionalism and talent.

Last, thank you to all the pilgrims who traveled the path before me and to the incredible people of Spain who, for over a thousand years, have protected the Way of Saint James and provided for those who endeavor to walk it so people like me can wander, experience, and grow.

DISCUSSION QUESTIONS

1. Reina lost her dad when she was eight but still strongly feels his presence and often believes he is guiding her. Do you believe spirits watch over us, or is it just our longing and memory of them that makes it seem that way?
2. Reina's entire life is altered when she takes a chance and sends the email to Brenda, saying she will go on the Camino in Matt's stead after he loses his passport. It was a "sliding door" moment—a single small decision that changed everything. Have you had a moment like that, an opportunity you seized that determined everything that came after?
3. "The Camino has absorbed many tears, and it is a keeper of secrets." Do you think there's something specifically mystical about the Camino de Santiago, or do you think any extraordinarily physical challenge where one is left alone with their thoughts for an extended period would have the same cathartic effect?
4. The pilgrimage is steeped in religious history and symbolism, and part of Isabelle's journey is a coming to terms with her relationship with God. Ted, Ned, and David also have a conversation about whether existentialism and God can peacefully coexist. How do you feel about Isabelle's reconciliation of her knowledge of evolution and her faith?

5. Was there one specific moment in the story when you decided Reina and John weren't meant to be together? Do you think if they married that they would have had a life that "would have continued in its imperfect-yet-entirely-acceptable way?" What do you think her future looks like with Matt?
6. Nicknames play an important role in the story. Reina is "Velma," "Little Buddy," "Doc," and "Rainbow." Isabelle is "Mi Geni," "My Masterpiece," "Billy Goat," and "Bella." Do you have a pet name and what is the meaning behind it?
7. Reina discovers her long-lost uncle on the trail. How do you feel about David? Do you think Reina was right to forgive him? Do you agree with David when he says, "Every morning we are born again, and it's what we do today that matters most?"
8. Reina discovers she is Andorran not Portuguese, and the revelation is stunning. After learning what she does about her mom, she sets off to discover more. Do you think it's important to understand where you come from, or does it not really matter?
9. The deal Isabelle strikes with Senor Sansas comes at a steep price—her home, her identity, seeing her family again, the future she dreamed of with Peter . . . and ultimately, her pa. How do you feel about the deal she made with Senor Sansas?
10. Isabelle understands what it means to give up your family and ultimately decides she can't ask Peter to do that for her. "True love means putting the other person first." Do you think she did the right thing? Should she never have gotten involved with him in the first place, knowing the jeopardy she put him in and that they had no future together?

11. Before reading this story, had you heard of the Camino? Does the story make you want to experience it?
12. How do you imagine the future unfolding for the characters?
13. Who was your favorite character? Why?
14. Movie time: Who would you like to see play each part?

ABOUT THE AUTHOR

Photo © 2020 April Brian

Suzanne Redfearn is the award-winning author of six novels: *Hush Little Baby*, *No Ordinary Life*, *In an Instant*, *Hadley and Grace*, *Moment in Time*, and *Where Butterflies Wander*. In addition to being an author, she's also an architect specializing in residential and commercial design. Suzanne lives in Laguna Beach, California, where she and her husband own two restaurants: Lumberyard and Slice Pizza and Beer. You can find the author at her website, www.SuzanneRedfearn.com, or on Facebook at www.facebook.com/SuzanneRedfearnAuthor.